12/29/09

Nopo San

The Life And Times Of A Well Seasoned Nut

Introduction

By

Robert P. Herbst

What I have set down here in these pages, will come as no surprise to anyone who has served in any branch of the Armed Forces. It was an experience I shall never forget. Nor do I think anyone who has lived through any part of an experience like this, should forget.

I do however, think one should try to remember the experience in its proper light. We can't change it anymore, so why not look at the lighter side of it. I have tried to do just this in the following pages.

Figure 1 Myself at 63

We all know it wasn't all fun and games. It was hard work. In some cases, most unpleasant work. There were those times I thought I might die. There were times I wished I could have died. Then there were always the other times when I can laugh myself silly about it. Fortunately for me, most of the time I had a ball. There were those who weren't as lucky.

There is no way I can remember all the facts and the exact time line involved in this story. There are parts I remember quite clearly. There are parts I don't want to remember. Then there are those parts I wish to God I could forget. So with this in mind, I'll call it fiction.

I have changed some of the names, places, and times to protect those of you who don't want to be remembered and to protect me from those few who are still looking for me.

However, for any of you who would like to write my address is in the book.

With great reverence, I dedicate this story to those I had to leave behind.

Illustrations

A Much Older Me	First Page
My Camera	Page # 40
Me At Tech School	Page # 41
Myself In A Typical 36-93 Portrait	Page # 42
The Beach At Okinawa	Page # 53
The Village Of Kadena	Page # 54
Another Shot Of Kadena	Page # 55
A Hill And Path In The Woods	Page # 56
A Bar On Okinawa	Page # 60
A Sign Painter In Kadena	Page # 61
My Avocado Tree	Page # 62
An Old Lady Picking Up Salvage	Page # 63
The Big Rock	Page # 64
Main Street Kadena	Page # 65
Delivery Wagon	Page # 65
Dust Control On Main Street	Page # 66
My Favorite Kids	Page # 67
Judy	Page # 68
Intense Negotiations	Page # 68
A Civilian Guard On Duty On Okinawa	Page # 69
A General Store	Page # 70
An Okinawan Farm	Page # 71
Plowing The Field	Page # 72
A Movie Theater	Page # 73
Kids At Play	Page # 73
Kids Outside School	Page # 74
An Okinawan Family	Page # 75
An Okinawan Shrine	Page # 75
Walter Ready For Base Alert	Page # 82
Classified Trash	Page # 87
Transportation To Tokyo	Page # 90
Ready To Take Off	Page # 91
A Picture Of The Base	Page # 94
The Oki Steel Works	Page # 95

The Base Photo Lab	Page # 98
A Japanese Benjo	Page # 99
Entrance To The Mitsubishi Fighter Plant	Page # 100
Moustache	Page # 101
Front Of Fuji View Hotel	Page # 101
Tree Care Japanese Style	Page # 102
Garden Behind Fuji View Hotel	Page # 103
The Kamakura Di Butsu	Page # 104
Back Of Di Butsu	Page # 105
The Front Of T. Sakat's Business	Page # 106
Sakata And Wife At Sun Dial	Page # 107
Sakata And Wife In Greenhouse	Page # 108
Sakata's Office Workers	Page # 109
5 Of My Fathers Pictures From 1924	Page # 110
2 My Fathers Pictures From 1924	Page # 111
The Last Of My Father's Pictures	Page # 112
The Worlds Only Three Roofed Bogota	Page # 113
A Tea House With Pond	Page # 113
Tea House And Crowd	Page # 114
I Have Absolutely No Idea What This Is	Page # 115
The Fishing Fleet	Page # 118
Japanese Fire Fighters	Page # 122
Magic In Japan	Page # 123
More Magic	Page # 124
Civilian Guard And Jeep	Page # 125
Geishas At Work	Page # 126
Honey Bucket Man	Page # 128
Osoba At The International Air Port	Page # 131
Picture Of Samurai Shrine	Page # 142
2 Pictures Of Kiyoko And I	Page # 147
Oki Steel Works And Barges	Page # 156
Quiet On The Day Before May Day	Page # 171
The Military Bridge	Page # 174
Cast Iron Pete	Page # 176
Pancho	Page # 181
Pancho At Bay	Page # 182
It Was All A Joke	Page # 183

Civilian Guard Headquarters	Page # 184
Peters At The Ready	Page # 185
Spirit Face	Page # 188
Japanese Ant	Page # 189
Service Club Workers	Page # 190
Fuji Musume	Page # 191
Kids At Accident	Page # 193
Kids Boxing	Page # 194
Experiment In Lighting	Page # 199
A Typhoon Jug	Page # 246
My Old Crash Pass	Page # 247
News Clip - Stas, Roger & Jane	Page # 253

INDEX

Chapter 1	The Air Force	Page # 1
Chapter 2	Basic Training	Page # 5
Chapter 3	Bivouac	Page # 13
Chapter 4	Fire Guard	Page # 20
Chapter 5	Fire Guard -- Again?	Page # 29
Chapter 6	Sick Call	Page # 34
Chapter 7	Tech School	Page # 39
Chapter 8	The Troop Ship	Page # 47
Chapter 9	Okinawa	Page # 53
Chapter 10	The F-86	Page # 77
Chapter 11	The Base Alert	Page # 82
Chapter 12	The Trip Over	Page # 89
Chapter 13	A Whole New Way Of Life	Page # 94
Chapter 14	The First May Day	Page # 116
Chapter 15	Fatso	Page # 126
Chapter 16	Osoba	Page # 131
Chapter 17	Culture Shock	Page # 137
Chapter 18	Kiyoko	Page # 146
Chapter 19	JP-40	Page # 151
Chapter 20	The Big Splash	Page # 156
Chapter 21	Typhoon	Page # 161
Chapter 22	Dumb Luck	Page # 167
Chapter 23	May Day Comes Again	Page # 170

Chapter 24	The Second May Day	Page # 176
Chapter 25	The Base Photo Lab	Page # 180
Chapter 26	The Shrine At Haneda	Page # 192
Chapter 27	The Flight Over Korea	Page # 202
Chapter 28	The Horrors Of War	Page # 211
Chapter 29	Three Weeks With The Marines	Page # 221
Chapter 30	The Reason Why	Page # 233
Chapter 31	The Dark	Page # 238
Chapter 32	The Last Typhoon	Page # 242
Chapter 33	Jane	Page # 247
Chapter 34	The Trip Home	Page # 255
Chapter 35	New York A.F.B.	Page # 260

Nopo San

Chapter 1

The Air Force

After all was said and done, the question upper-most in my mind after high school was, which branch of the service should I enlist in? I didn't want to be drafted so I began a systematic appraisal of the various branches of the armed services which were open to me.

There was no way I could stuff my six-foot four-inch frame into a "Pup-Tent" or an Army sleeping bag. The Army was definitely out. At least as far as I was concerned. Besides the sleeping arrangements, the Army was expected to fight and this was definitely not my bag.

Somehow, the idea of getting shot at, while laying face down in the mud, just didn't turn me on. If I was going to have to go to war, it would be in a civilized manner or not at all.

The Navy looked great, I had always loved boats and was only seasick once in my life. A friend took me down to the Brooklyn Navy Yard and used his influence to get me on board a Destroyer. To him, this was the Ideal Duty. Loose protocol, and lots of good clean hard work with a minimum of Chicken ----.

I had almost made up my mind to follow his advice, when I got a good close look at the sleeping arrangements on the ship. Suddenly, I had a mental nightmare of trying to get a good nights sleep with my oversized six foot, four inch, frame draped over either end of a six-foot long hammock. Much as I loved the sea, I regrettably ruled out the Navy.

The Marines were out, because they did the fighting for the Navy. I really wasn't mad at anyone and I had always found fighting was best left to someone who knew more about it than I did. Preferably, someone much shorter and more aggressive than me. Once again, the Marines did a lot of sleeping in pup-tents, and hammocks. I just simply didn't fit in there either.

This left the Air Force. Now here was an outfit I could relate to. They slept in buildings, on real beds and from what I heard, the food wasn't bad at all. They appeared to have all the comforts of home. To make the package complete, the Air Force was not expected to fight. They dropped bombs and sent up fighter planes.

This was a much more civilized way to fight a war, no nasty hand to hand combat stuff and no pointing guns at one another. This was definitely the branch of the Branch of the Armed Service for me.

It was the first major decision I had made totally on my own. Unfortunately, it went completely against what my father had in mind for me. As a matter of fact it went against what the entire family wanted me to do.

All too soon it was September. Summer vacation was over and it was time to take the plunge. I marched myself into the recruiting station in Mt. Vernon, New York, filled out the paper work and signed my name on the dotted line. This part of the process was quite simple.

In a fit of rage my father disowned me forever. I had never seen him so mad in all my life. Except possibly, the time I had tried to climb a tree with the family car. The car failed to climb the tree. Upon reaching the stump of the tree the car stopped, through to no lack of effort on my part. With a loud crash, it stopped and refused to move any further up the tree.

I have often wondered if he would have been quite as mad if the car had made it to the top of the tree. Oddly enough, I never got up the nerve to ask him this question. At the time the situation seemed best left alone to quiet down.

I never quite understood his attitude. He was rid of me for four years. He should have been happy. I was part of the Air Force now. I have often wondered if he thought the Air Force might hold him responsible for what he thought I might do. In my opinion, he should have been glad to get rid of me.

My mother, on the other hand, bought a bottle of champagne and together we had a champagne breakfast on the day I left for my first day in the Air force. Just between you and me, I think she bought the champagne to celebrate getting rid of me. She was just a little too happy to see me go. Whatever the case, both of my parents would now get some much needed rest.

I took the train to New York City, arriving at the induction center right on time. I was sworn in with a bunch of other guys from the New York area and we all took a few minutes to get acquainted.

Then I got sick. It was just my kind of luck. The rest of the bunch, I had been with, moved on to basic training in Texas without me. I was left alone at the mercy of my first military doctor. I had the most awful stomach pains, I felt like I had swallowed a watermelon and it was growing inside me, it was either this or I was pregnant and about to give birth.

At any rate, I was sure death was only moments away. The only good part of it was, I was now the property of the U.S. Air Force and it was up to them to set about fixing me.

The doctors poked and probed for a few minutes before telling me I had, **Acute Gastritis**. Never having even heard of Gastritis before, much less Acute Gastritis, I was convinced I was terminally ill.

I had visions of the doctors standing over my prostrate body as I lay on an operating table. They were about to remove the gastritis, or whatever it was. It was to be a long and painful operation during which, no anesthetic of any kind could be used.

The Gastritis felt so large, I knew in my heart, it couldn't be removed any other way but by surgery. Pasted on the ceiling over the operating table was a document proclaiming the doctor was a graduate of the Marque DeSade School of Internal Medicine and Surgery.

Just about the time I had convinced myself the Gastritis was incurable and Acute Gastritis meant a long painful death was eminent, I gave up a mighty belch. The doctors all turned toward me and stared. I was sure the end was near. A funny thing though, I suddenly felt much better. It was only then, one of the doctors explained to me just what gastritis was.

Thus, my first day in the Armed Forces was spent on sick call. I was off to a great start.

Later, I realized the gas from the champagne my mother had given me, had become trapped under the greasy eggs and bacon I had eaten for breakfast. All this greasy food had fused together like a giant cork in my stomach and had remained there, until I went on sick call. To this day, I drink champagne only with the utmost care and only after meals.

On my first leave from the service I went home only to be physically attacked by a man I had thought was my friend. I have often wondered if my selection of the Air Force over his desire for me to go Navy is what triggered my friend's attack on me. I never did find out exactly why he attacked me.

He had been hired by my family as a companion for my younger brother who had been stricken with Polio. He left shortly after the this and we never heard another word from him.

Nopo San

Chapter 2

Basic Training

I was thrown in with a new group of recruits headed for Williams Air Force Base in Upstate New York. These guys were all strange foreigners from a land far, far away called, Chicago. They were not a bad lot, just different.

Basic training was to be carried out at Williams Air Force Base, in the scenic Finger Lakes Region of Mid Western New York State. I think Williams was the only Air Force Base in the world which had no runway of any kind. There were a few planes scattered about which had been brought there by truck. Their wheels had been cast into cement pads and their engines removed. The poor planes were doomed to stay on Williams A. F. B. forever. I truly felt sorry for them.

Looking at those planes standing there, their wheels sunk deep into the concrete and their engines gone. It made me wonder just whom the Air Force thought was going to steal the planes? Much less how they thought, the perpetrator was going to get them off the base? A T-33 air craft is a little hard to hide under your coat.

Then again, what would you do with it if you did manage to swipe one? It's kind of like a dog chasing a car, what would he do with it if he caught it?

I knew the area well. I had attended a boarding school on Seneca Lake several years before. My biggest fear was, the railroad officials might remember my name or face if I ever got anywhere near town.

While at the boarding school, a few of my friends and I greased about a half mile of up-hill rail-road track. Even though the school made us clean the grease off the tracks, the railroad officials and the school officials still failed to see the humor in our prank.

I even knew a few girls in the area, but I would have no opportunity to call them during Basic Training. Besides, I had a girl friend from High School. I had intended to ask her to marry me, as soon as I got out of Basic Training.

According to history, Williams was originally an Army training base. The Army used it all during the Second World War. Then they decided it was unfit for human habitation.

They gave it to the Navy. The Navy promptly painted it grey. After a year or so of trying to use it as a training base. They also decided it was unfit for human habitation. The Navy abandoned the place, shortly after they finished painting it all grey.

No one else wanted the place, so they made the Air Force take it. The Air Force had just separated from the Army a few years prior and it was going through growing pains. Getting the base handed over to the Air Force must have been the Army's revenge for the Air Force leaving their fold.

The Air Force wasn't sure whether or not Williams was fit for human habitation either. However, it was all they had at the time. In their infinite wisdom, the Air Force sent me and a lot of other guys there to find out if it was fit for human habitation for them. From day one on, the situation was in serious doubt.

Of course, I had lots of good company, there were thousands of other guys there with me. We were all equally convinced the Air Force had singled us out for cruel and inhumane treatment.

No matter how hard you stretch the truth. I don't think there is any way you could come up with the idea this attitude put me a notch above any of my fellow sufferers. We all did as we were told to do, or else, and we all suffered alike.

We were issued Army, olive drab blankets to put on the things we had to use as bunks. We had to scavenge around to find the parts needed to make one complete bunk if we wanted to sleep comfortably. At least comfortable by Air Force standards. Everything else we were issued had been very well used.

By the grace of God and little else, we all made it through Basic Training. Just like those who went before us and like those who were destined to follow. Little did we know, the Air Force was about to abandon the place and we were among the last few recruits to be put through Williams Air Force Base, before they closed it.

Shortly after they closed Williams Air Force base, they gave it to the Boy Scouts for a summer camp. Of course, they waited until after we finished Basic Training. It seems even the Air Force thought the place was unfit for human habitation. We could have told them if only they had a mind to ask us.

Basic Training was not really hard to take, but one did have to work at it to stay up with the other guys. It was kind of like a boarding school where you were told what to do and when to do it every moment of the day and night. This was Old Hat to me, I had been to tougher boarding schools than this was.

The purpose, of all this, was to get the new recruit used to taking orders without question. In most cases it worked. There are, however, those of us who were by some divine decree, destined not to fit in. In our group it was, Billy Howard.

Billy was about medium height, maybe one hundred ten pounds. Brown unkept hair and big thick glasses. I think it was because of the glasses, I can't remember what color his eyes were. Looking back through his glasses you could just barely see his eyes in there. They were just little tiny slits. He almost looked Oriental, but I'm quite sure he wasn't. Maybe the fact I'm color-blind had something to do with it. Somehow I just can't remember his eyes, just those huge thick glasses.

His voice was a piercing high-pitched whine. It penetrated even the most carefully placed ear plugs. He whined all the time. Not just once in a while like most of the rest of us did. This guy never shut up.

The most striking feature about Howard was his face, it was round. Not oval or long like most faces, his was round. From the sides of this round face, huge ears protruded. They stuck straight out from his head. He almost looked like he could fly in a good wind storm. He looked a lot like the "What Me Worry Kid" from "Mad Comics", way back in the old days.

Howard joined our little group after being thrown out of another group. It seems the other group was going to kill him. Just why the Air Force thought our group was going to be any different, is something I will never understand.

The reason Howard was so unpopular, was because he would not change his clothing, bedding, shoes, socks, or underwear. He would not wash, shave, comb his hair or make up his own bed. In short, he would do nothing to help himself or anyone else.

Under ordinary circumstances and in civilian life, Howard could have been ignored. Unfortunately for Howard, during basic training, punishment for the sins of one are visited on the group. We all had to pay the price for his sins.

The rest of the group tried to help the Howard at first. Then, when it was obvious no amount of help was going to do any good, the rest of the group turned to violence. I abstained from this part of what was hoped would be Howard's education.

Unfortunately, violence didn't work either. Howard hung in there, like grim death. I had to admire the guy for this alone.

I even tried to help him fit in, but Howard was determined to pull in the opposite direction. He was a sad case if ever there was one. How he ever got into the service in the first place, is still a wonder to me.

Unless of course, someone paid big bucks to buy him a place in the service just to get him out of the house. There was always the remote possibility someone had abandoned him on the front doorstep of an Air Force recruiting station.

One day I sat down with Howard and tried to help him. I made a genuine effort to try to help the kid. I asked him why he wouldn't get involved like the rest of us. He told me his mother had always done everything for him. His mother had apparently done all the things for him, he was now expected to do for himself.

Somehow, he just couldn't get it through his head his mother was no longer there to do these things for him. He would now have to start doing them for himself. In all, I spent several hours talking to him over a period of several days.

The upshot of the whole thing was, he just wouldn't change his ways. He seemed to be convinced if he didn't do for himself, someone would come along and do it for him. This, of course, was not the Air Force way.

Poor Howard, his life during Basic Training must have been a nightmare. The other fellows, unable to stand the smell, gave him a G.I. Shower about once a week. Using scrub brushes, they would hold Howard down on the shower room floor and scrub him from head to toe.

Then there were those other unpleasant things done to try to get Howard out of our group. He was isolated. No one would talk to him. His bunk would be turned upside down in the middle of the night, with him in it. He was doused with buckets of water as he slept, and so on. Nothing worked. Howard was destined to be with us, unchanged, until the end of Basic Training.

It would be unfair of me to say Howard never tried to fit in. He wasn't a bad sort, just misdirected. I can remember one time, just before a big inspection. Howard decided the walls of his room were dirty. Indeed they were dirty, as were the walls in all the rest of the rooms.

Howard decided to wash his walls and show the rest of us up. What he didn't know was, the paint on the walls was a poor grade of water color. As were the layers of different colored paint under it. He apparently worked very hard during the night while the rest of us slept. The old paint flowed off the walls and onto the floor in a technicolor nightmare.

By morning, his multi-colored footprints led back and forth to the bathroom, where he had gotten the soap and water to do the job. There were blue footprints, brown footprints, yellow footprints, and so on, all up and down the entire length of the hallway and into the bathroom.

The end result was a psychedelic nightmare. It flowed down the walls onto the floor and out into the hall, the rest of us had worked so hard to get clean.

The bathroom fortunately, had a cement floor and could be cleaned up before the inspection. The rest of the mess, to the best of my knowledge, is still there.

Howard had apparently tried to wash some of his paint spattered clothing before the inspection. The laundry room was also a disaster area. Paint had been splattered everywhere. Exactly what was going through Howard's head while he made this mess is still unclear. Obviously he thought he was helping and trying to fit in with the rest of us.

The Hall Guard told us he had gone down stairs for a cigarette and gotten involved in a conversation with the downstairs hall guard while all this was going on. When he saw the mess Howard had made, he woke the rest of us up. But it was simply too late to do anything about it.

Personally, I think maybe the Hall Guard had found himself a nice quiet corner and gone to sleep. There was just too much of a mess to been made in the five or ten minutes it takes to smoke a cigarette.

I will never forget the expression on the face of the inspecting officer. When he got to Howard's room his jaw dropped open, his eyes grew wide with a totally incredible expression. He muttered loud enough for all of us to hear, "What in God's name happened here?"

I have always considered myself to be a reasonable tolerant person. But as I looked out of my room at the mess Howard had stayed up all night to create. I have to admit, as tolerant as I tried to be, even I was seized with the urge to destroy Billy Howard.

I couldn't help wondering what kind of punishment the Air Force would heap on us, if we severed Howard's head, mounted it on a long pole and marched around the area with it. It would have been just like they did in the movies about the French Revolution.

There were others among us, who had gone on beyond the

wondering stage and had to be restrained. In our ranks, I'm sure there would have been a medal in it for the perpetrator. The Air Force unfortunately, might just see things differently.

Howard, on the other hand, couldn't understand why the rest of us were so mad. After all, hadn't he gone "beyond all expectations" and washed the walls of his rooms, all by himself? The rest of us were all very happy to see he was so willing to take all the blame. However, this was the **only** thing we were happy about.

Little did I know, in the end Billy Howard, would go on to Tech School and I would be left sitting by myself in an empty barracks. Such is the way of life in the Military.

Now mind you, this didn't mean we didn't have any fun during Basic Training. There were the standard things everyone does. I will limit this story to the spectacular and leave the mundane to your imagination.

I remember one incident when some **unnamed person** dumped a whole box of **Super Soap** into one of the tumble action, washing machines in our barracks. Now this was spectacular!

Picture, if you will, the expression on the Sergeant's face when he stepped out of his room, on his way out to a date, without looking. By the time he realized what was happening, he was belt deep in the suds. His dress uniform was instantly soaked with soapy water from the belt down. He was one unhappy Sergeant.

His girl friend was not at all happy about the situation either. They were to have met at a secluded location, with no phone. We found out later she had waited a whole hour for him before she stormed off never to see our Sergeant again.

Believe it or not, the Sergeant wasn't mad for long. In fact, he threw a party for us. It was called a **G.I. Party**, and it lasted all night long. For those of you who have never been to one, a G.I. Party is where you are told to clean every inch of your barracks, usually as a punishment, and usually with your toothbrush.

The experience was designed to teach the recruit any transgressions against authority was not permitted. Loading the washing machine with a whole box of Super Soap was considered a transgression against authority, especially when the authority got his best uniform soaked in dirty soap suds.

By morning, everything which could be cleaned, had been cleaned, and we were left with about fifteen minutes to clean out what was left of our toothbrushes before breakfast. It was a learning experience.

Nopo San

Chapter 3

Bivouac

I guess, after learning a bitter lesson in Korea, the Air Force decided to follow the Army way of training a bit more closely. With this idea in mind, we were to be subjected to the rigors of a real Army type **Bivouac**. It was supposed to toughen us up a little and prepare us for the hardships of actual combat conditions.

It was getting close to the end of my basic training period, but if bivouac was anything like the rest of the training I had received to date, this was going to be a snap.

I had been a Boy Scout under an ex-ranger, who had lost an eye at the Normandy landing. When my old Scout Master said we were going to Bivouac, it was a lesson in survival. At least, in this one area, I felt I was better prepared than most of the other guys. As a matter of fact we got more training in hand to hand combat in the Boy Scouts than I ever got in the Air Force.

Unfortunately, our beloved Scout Master was forced to leave the Boy Scouts. He was told it was inappropriate for him to be teaching us Commando Tactics, Judo, Knife Fighting and Hand to Hand Combat in the front yard of the church where we had our meetings. If I do have to say so myself by the time he was finished with us, we were pretty darn good at it all.

Most of the other fellows in my group had never slept outside a house before, much less, on the ground without a bed. As a matter of fact as I listened to the other fellows talk, I got the impression there was no unpaved ground left in Chicago.

On the chosen day, we all packed our gear and made ready for what appeared to be, a glorified Boy Scout camp-out. I was really looking forward to the experience. It was my first opportunity to do anything that even smacked of hardship since joining the Air Force. Except maybe the time on sick call my very first day in the Air Force. Or possibly avoiding food poisoning at the chow hall in our area.

At four o'clock in the morning, we formed ranks and headed out to the bivouac site. Aside from the early hour, it looked like it was going to be a fun day. The weather was overcast and there was a light-drizzle. A little rain never hurt anyone. We were going to play Army with real soldier stuff.

There was no way I was going to fit into this stuff but it was going to be a good time anyhow. We marched to an isolated area of the base, where we unpacked our tents and made camp. Due to my size, I had been assigned to sleep with three other guys in a four-man Pup-tent.

Of course, there was no way the Air Force could stretch the blankets, so I was going to have to sleep with my shoes and socks on. I had anticipated this and brought extra dry socks with me. Just like any good Ex-Boy Scout, I was prepared.

By eight o'clock, we were attending classes again, only this time we were wearing steel helmets and the classes were out of doors in the rain. This was real Army stuff, and it was fun.

We got to see explosives at work. An Explosives Expert wound some Primer Cord around a one gallon can of gasoline and touched it off. I could just imagine a Fourth of July with this stuff. **Wow!**

I had never eaten in a Field Kitchen before. It's like an outside Chow Hall with just about the same associated risk of food poisoning. After taking your Mess Kit off your belt, you dunked it into a 55-gallon garbage pail of hot water. This was supposed to get any grease and the grey filmy looking stuff off it.

Then, you moved down a Chow Line where food was dumped, without ceremony, into the various compartments of your mess kit. I now know exactly why it's called a **mess kit**.

Breakfast was an experiment in culinary disaster. Greasy fried eggs, drizzled on by a cold, wet, rain seemed to turn to lead. Bacon, like wise drizzled upon, bore no resemblance to what it was supposed to look or taste like. The fried potatoes, fused together by the grease they were cooked in, could not be eaten. Eating Cereal Flakes and milk in a rain storm became an exercise in seamanship.

Lunch was a little better, it had warmed up just enough to keep the greasy blobs floating on the food from becoming solidified. It was still raining but what the heck, there was the whole out of doors to eat in.

The mashed potatoes became soup. Soup became, ----- I really don't know what you'd call it. The peas floated off the sides of the mess kit, as you tried to eat them. The coffee no longer looked or tasted anything like coffee. I didn't even try to save the Ice Cream.

Under actual combat conditions, if the enemy was simply to leave us alone. We would probably poison ourselves in a relatively short period of time. I now know for sure where the expression, "The Army moves on its stomach, the Air Force flies by the seat of its pants", comes from.

Eating all this cold greasy food was like swallowing a can of liquid pipe cleaner. The trail to the outdoor latrine was well marked by those who didn't make it in time.

We were even given carbines and real bullets to put in them. I suppose the idea was to try to get us to the point where we knew which end of the gun we were to put the bullets into. Here again, the boys from the big city hadn't had much experience with any kind of gun much less a military weapon.

The instructor told us to shoot toward the targets and try to hit them. Above all, **don't point your weapon at the guy next to you!** Somehow, I got the impression they didn't expect very much from us on the range. In actuality, it was only by the grace of God and not much else, no one was killed.

When it was time for Billy Howard to take his turn, I can remember watching as the Range Officer dove into the safety ditch with us. Suddenly, alone on the firing line with a loaded gun in his hands Howard panicked. He dropped the gun which promptly went off, the bullet narrowly missing his head. He then ran away leaving his weapon laying there on the range.

It took us several hours to find the guy and he had to be forced back to the firing line. This time however, someone else shot the gun for him. The poor guy was absolutely hopeless.

Last, but not least, we sat in a little room and the Air Force exposed us to some of the various gasses which might be used in warfare. Somehow I think their information was somewhat dated. They let us sniff Phosgene, Tear Gas, and a little Mustard Gas.

According to the military books I read, this kind of stuff went out with the First World War. The New Generation was into Nerve Gas, Germ Warfare, and other such agents designed to eliminate the enemy rather than just slowing them up a little.

I was not however, disappointed we missed exposure to these modern items of warfare. It was my firm opinion we already had enough exposure to modern germ warfare. After all we did have to eat in the chow hall each day. This should have been enough to make us fairly resistant to most of the more deadly forms of modern day killer bugs.

Later in the evening, the real fun and games started. We were given positions along a perimeter and told a password with a counter sign. According to our instructor, we were to maintain our positions until relieved and challenge anyone who approached us. This was supposed to show us what real warfare was all about.

After dark, we could hear people moving about out there, but no one ever came by our position. I was almost disappointed, I was really looking forward to catching someone.

In order to add a sense of realism to the situation, there was someone out there throwing fire crackers at us, when and if they could get their cigarette lighter to work in all the rain. I really got a kick out of it.

Our Boy Scout Troop used to do things like this way back when. Only we had other fellows from our troop out there trying to grab us. If caught, we were tied with rope and kept as prisoners. As a general rule, there was no adherence to the terms of the Geneva Convention by our Boy Scout Troop. I can safely say our Boy

Scout Troop Bivouac was one heck of a lot rougher than this Air Force Bivouac was.

At about twelve midnight, the order came through to head for the tents and some much needed sleep. The rain had stopped. But no matter how I tried, there was just no way I could get comfortable in the equipment the Air Force had gotten from the Army. It just firmed my resolve about the Army. Boy! Was I ever glad I didn't have to contend with this on a daily basis.

It was cold to begin with but as the night wore on, it got even colder. At last a jeep pulled into our area and there was a hushed conversation about the weather. There was talk about how the camp should be struck and the men sent to the Barracks.

The word spread like wild fire. We were going back to the barracks. Somewhere along the line the **word** became an order. Like a tribe of desert nomads we struck our tents and headed for the barracks without any official order being given.

The three fellows I was with split up the stuff and lit out with the rest of the guys. I was given the job of carrying the tent, as I was the largest of the group. I didn't mind, someone else had to carry all the rest of the gear. It had taken us several hours to set this site up. It was disassembled and packed away in less than five minutes.

Some of the other guys lost their way and had to be rounded up by the Air Police as they straggled about the base looking for our area. These guys from the big city were totally lost without street signs.

The Sergeant arrived soon after the last of our little group straggled in. To say the Sergeant was a little unhappy, would be the understatement of the year. He raged at us, telling us we had no business turning out and going to the barracks without orders from him.

He had apparently been out of the area when the orders came through. When he got back we were gone. I marked this one down in my book for future use, When a Sergeant loses his command and can't find his men, he gets testy. It was another learning experience.

Please don't ask me why, but at this point in by brand new military career, I decided to get drunk out of my mind. I had no real reason and I didn't like the taste of whiskey at all. Like I said, I don't know why, I just did.

While away from Base, on my very first three day pass, I bought a quart of whiskey. I brought it back to base with me and then all in one night, drank the whole darn thing.

I can remember being held down on the floor There were two guys trying to knock me out before the Sergeant found me. I was dragged up stairs to the shower and thrown into a shower stall. Then, while three or four of my comrades tried to hold me in, the cold water was turned on.

There was just no way I was going to take a cold shower. While trying not to hurt anyone, I bashed my way out of the back of the stall. There was very little left of the shower stall when I was finished.

Later in the night, I can remember having a call of nature. I got up out of my bunk and started for the bathroom. In the hall I was stopped by the Hall Guard, who's job it was to stand by in the hall and watch for fires in the barracks.

I think it only fair to point out at this time, it was estimated it would only take about three minutes for the entire Flight to get up out of bed, grab something to wear and get out of the building. It was also estimated, once started, a fire would burn the building to the ground in something like ten minutes. This really didn't leave a whole heck of a big margin of safety.

However, it did serve to make those who smoked, very careful with matches. I didn't have to worry about this, I didn't start to smoke until I got out of the service.

Anyhow, this Hall Guard stopped me and said, "I got orders. You are not to go anywhere. Now go back to bed and stay there."

I looked him straight in the eye and said, "It took at least two of you guys to knock me out while I was drunk. You saw what

I did to the shower stall. Now you're telling me, little old you is going to stop me from going to the bathroom?"

There was no further argument from the Hall Guard.

The next day, I missed a whole day of classes. I was so hung-over my comrades put me in back of a row of lockers to sleep it off. They told me to keep very quiet and no one would find me.

At one point, I woke up to find someone looking back in behind the lockers at me I think it was our C.O., but I will never be sure. It could have been a dream, but I don't think so. I never heard another word about it. Luck was sure with me this time. The next bout I had with whiskey, nearly killed me.

However, it wasn't until after Basic Training when things really got interesting. I had signed up for Weapons Maintenance and, like the others guys, sat around in the barracks waiting for orders, when basic training was completed.

One by one, the other guys packed their bags and left. Even Billy Howard got orders sending him on to some kind of school, I don't remember which one. At the end of two days, I found myself sitting alone in an empty barracks. There just had to be something wrong. I went up to the H.Q. and presented myself. I asked where my orders were.

Without any punch pulling, they laid it on me. I was told the records showed I had lied on my enlistment application and I was waiting to be discharged as an undesirable.

Nopo San

Chapter 4

Fire Guard

I couldn't believe what I was listening to. These people said I had a criminal record a mile long and I had lied about it when I enlisted. There was no question about the fact I was never known as a great student but to call my efforts in High School criminal, was going too far.

I called my mother and told her what was going on. My father, who by this time was no longer mad at me, hired a lawyer. After a long and difficult investigation, it was found some clerk somewhere had attached the wrong record to my file. Poor dad, I guess once I was out of the house he found the peace and quiet was so nice , he would go to any lengths to keep me in the service.

The way I understood it, there was another person with the same name as mine who enlisted about the same time as I did. Somehow, our records got switched somewhere along the line. As soon as the error was brought to light, my orders were cut on the spot and I was off to Tech School.

At least, this is the way the official record reads. There were, however, a few months spent in limbo waiting for all this investigation and stuff to take place. It was during this time, my real Air Force career began.

I was made a Fire Guard. I bet you're thinking being a Fire Guard means you stand around with a hose in your hands and watch things burn up. No such luck. It meant I was to service several coal fired boilers which heated the barracks my comrades and I lived in. Now this could get interesting.

In the beginning, I was given a line of six buildings to take care of. I didn't mind. What the heck, I had nothing else to do. At least, I would be warm and I wasn't on K.P. It was kind of fun.

I had never even seen a coal fired boiler before in my life.

Now, here I was, in charge of six of the things. I had absolutely no idea what to do with them and no training. I kind of figured things out quickly.

The idea was to keep shoveling enough coal into them to keep the fires going and haul the ash out in the cans provided. Even though the furnaces had automatic coal feeders on them, the coal would freeze solid in the bin and have to be broken up a bit before it would go into the feeder.

One of the other fellows finally told me, two or three times a night I had to make the rounds of each building, knock the "clinkers" off the grates, carry out the ashes, and in general make sure everything was running okay, it was really quite easy. Although I had no idea what a clinker was. I managed to figure this one out quickly.

If the fire looked bad or was out, I had to restart it before the barracks got cold. If the barracks did get cold, I would be moved from the Fire Guard, to the K.P. roster. This would never do.

Now the Navy, in their infinite wisdom, had left several little surprises for us. For instance, there were two boilers in each building. One to make heat and the other to make hot water. The cold water pipe which supplied the toilets, drinking fountains, and other cold water applications ran right over and close to the heating boiler. On cold days, and nights, the heating boiler had to really be fired up, because none of the buildings were insulated.

The heat rising up from the un-insulated heating boiler, would super-heat the cold water pipe while the water was not being used. Fun city came, when the new recruits returned from training, or got up in the middle of the night to get a drink of water. Anytime the cold water had not been used for a while, the heat from the heating boiler would turn the water in the pipe to super heated steam.

The water pressure kept the super-heated water from becoming steam until it got to the valve. Then when the poor soul tried to get a drink of cold water from the drinking fountain, or worse yet, flushed the toilet while still seated. A blast of live steam would come out instead of cold water. I kid you not, there were times when those furnaces glowed red hot when the weather got really cold.

After several weeks of taking care of the six buildings, I was taken off this assignment and put in charge of one big building. This new building housed four groups, or flights as they were called, instead of two flights as in each in the other six buildings. I don't know why they did this but it made little difference to me. The one big building did have to be serviced more often. I suppose as they were closing the base down, they just didn't need all those buildings heated any more.

In this building there was a boiler instead of a hot air furnaces as had been in the other six buildings. In this one boiler, the coal had to have the coal shoveled in by hand. In all the boilers there was an automatic coal feeder. It was a neat thing to play with but it did cause problems when the fire went out and the coal continued to feed into the furnace.

This new boiler was so big it took more coal and burned it faster, than its smaller counterparts. I kind of enjoyed taking care of this one huge boiler. I made a pet out of the thing. I even polished all of the gauges. I kept the fire in the boiler as perfect as I knew how to. No one had ever taken the trouble to explain the operation of a boiler to me, so I had to learn as I worked. Playing with a boiler was a lot more fun than fooling around with those hot air furnaces.

Things went along just fine for about two or three weeks Then one day when I arrived to service the boiler, I found the coal-bin full to overflowing with a bunch of dirty looking stuff. It wasn't a clean black, like the other coal had been. This stuff was a larger lump and it looked like it had soot all over it.

I took a lump over to the H.Q. and attempted to hand it to my C.O. "What's this stuff?" I asked "It doesn't look like the other coal I was using."

"It's soft coal, dummy. Figure it out for yourself. Now, get back to your boiler and leave me alone, I got work to do." was the reply as he backed gingerly away from the lump of coal in my outstretched hand.

I looked around, everyone in the office had heard what he said. They looked at me though sorrowful eyes but no one offered to help. His attitude was one of complete indifference. However, it made no difference to me, it wasn't my boiler.

Returning to my building, I threw the dirty lump into the fire box and watched it burn. It burned with a pretty yellow fire but it sure didn't look like it was giving up much heat. I knew if the building got cold I would go on K.P., this I didn't want. I had been told to figure it out for myself, and this is exactly what I did.

Bear in mind, I had never in all my life even seen soft coal. I had no idea what it was supposed to do. Going on sheer instinct, I got out the shovel and heaped the new soft coal into the furnace, until there was a unbroken line of coal from just inside the fire door to where the flue pipe exited the furnace.

I then closed the fire doors and opened the ash-pit door. This bypassed the damper control and allowed a full un-obstructed flow of air to pass up through the coal. The fire could now burn as fast as it wanted to and would not be restricted in any way. In other words, it was now totally out of control. As I left the boiler-room, I thought to myself, "This will keep-um warm!"

In retrospect; if I had left the ash pit doors closed, I would have been alright. The damper control was attached to the ash pit door. But I figured this new coal would need all the air it could get, so I left it open.

After seeing to my boiler, wiping down the gauges, sweeping the floor and blowing down the automatic water feeder, I took one last look into the fire box. The fire had not yet come up through the coal. I closed the boiler-room door and went to chow. I figured by the time I had finished the evening meal, the boiler would have done its thing. Then I would have a much better idea of just how often I would have to put more coal into it.

I really enjoyed going to the Chow Hall on Williams

A.F.B. It was a true life threatening experience, day after day I survived it. After all, would you voluntarily go to a restaurant, which had an ambulance on permanent duty station right outside the front door? Well this place had one. Unfortunately, it was the only game in town.

There was at least, one case of food poisoning at each meal, sometimes more. The ambulance drivers were never bored. After each meal, it gave me great pleasure to walk by the ambulance and know once again, I had cheated death.

Today however, as I left the Chow Hall a fire truck flew past the place going in the general direction of my one big building. I thought to myself, "Sure hope it isn't my place burning down."

Turning the corner on the street which led up to my building, I was greeted with a unique sight. In spite of the cool ten degree temperature, people clad only in their underwear, towels, or even less, were streaming out of the building in panic. They were diving headfirst into the ditch across the street. The ditch was full of ice and snow but no one seemed to care. To me it looked like a full scale route.

There was live steam belching from all the open windows. Occasionally something inside the building would burst with a loud **boom!**. Although the word boom seems kind of pale when compared to the real thing. More steam would then belch out from some new point. It was obvious now, the low rumbling noise was coming from my boiler.

Picking up my pace, I arrived on the scene, just as one of the firemen said, "Get out of here quick! It's going to blow at any moment!"

There was a red glow pulsating from the boiler room and huge bursts of steam streamed out of the boiler room door-way. The door had apparently already been blown clean off its hinges by the force of some earlier happening.

This would not have been hard, as the door had seen better days many moons ago. Now, judging from the pile of wreckage at the bottom of the stairs, the only thing left for this door was a decent burial.

As I started toward the boiler-room, a fireman grabbed me and said, "Don't go down there! It's ready to blow! Can't you see all the smoke and steam?"

At the time, I had nothing better to do, so I shrugged him off and proceeded down the stairs toward the boiler room. After all, it was my pet boiler and I wanted to see what was going on.

At the top of the stairs leading down to the boiler, it was obvious I would need something to keep the steam off me. Although there was there was lots of steam billowing up the stairs there seemed to be a clear area down close to the ground. I peeled off my field jacket, put it over my head and fumbled my way down the steps on my hands and knees through the steam. It really looked a lot worse than it was. I was quite safe because of the cold air near the floor.

Once inside the boiler room though, I was treated to a scene straight from Hell. Parts of the outside walls of the boiler, had been blown off and the inside walls were cherry red. There was water dripping from everything, and as the drops hit the glowing boiler, they flashed into steam with a bang.

Water was dropping back down through the main steam header. When it hit the red hot top of the boiler, it was blasted back up the pipe with a loud roar. I guessed this was what had been bursting the radiators in the building. Everything was so old, it wouldn't take much to burst them. According to the gage on the boiler, anything over five pounds of steam pressure was considered dangerous.

There was about an inch of rusty mud on the floor. The stuff was so slippery all I could do was crawl along on my hands and knees. It's probably a good thing I stayed down. If I had tried to stand I would have gotten a face full of live steam as the water dropped back down the steam header and flashed on the top of the boiler.

Crawling along on the floor, I got to the ash-pit door and

pushed it closed with the coal shovel. Then, I opened the fire box door with the shovel and looked inside.

The grates were gone. They had melted down into the ash-pit. All the soft coal, which had burned with such a pretty yellow flame, was now a white hot mass projected such heat, it singed the hair on my hands and face from a shovel length away.

Almost at once, the change in draft began the long process of cooling the furnace down to its normal temperature. One thing was very obvious right from the start, this piece of junk would never make steam again.

It took about two hours to get the fire banked back and the rest of the things back under some sort of reasonable control. Then I killed the fire in what was left of my boiler with water from a short garden hose I kept in the boiler room to control the coal dust.

As I left the boiler room for the last time, I couldn't help wondering what the Air Force was going to do to me for this.

There was no electricity in the building and the recruits had long since packed up and moved to another barracks. As I stumbled up the stairs from the boiler room in the dark, I almost ran headlong into my "friend" the C.O., the man I had spoken to earlier in the H.Q.

His eyes were round with fear, as he looked at me through the dark. He was looking at me as if he were looking at a ghost. "Are you going to tell them what I said to you about the coal?" He mumbled on, in a croaking voice, "If they find out how this happened I'm finished in the Air Force."

Looking through the darkness at this hapless hunk of humanity, I experienced the power of life of death over an individual, whose rank was higher than mine. I smiled my kindest smile. Then through clenched teeth, I asked quietly, "Are you going to cut my orders and get me off this God Forsaken Base? There were witnesses to what you said!"

There seemed to be a mutual understanding between us, so I left him standing there in the dark with his thoughts. I returned to my building, took a shower and hit the sack. Frankly, I was all used up for the day.

The year I went through basic training was the year, fifty percent of the male population on the base came down with Pneumonia. The other fifty percent, which included me, wound up with Chronic Bronchitis. It became a living memory of my first few months in the service of my country. I am not bitter about this. It's the chance one takes in the service. In fact, I consider myself lucky. There were a lot of other guys who didn't get back at all.

During the months of January and February, the word cold took on new meaning for the personnel at Williams. It was not unusual to wake up in the morning with as much as two inches of snow on top of the blanket on your bunk with the window closed.

There was one formation called at four o'clock in the morning. We stood waiting in a drizzling rain and sleet storm for over an hour. At last we were informed the officer who was supposed to inspect the formation had overslept and we should all go back to our barracks.

After standing still for so long, our uniforms had frozen in place and as we tried to move out the whole group of us made the strangest noise. If I remember correctly, there were over one-hundred cases of frost bite on sick call on this one day. Nothing major, mind you, just superficial and painful.

About the only way to keep warm during the months of January and February, on Williams A.F.B. was to sleep between two mattresses. I was lucky enough to have a spare key to the supply barracks. Getting the extra mattresses was no problem for me. The two blankets we had been issued simply were not enough to keep warm with.

The big trick was to keep the top mattress from falling off while you slept. It was not at all unusual to find snow on top of the mattress in the morning, even if the window was closed. Snow blew in freely around the window, with just the slightest breeze. It was at this point in my Military Training, I learned the "Secret of the Soda Machine". Over in the supply barracks, there was a Soda Machine it hardly ever had any soda in it. I couldn't understand why in the world a Soda Machine in a locked barracks was always out of soda.

There was a red light, at the top of the machine which indicated the machine was out of soda. The light was always broken out and again, I couldn't understand why. Then one day, an unnamed friend of mine explained the thing to me.

It seemed if some, unnamed person was to take the wooden rod from the bottom of a wooden coat hanger. This unnamed person could poke it into the machine through the broken light just far enough to push the reset button.

Each time the reset button was pushed, the pusher got a free soda and fifteen-cents change. I had never liked the brand of soda very much but if someone was going to give me fifteen cents to drink it, why not? If all you wanted was a soda, there were several cases of the stuff stacked right next to the machine. It was warm, but it was free.

The morning after the thing with the boiler, I woke to find three inches of snow on top of the mattress I was sleeping under. Someone was shaking my bunk. It was my C.O. and "friend" from the H.Q.

Without a word, he handed me a stack of papers with my name on them, and left. My bag was already packed and I was ready to go. I kicked the snow off my top mattress and got dressed. On my way out the front door, I gave my room to some worthy soul who was just moving into the barracks.

By noon I was on a train headed home for ten days leave. They gave me the leave before I had to report in at Lowery A.F.B. in Denver, Colorado, to begin training in Weapons Maintenance.

Basic Training was finally over. The Air Force closed Williams A.F.B. and gave it to the Boy Scouts. I never saw the C.O. again nor did I ever hear from or about him. No one ever even asked me how the boiler blew up, but then again, I really didn't expect them to. This part of the fiasco would have been taken care of by my friend the C.O. He would be very careful not to let anyone get to me for my side of the story.

Nopo San

Chapter 5

Fire Guard --- Again?

I arrived at Lowery A.F.B. in Denver, Colorado, in March, of 1950. It was still cold, but unlike the northern Winters I was used to. It was a dry cold which cracked the skin and gave new meaning to the words, Static Electricity. Rugs, when and if found, were carefully avoided. It usually took at least two men to separate the laundry after drying, static cling really clung.

The wind howled about with a vengeance at this mile high altitude. I experienced my first dust storm. It was an experience will live forever in my memory. It started early in the morning, the wind picked up and the dust begin to blow. There was just no way to keep it out of the barracks. It came in around the windows and doors no matter what we did. We found the dust in our food. It was in our beds, foot lockers, shaving kits, and so on. We slept in it at night.

Then, in the morning the Sergeant would show up and for the rest of the day we cleaned the dust out of the barracks. In the end, I can safely say without fear of contradiction, "I hope I never see another dust storm as long as I live."

Then on clear days you could see the Rocky Mountains rising majestically out of the flat plains. It was a sight to behold. At one time, I was able to count four thunder storms out on the plains at the same time. The only other place I can think of where you might be able to do this would be in Florida.

Due to the altitude, it was just a little hard to catch your breath for the first few days. This was not really a problem. I was young and adjusted quickly. Unfortunately, my bronchitis was beginning to limit my ability to physically exert myself.

My first stop was the H.Q. where I checked in with a Master Sergeant who was the image of all Master Sergeants. He was short, round, red faced, and he swore like a sailor at the slightest infraction of Military Protocol. All in all he was a fine soldier or he never would have made it to Master Sergeant. I liked the man at sight.

Once away from Basic Training the attitude of all the people in the Air Force Seemed to change. It was more like a business relationship. People worked together to get the job done.

His gruff attitude abruptly changed when I handed him my orders. He stopped what he was doing and looked at me with great interest. Then rummaging through a pile of papers on his desk he said, "We have heard all about you and the job you did as Fire Guard on Williams."

"They said you did a great job up there. So we thought while you are waiting for your group to form for Weapons Maintenance School, you might like to take care of a few of our boilers here at Lowery." There was an evil grin on his face as he went on to say, "We just love volunteers here, and you **did** just volunteer, didn't you?"

What else could I do? I swallowed hard and nodded my head yes.

The tension was beginning to ease and I felt a little better about the situation. Fire Guard wasn't at all bad and at least this time, I knew a little something about boilers. I felt even better about it when I realized all the rest of the new men were being assigned to K.P. Once again, the Herbst luck had prevailed. Still, I had this nagging feeling my old C.O. from Williams had something to do with this.

The Sergeant pointed across the street and said, "You **will** take care of those buildings over there."

There were eight of them. I thought to myself, "Here we go again."

The service was really great for this one thing, if for nothing else then for this one thing alone. Every time they told you to do something they put it this way, "You **will** do this!" or "You **will** do the other thing!" It kind of took all the guess work out of just exactly what it was they wanted you to do. Of course, sometimes they went even further and added the word **now** to the thing, thus removing even more of the guess work.

On my way out to my new hone, which just happened to be one of the barracks I was to take of, I stopped by the boiler room to take a look at my new charges. As boilers go, they were nothing special, but the coal. **Wow!** Now this was something I would have to find out about. The lumps of coal were a foot or more across. I would have to break some of them just to get them into the boiler.

I turned around and marched straight back to my new friend the Master Sergeant, with a lump of coal in my hands.

"What is this stuff and how do I handle it?" I asked, as soon as I had his attention. I wasn't about to take any chances on my new base.

It turned out to be soft coal of a local type and it also turned out to be a lot of fun to play with. I could stuff a large lump of the stuff into the fire box and it would break up all by itself. It was fun to watch as it split this way then the other way.

I had to be very careful no one saw me having fun. If they saw me enjoying this new job I was sure they would move me onto the K.P. roster. I made it a point to always look dirty, annoyed and tired. This seemed to put them off quite nicely.

Once again, I watched as all the men I came in with moved on to Tech School, and once again, I found myself sitting alone in an empty barracks.

I went to the H.Q. and asked why, once again I was told I had a criminal record and I was to be discharged. I called my father and asked him to have a talk with the lawyer he had hired. Then I sat back to wait. There was nothing else I could do but wait. Time dragged on and Spring arrived with its hot dry weather.

I have to back track at this point, to fill you in on one very important detail; One of the barracks I took care of was an In Training Flight Officers Billet. They didn't live in Barracks like we did, they lived in billets. For the life of mc I couldn't tell the difference, the buildings all looked the same, but the Air Force knew the difference and this is what counted.

Since my first days in the military I didn't like officers, not because they represented authority, but because one of them told me he was my superior. After a brief scuffle, I was able to convince this worthy soul he might out rank me but he was in no other way my superior.

No, I didn't hit him. It's against my nature to run around hitting people. I just grabbed him by the front of his shirt, lifted him up until I could look him straight in the eye and asked, "Okay, tell me. Just how is it you feel you're my superior?"

He muttered something about referring to rank only and reminded me it was against Military Regulations for an enlisted man to squash an officer. I really didn't want to hurt the little fellow so I put him back down and walked away. It was kind of like game fishing, you let the little ones go.

The female officer was something else again. Just having to salute one of them caused the hair on the back of my neck to stand straight up. Thank the Lord I never had to serve under a female officer.

Anyhow, officers were never my favorite people, especially the C.O. I had up on Williams. Now here I was, having to take care of a whole building full of them. To make matters worse they were trainees just like me. However, they were going to Flight Officers School and to hear them talk, they were second only to God himself. Well, I grit my teeth and did as I was told, but I didn't much care for it.

Then one day late in July, I was seized by an irresistible urge. I had one Cherry Bomb left over from the 4th. The Officer Trainees were all in the shower after a grueling day of flight training naked as "J" birds.

The latrine itself was a dug out affair like a swimming pool. It had a small slit type windows about six feet up on the wall which opened out at ground level. The rest of the place was open with no partitions. The sinks were on one wall, the showers on another, and so on.

I lit the fuse on my Cherry Bomb and pitched it into the latrine while I hollered as loud as I could,"**Grenade!**" I really had no intention of waiting around to see what would happen, but as I turned to leave I was confronted by an officer who had walked quietly up behind me.

He didn't say a word, he just motioned for me to follow and led me back to my "friend" the Master Sergeant. The two of them spoke briefly and then the officer left, without a backward glance.

Somehow I knew I was in big trouble.

The Sergeant walked slowly over to me and said, "I'm going to give you a choice. Stand for a general court martial and get thrown out of the service with a dishonorable discharge --- or --- pull K.P. till you drop." The choice was easy, I kind of liked the service so I picked the K.P.

I won't bore you with the gruesome details except to say I went on for twenty-eight days, working eighteen hours a day, until I finally dropped into a huge pot of vegetable soup and nearly drowned.

There may indeed be others out there who had fire crackers left over from the 4th. of July. Somewhere there must be someone who used their fire cracker as I used mine. I am just as sure they paid a similar price but, I am told, twenty-eight days is a kind of unofficial record.

After I had sufficiently recovered from my ordeal, I was told my good name had finally been cleared by my father's attorney and I was to go on to Tech School.

Nopo San

Chapter 6

Sick Call

The first thing the Air Force did, before getting around to training me for Weapons Maintenance, was to give me a complete new physical examination. As part of this examination, I again had my vision tested. Apparently, I would be working with electronics and this involved color coded wires and components.

No longer did one just pull a trigger to make the gun go, **bang!** Today you push a button. Now this was a twist I hadn't expected. I had always been good, working with my hands, and wiring in the average household was no problem.

Suddenly they were talking about huge cables with hundreds of pairs of brightly colored wires, all of which looked grey to me. I had really wanted to get into the Air Force and I knew I was color-blind. Way back in the early days of my schooling, I had been found to have a rather serious problem with color. In fact, I had been told by several doctors I was quite color-blind.

Now hold on right there. I have been asked this question so many times, I know it by heart. You're saying to yourself, "What's it like to be color-blind?" This is what your thinking, right?

OK, here it is for the record. "It's like watching an old black and white TV set." Remember black and white TV? No color at all. Well this is how it is to be color-blind.

Yes, I have learned through the years to identify some colors but I have no idea what they actually look like. Confused? Good! Now maybe you know how I feel when you hold up a colored object and ask, "What color does this look like to you?" I'm color-blind, it's **grey!** Are you happy now?

To get into the Air Force back in those days, one had to pass a color vision test. I just happened to know where I could buy a real doctors, color vision test kit. I bought the thing and practiced day and night until I could identify the numbers in all of the spotted circles. I even knew about the one which had no number. The one the doctors relied on to trip up guys like me. Needless to say, I made it into the Air Force.

Now here I was getting a new color vision test, and this time they used colored lights. After a few minutes of testing, the man giving the test pointed his finger at me and said, "You're color-blind! How the heck did you get this far without anyone finding out?"

I was sent back to the barracks to wait again. This time I had to wait to see what schools I could go to. I was told there were not many who didn't need, at least a little, color vision.

About this time, I got sick again. I don't get sick very often but when I do it, I really go all out. I woke up in the morning and had great difficulties getting the room to hold still long enough for me to plant my feet on the floor. I had never in my whole life, been this sick.

Somehow I reported for sick call. Sick as I was, I was placed in a formation and marched to sick call at the hospital about a quarter of a mile away. I am not really sure just how I got there but I did.

Marching was no real problem but when the formation turned to go in a different direction, they would have to send someone back to get me and lead me back to the rest of the group.

At the hospital they found I had Amoebic Dysentery and I was running a fever of about 104 degrees. Once again, I had no idea what Amoebic Dysentery was. All I knew for sure was what I had learned in High School Biology Class. An Amoeba is a little one celled critter who's real tough to kill. I must have had a whole gang of the little things in me, because I was one sick kid.

I was placed in an isolation ward because this Amoebic Dysentery was highly contagious and they didn't want me infecting everyone on the base with it. This left me with a rather uneasy feeling. Where was the guy I got it from? Amoebic

Dysentery is a strictly tropical item. How the blazes did I get it in Denver, Colorado, during the early spring?

Here I was in an isolation ward with Amoebic Dysentery. This whole, huge ward of about thirty beds, I was the only person in it, it was kind of scary. It didn't matter though, I felt so terrible I just didn't care where I was.

I didn't know just how long I was there all by myself when a cheerful orderly showed up with several bottles and lots of tubes. "**Lunch!**" he said with a big smile. "Eat it all up."

With this, he stabbed a needle into my arm and connected me to one of the bottles. Through bleary eyes I watched what was going on. I felt so bad, I didn't even feel the needle.

As the man finished, I asked what I was supposed to do while all this was going on. With a smile he said, "Just count the drops," and pointed to a little bulb in the tube where a clear liquid had begun to drip. Then, without any further word, be left. I was alone again.

I lay there and watched the drops and wondered what was going to happen to me. The first bottle was almost empty when the man came back and switched bottles. "Dessert!" he said with a smile.

Strangely enough, I felt better already. But now, a new and even more gruesome horror befell me. As I watched the drops, I began to feel the need to get to a bathroom.

The bottles were attached to me through a tube and needle, which I dared not remove. The rack which held the bottles was fixed to my bed and would not come off. I rang the buzzer but there was no one in the office to hear it. I was alone to face this menace all by myself.

Now as my need to get to the bathroom intensified, I could feel each drop as well as see it as it fell in the little bulb. The bottle was still half full.

I yelled for help but there was no answer. I threw things at the door in a vain attempt to attract attention. Still, no help came. My bladder was ready to burst and still the drops fell in the little bulb. The pain in my bladder mounted with each drop. Talk about the Chinese Water Torture, WOW!

Just about this time I had decided relief was the better part of valor. I was going to let go in the bed and bear the shame. A nurse suddenly appeared to get some papers out of the office at the end of the ward."Help!" I yelled, "For God's Sake, **HELP!**" She froze in her tracks. I don't think she knew there was any one in the ward until I yelled.

I explained my problem as best I could under the circumstances. Being a nurse of exceptionally high caliber, she understood instantly what the problem was and provided me with the desired item. Life slowly returned to normal as the urinal filled. I set the full urinal by the side of the bed and finished counting the drops as I waited patiently for the orderly to return.

When the orderly arrived to remove the bottles and the needle from my arm, I asked him why he had left me in such an uncomfortable situation. He smiled at me and said, "Hey trooper! War is hell."

Waiting until he was about halfway back up the ward, I threw the full urinal at him. It hit him square in the back between his shoulder blades. The force of the blow knocked him clean off his feet. It was one of those rare simple pleasures in life, which gives one such a warm feeling of accomplishment.

Naturally the guy was mad as a wet hen. He was indeed wet from head to toe and he smelled awful. He came back to me all set to bash my brains in with the empty urinal. I looked at him sheepishly and said in a weak voice, "You wouldn't hit a sick fellow Airman, would you?" I could see him grit his teeth as he suppressed his rage. He muttered a vile curse, swore vengeance on me and left the ward. I never saw him again.

A few days later, I was sent back to my barracks, completely healed. I was warned however, Amoebic Dysentery never really goes away. I have found, through the years, this is quite true. It seems to come back about every other year, regular as clock work.

Now however, for the moment, I was well again and I do mean the Air force did a great job of putting me back on my feet. It was time to sit down with the powers who controlled my life, and figure out just which Tech School I was going to attend. Knowing the extent of my color blindness most of the schools were ruled out. I asked the officer who was interviewing me, "What are my options?"

He told me I had a choice, Heavy Equipment Operator, or Cook. Everything else was out of the question because of my color blindness.

The idea of driving a huge piece of heavy equipment was kind of intriguing. I pictured myself riding atop a huge bulldozer as it crashed through all obstacles and crushed everything in its path. I could just picture in my mind the path of smoldering wreckage I would leave behind me every where my machine and I traveled. It was something only I could imagine. It was a kind of death wish.

I picked Heavy Equipment Operator. "Okay!" The officer said, "You got it!"

Nopo San

Chapter 7

Tech School

On my first day of Tech School, I was in "Seventh Heaven". I had made it to the big time. At last, my father's lawyer had been able to convince the Air Force I did not have a criminal record. No one knew about the boiler on Williams A.F.B. except my old C.O. and myself. Last but not least, I had been forgiven for the fire cracker incident.

Now, I was about to learn how to drive a monster bulldozer. I would crush all that stood in my way. Nothing would remain where I had been but flattened smoldering rubble. I could picture, in my mind, huge smoking, flattened, fields of devastation where ever I'd been. I was sure glad there were no mind readers about, I would have scared them half to death.

Now here I was standing in a formation with a lot of other guys I didn't know. We were waiting to be marched off to our first day of Heavy Equipment Operators School, or so I thought. I had not seen my orders but I knew what the officer had told me. I was to be trained as a heavy equipment operator because of my color blindness and this is all I really had to know.

We marched about half a mile to a small building somewhere on Lowery A.F.B. in Colorado. I can remember thinking to myself, "This is an awfully small building to teach Heavy Equipment Handling in." But then again, I was new here. What did I know? Maybe the first few classes were some kind of movie.

I still had this mental picture of myself riding high atop some monster earth mover as it crushed all obstacles in its path. This was going to be a ball. I could almost feel the impact as huge trees fell like matchsticks before my bulldozer.

We filed into a classroom and sat down. After a brief wait a

Sergeant appeared with a large black box, which he put on the table before us. Assuming the teacher was going to introduce himself I paid close attention. He proceeded to tell us, "This gentlemen, is a camera. By the time you finish this school, you **will** know everything there is to know about this camera and any other camera you will ever need to use in the Air Force."

Figure 2 The Kind Of Camera I carried.

I put my hand up and when he recognized me I said, "I think there has been some kind of mistake. I was suppose to go to Heavy Equipment Operator. I'm color-blind."

He looked long and hard at me. Then in a patient voice said, "You don't look color-blind. Is your name Herbst?" I nodded yes and he went on, "Sit down, you are about to become a Photographer." Then, almost as an after thought he added, "You

will become a Photographer!"

I was kind of glad he didn't say now along with it. This meant they were at least going to give me time to learn. As I said earlier, I had long since made up my mind to go along with whatever they told me to do. Looking around at my class mates, I figured if these other guys could do it, so could I!

Like the man had said in the beginning, we learned everything there was to know about a camera in those few months. I found, in spite of my color blindness I was becoming a reasonably good photographer. In fact, my grades were second only to one other guy in the class. He had seven years prior experience as a commercial photographer.

In the beginning, the ex-commercial photographer and I didn't like each other very much. However, as time went on, there developed a kind of good natured rivalry between us. We each began working for the highest mark we could get.

Figure 3 We Had Time To Fool Around With The Equipment.

We got a chance to play with some pretty sophisticated equipment which of course we made good use of. As you can see to the right.

The red tag is a reject tag. This photo was taken with an 8"X12" Portrait Type Camera complete with dark cloth and tripod. Anyhow, this is what I looked like in Tech School.

In the end, the ex-commercial photographer graduated with a 96. I was only able to get a 94, but we had become the best of friends. We had the two highest marks ever achieved in the school up to the date we graduated, so I couldn't complain. In the history of the school, I was second only to a man with seven years prior experience. I was very proud of this.

We also did a lot of what was called a 36-93 portrait. Obviously, we had to use ourselves as models. Therefore we wound up with a lot of really nice pictures of each other.

At the end of Tech School, we were told we would be able to pick out our assignments in order of the grades we had made in school.

There were fourteen of us. There were seven openings in Germany, four in France, two on the island of Okinawa, and one in Korea.

Figure 4 A Typical 36-93 Portrait

Having the second highest mark in the class I picked Germany, my grandfather's homeland. I just knew, once there, I would be able to look up some of my distant relatives. I wrote to my father with great pride, I was to be sent to Germany and I asked him to send me all the addresses he had for our distant relatives.

We had about seven days to kill while our orders were being typed up and confirmed with Washington, so they put us on K.P. one last time. We were all so excited about our assignments no one really minded.

At last the orders were posted. There was Germany right at the top of the list. I ran my finger down the list looking for my name. It wasn't there. I went on to France, still no Herbst. Then I found it, I was to be sent to the island of Okinawa.

I raced into the H.Q. and demanded an explanation. A very patient and sympathetic Sergeant explained things to me. Most of the other fellows in my class were re-enlistee's and as such had first choice of assignments. Now they tell me!

I was hurt and angry but there was nothing I could do about it. I made up my mind to live with it and have as much fun as I could. Okinawa just couldn't as bad as I had been told it would be. If there was a bright spot anywhere on the island, I was determined to find it.

We were given a thirty day leave. After our leave we were to report to our various debarkation points. I teamed up with three of my former class mates and chipped in for a car ride home. The car was an old clunker. It was owned by my friend, the former commercial photographer. The thing looked like it still had some life in it so off the four of us went on a cross country ride I will never forget.

The car ran fine, but the tires blew out at regular intervals. We rotated drivers between the four of us almost as fast as we changed tires. Finally we were all so tired we just pulled over to the side of the road. I slept on the bare ground under the car. The trip took all of four days, but we all got home safely. Mine was the last stop as my home was the furthest out.

When I got home, the first thing I did was to shower and the second thing was to crash into my old bed and sleep for 18 hours. When my father got home and saw the things strewn about in my old room he nearly called the Police, thinking the house had been vandalized.

I spent my leave time with the family out at Wainscott, Long Island. This was done much to the consternation of my girl friend. She naturally thought I should spend all of my time with her. I had wanted to take her to Wainscott with me, but she refused. She didn't like it out there for some reason.

There have been many times since then when I have wondered what would have happened if I had spent my time with her. I loved her very much, but the family ties were stronger. I had even bought a ring for her at the end of Basic Training.

I have been told all my life , "Hind sight is 20/20." Now I know why. Looking back over my life, I think I could have spared myself the agony of twenty years of unhappy married life if I had just stayed with my girl friend and married her. But I didn't.

My leave ended all to quickly. Once again I was off and running for my next duty assignment. My girl friend was only a fond memory now but we still wrote to each other trying to mend the widening gulf between us.

I would only hear from her one more time after I had arrived on Okinawa. She send me a "Dear John" letter. I guess she felt she had to make it official. I heard later she had married a banker and had several kids. I sure hope she had better luck with married life than I did.

I flew on a commercial Air Plane out to California and spent a short time visiting family out on the West Coast. It was a nice visit but like all visits, it was too long for the host and not long enough for the visitor.

At the end of my visit I was given a pair of military hair brushes as a going away present. I have carried those brushes with me all these years and to this day I still use them. It could well be one of the main reasons I still have all my hair.

In August, I found myself on Parks A.F.B. in California. I was awaiting transportation to Okinawa. I can remember thinking to myself as I looked around Parks A.F.B. It was just like the

Military to find the most terrible spot on the face of the earth, then build a base on it. It was terribly hot. The ground was so parched it cracked. It was the first time in my life I had ever seen ground get so dry it cracked.

There wasn't much else about Parks which really stuck in my memory. Today as I look at the news on TV, I see the reports on all the terrible fires which regularly sweep California. I can understand how they happen.

I was at an Air Force Base on the West Coast. This had to mean they were going to fly me over to Okinawa. This was great, my first flight in a Military Air Craft, I could hardly wait. But first, I had to pay my dues, seven more days of K.P.

In looking back I really think I must have made some sort of record. I don't think I have ever met anyone who has pulled a total of fifty days of K.P. during the course of only one year in the service. It just had to be a record some place.

At long last, my orders came through. I was loaded onto a bus headed for the State of Washington. They must be going to send me out by plane from there after all this was the Air Force we went places by airplane.

Once again, the Herbst Luck prevailed. I found myself standing on a dock, in the cold, wet early hours of the morning, waiting to board a huge grey troop ship.

There was one bright spot, the Red Cross was there with hot coffee and doughnuts for every one. Every one, that is, who had twenty five cents for a five cent cup of coffee and twenty five cents for a five cent doughnut.

There was no competition so if you wanted the coffee and doughnut, there was only one game in town. To this day I think of this situation every time I see anything about the Red Cross. I didn't have fifty cents in my pocket. So I stood there cold, wet and miserable, with a lot of other guys in the same situation and watched those who had the cash, chow down.

I think the part which really stirred my anger the most was; right across the street from us there was a coffee shop advertizing coffee for five cents a cup and doughnuts for five cents each.

    We couldn't walk across the street to take advantage of it. Ten cents I had in my pocket, but not the fifty cents I needed for the coffee and doughnuts the Red Cross was handing out. Now this hurt! I never forgave the Red Cross for it. To this very day, every time I see a Red Cross emblem I think about how cold and miserable I was standing there on the damned dock in the rain.

Nopo San

Chapter 7

The Troop Ship

Standing there on the dock, looking at this huge grey ship, there were no words to express just how I felt. I would be traveling with 800 other Air Force personnel, most of them officers, and 4000 soldiers. The ship simply didn't look big enough to fit us all in. Then again, I was still quite new to the Military. I should have had more faith in their ability to pack a human cargo.

As our names were called, we filed silently on board the ship. Once again, the Herbst Luck took over. All the Air Force enlisted men were assigned to the forward hold, all but me.

There were not enough bunks up forward for all of us, so for some strange reason my name was picked out as the one lone Air Force enlisted man to be thrown into one of the midships hold with the soldiers. Now I know exactly what it feels like to be the lone Republican at a Democratic rally.

We were a miserable lot. Talk about your sardine cans, I could lay down in my bunk and with little or no effort reach out and touch twenty-six other bunks. The air was foul and all the soldiers were sea sick. I never understood how they could be so sea sick while the ship was still tied to the dock.

Since this time, I have had a chance to examine many Sardine Cans, I can tell you without fear of contradiction; the lowly Sardine fares better in its can, than we did on the troop ship. There were two things the Sardine had which we didn't have; **more room and oil.**

As I read the history books about the slave traffic between Africa and the States, I can't help thinking the slaves had it better on those old sailing ships than we did on the Troop Ship.

They may have been stuffed into the cargo hold so tight they had to sleep side by side, but at least they weren't stacked one on top of the other. History tells us the slaves were transported at the rate of so many per square foot, the Military deals in so many per cubic foot.

My bunk was the third from the floor, for which I was very glad. The fellows on the bottom bunks got all the splash from when the fellows on the top bunks got sick and heaved up all their good second hand **Yum Yum** from the mess deck.

I have to admit the food on the ship was great. Once again, there was plenty of it. What, with so many of the other guys being sea sick all the time. There were always seconds for me. I never got seasick so I had a ball.

While I am on the subject of, **The Mess Deck** let me explain how this method of eating works. It's a lot like the land type Base Chow Hall, except there are no chairs to sit on. In order to save space, one stood at a long counter like thing made of stainless steel and ate off the same kind of stamped stainless steel tray used by the entire Military in all of their Chow Halls. There are those things in life one can rely on to never change, the stamped out stainless steel mess tray was one of them.

The counter like thing had edges which were built up about an inch, I suppose it was to catch things which slid back and forth on the counter in rough weather. It also kept food from spilling on the floor.

This was great for me. In rough weather, I could stay right at the middle of the counter like thing and grab special treats off other peoples trays as they slid past me.

It did, of course, have its draw backs. If your tray got away from you and wound up in front of someone who was seasick, you could wind up with a whole new selection of goodies on your tray when you got it back. This became even more interesting as the grease from the food coated the steel table. Things began to move faster and it became even more of a challenge to sort things out in your mind as the **buffet** slid past. I usually tried to stand where I could see what was going on at both ends of the table and I kept a firm grip on my own tray.

Obviously, the sleeping conditions were the pits, so after a few night of trying to get some rest in the midships hold. I wound up sleeping on the floor in the forward hold with the rest of the Air Force guys.

There was no bunk for me so I slept on the steel floor and used my hat as a pillow. I was so tired by this time it didn't make any difference where I was, just so long as it wasn't down in the hold with all the vile smell. The Air Force hold, up in the front of the ship, seemed to be better ventilated somehow. Later, as the weather got better, I moved out onto the deck to sleep.

The whole aft, or Fan Tail, of the ship was one great big, huge latrine. I was assigned to the job of keeping it clean. Somehow this didn't surprise me. There were supposed to be four other fellow sufferers to help me along with the job but after only one day they all got Sea-Sick and the job fell on my shoulders alone.

It was then I got my first lesson in Naval Engineering. The floor drain in the aft latrine was located at the highest point on the floor. Everything had to be pushed up hill to the drain with a squeegee. This was a long pole with a piece of stiff rubber fixed to the end of it. As you pushed it along the floor, it pushed all the liquid before it, except for the part which ran around the ends and back down hill to the low spot in the floor again.

The job was a real stinker but it did have its light side. There were about 120 toilets in the aft latrine and they were drained into pipes which exited the ship by way of Scuppers. A scupper was nothing more than a hinged plate which opened when the aft of the ship came out of the water and closed again when the aft of the ship went back down in the water. It worked like a giant check valve.

It was simplicity itself, except one of them didn't work. It was attached to the first line of toilets you came to, as you walked through the doorway to the latrine. While the fantail of the ship was up out of the water, everything looked quite normal.

But as the aft, of the ship, fell off the top of the wave and went back down, the water ran back into the pipe through the broken scupper. The resulting backwash would spray up about three feet over the top of the toilet.

It didn't get really interesting until we hit rough weather. Then these poor seasick souls would race into the latrine and heave their guts out into the first toilet they came to. Only to have it driven back up the pipe, out of the toilet, and into their faces, by the water coming back up the pipe through the broken scupper.

In really rough weather the force of the back wash was enough to knock these poor souls clean over backwards. It was a sight to behold. I really felt sorry for the Beetle Crushers.

During this whole time, it was my job to keep pushing the water up hill to the drain as fast as it came back in through the toilets. It was kind of like trying to hold back the tide with a tooth brush. I liked to think I was saving the lives of all who used the Aft Latrine. After all, if it hadn't been for me, there would have been enough stuff sloshing around back there to swim in or drown, as the case may be.

Somewhere along the line, I was relieved of my job and some other worthy soul took over. For the rest of the trip, I was allowed to lounge about on deck and sop up the sunshine. This is, when the Navy wasn't cleaning the decks. They had a nasty habit of moving quietly up on the deck and then without warning, washing the deck and everyone on it clean with a high pressure salt water fire hose.

There was really no place to retreat to when this happened so we just sat there and got clean right along with deck. The sun dried us right out again, so no one really got too upset about it. One day there was a minor revolt when the Army took the fire hose away from the Navy and washed sailors for a change.

As I said earlier, as soon as the weather got a little warmer, I moved out onto the deck to sleep. In my travels about the ship, I had found a great place to sleep. There was this neat little place right up in the point of the bow. It was full of ropes, canvas and other junk but with just a little adjustment, I made a comfortable bed out of it and had my own private bedroom. This all worked out fine until we hit the Typhoon.

The Captain had been trying to avoid the Typhoon by sailing around it. The effort had added a couple of extra days to our trip. The Captain tried hard to get out of its way, but he failed. We wound up going right through the middle of it.

We all knew there was a Typhoon nearby, but we all thought we were going to miss it. No one had said anything to the contrary until we plowed into the thing. I found out about it when I woke one morning. When I looked out of my private bedroom, all I could see was green water. The whole bow of the ship was under water and I was cut off from the rest of the ship.

There was no way to get from the rope locker to the rest of the ship without going out on the unprotected deck. As I crawled out of the rope locker between waves. I could see the whole aft end of the ship was now under water. I couldn't help wondering who was down there in the aft latrine getting a face full.

As I stood there wondering what to do next, my attention was attracted to the bridge of the ship. The Captain was up there pointing at me or at least in my direction. It was plain to see the poor fellow was quite upset. Just about then, I turned around to see what he was so excited about. All I could see was a huge mountain of green frothy water coming at me like a freight train. The water hit me and carried me along the deck like a cork. Only luck saved me from going over the side.

As I was washed past a railing on the officers deck, one flight up from where I was standing. I managed to grab hold of a part of the railing and hang on for dear life. It was no easy task, I never knew water could have so much force. I hung on like grim death.

As soon as the water washed on by, rough hands grabbed me. I was dragged back into the ship. I was made to confront a very angry ship's Captain. He yelled at me, above the howling wind, "You ------- idiot! What the Sam ---- were you doing out in the ------- rope locker?"

I really intended to answer him, but he went on before I got a chance, "Get this ------- idiot out of my ------- sight and make sure I never see him again!"

Again, rough hands grabbed me. Again, I was placed back in the mid ship hold and told, in no uncertain terms, I should stay there. No matter what. Even if the ship went down.

It wasn't so bad though, we made Okinawa two days later and I was escorted off the ship by an armed guard. The guard told me the, Captain wanted to be sure I got off and there was no way I could get back on board. I had arrived at Okinawa.

Nopo San

Chapter 9

Okinawa

I don't think there are any words to describe just what it's like to tramp off a stinking troop ship onto the pristine, sun bleached, clean of an Okinawan beach. I don't remember any buildings, although I am sure there were some. I do remember a long concrete quay the ship was tied to. It was bleached white by the sun and the light hurt my eyes.

This beach is typical of Okinawa. As a general rule, when we went swimming we posted a shark guard with a rifle at just about the point I'm taking this picture from. It was on a beach such as this where I was introduced to Okinawa.

Figure 5 An Okinawan Beach

We were loaded into a truck and it went inland from the beach. At a place called Kadena, my name was called off and I got out of the truck. I waved good-bye to the only other man on the whole ship I knew. He was going to Naha, the other Air Force Base on Okinawa.

Someone pointed me toward a building and told me I was

home for the next year and a half. It was hot, and I smelled bad after being cooped up in the midships hold for a day or so. The first thing I did when I got to my barracks, was to take a long, hot, refreshing, and much needed, shower and shave.

After the shower, I stepped across the street to the chow hall for something to eat, I had a chance to look around at my new home. It didn't look at all bad. I found I liked Okinawa.

In the chow hall we ate off plates and got soup in bowls instead of stamped out compartments in a cold steel slab. The food was served to us by Okinawan civilians. Even the coffee came to us in ceramic mugs. I remembered now, this was called civilization. I was suddenly being treated like a human being again and I liked it.

Figure 6 Kadena Village

On the way inland I got my first look at Kadena Village. This is the village just outside the main gate to Kadena Air Force Base. This part of Kadena is the "Residential Area" and we never wandered too far into it. There were still a lot of people who still harbored deep resentment toward Americans.

Figure 7 Kadena's Residential Section.

    I had found, during Basic Training, it was easier to shave while I was in the shower than it was to try and wait for a sink and mirror later. It's a habit which stuck with me right up to now. No one has ever been able to show me a better way. After all, it doesn't make much sense to get out of the shower, dry off, then put water and soap back on your face, does it?

    There were little green lizards of several different types running around all over the place. Any place which had live lizards running about, couldn't be all bad.

    There were a lot of very picturesque spots on the way to the base. This little path, on the right, wandered up into the hills for miles. There wasn't much up there but it was a nice quiet place to walk.

The next morning, I got up and walked across the street to the Chow Hall. This was going to be great. Food was only a few steps away and I was hungry enough to eat a horse. Much to my delight, I found the Chow Hall on Okinawa was fully staffed with Okinawan civilians. There would be no K.P. here. It was almost too good to be true. The food was good to excellent, on a scale of one to ten, about eight.

Figure 8 Okinawan Country Side.

The Photo Lab was about a quarter of a mile from my barracks, well you can't have everything. A little walking is good for you, I just had to remember not to over do it. Okinawa was truly a wonderland with Banana Trees, Palm Trees and lots of other great things, I had never seen before. As I walked to the Photo Lab the first morning, I must have looked like a wide-eyed New York tourist.

I reported to the Base Photo Lab and met the crew I would be working with for the next year and a half. They were a good lot and welcomed me into the fold with friendship. I was handed a big Speed Graphic Camera and told it was all mine so long as I was on

Okinawa.

I had hardly had time to thank the officer for the camera when a jeep pulled up outside, and Air Policeman burst through the door to the Photo Lab and said, "We need a photographer! **Now!**" He panted, "**Right Now!**"

Because at the time I was the only one in the room with a camera in his hands, he looked right at me. I looked over at my new C.O. and he nodded approval. The next thing I knew, we were sailing down the road toward the Air Field and my first job as an Air Force Photographer.

On the runway there was this huge plane. I had never seen anything so big. It was a B-36 and believe me it was huge. The Air Police were setting up all kinds of guns all around it. There were even several light machine guns in sandbag pits here and there. They sure didn't want people anywhere near the plane.

We screeched to a stop at the foot of the ramp leading up to the door of the plane. An Officer told me there was some damage inside the plane and he needed pictures taken of it immediately. Well, this was my job so I marched up the ramp and into the plane with him, camera in hand.

Inside this huge plane, there was only one large crate. It had apparently broken loose from its tie downs, slid about on the floor, and had sustained a little damage to one corner. I took a few pictures of it and then explained to the officer in charge what I had done.

I wanted to be absolutely sure I was doing everything right, so I asked if there was anything else he wanted pictures of. He told me there wasn't so I asked for a ride back to the Photo Lab. I wanted to get started processing my first job as an Air Force Photographer. I was really quite proud of myself.

As we stepped off the bottom of the ramp and started toward the jeep, the officer suddenly turned to me and said, "You're not wearing your flight line pass!"

I smiled at him as I said, "What's a flight line pass?" Almost at once, I had the old feeling I had once again said the wrong thing. People were pointing loaded guns at me from all directions. I had the most uneasy feeling I was suddenly the center of a whole lot of most unwelcome attention.

The officer scowled at me and asked again, "Where is you're flight line pass?" The people with the guns began pulling the slides to put bullets in the chambers. These guys didn't like me and I had no idea why.

Placing my camera on the ground, I raised my hands slowly in the air, I repeated, "I don't know what a Flight Line Pass is. I just got off the boat yesterday."

The officer instantly turned beet red, "You mean you don't have your security clearance yet?" and with this he grabbed my camera.

I was all set to demand the return of my camera when I became aware there was the business end of a pistol only inches from my nose. A harsh voice said, "Don't even think about moving."

Much as I hate to think this, these guys were actually looking for an excuse to shoot me. It was a really weird feeling.

The next two weeks were spent in the stockade. Although I was not treated as harshly as the others in there, I was quietly informed, if my security clearance did not show up, I was going to be in big trouble. Obviously this guy had no idea what big trouble was. He hadn't been out on the flight line with me when all those guns pointed in my direction. Now that's my definition of big trouble!

Fortunately, my security clearance showed up in good time. I was sent back to the Photo Lab for more fun and games. I never did find out just what was inside the crate. I guess there was no need for me to know, so no one told me. I would be just as happy if I didn't know. This way no one could accuse me of talking about it.

Much later, I heard a rumor the Air Force was secretly hauling Atomic Bombs over to Japan and storing them somewhere. They were supposed to be stored in Japan just in case they were needed in Korean. I will never know for sure. Quite frankly, I don't want to know.

Once having been to the flight line I became a constant visitor as something was always breaking or falling apart out there. One particularly gruesome thing was the day the fuel truck caught fire. It had been on its way out onto the flight line to fill up one of the prop driven aircraft which were still quite common on our runways.

A little way from the plane it was to fuel, the truck stopped short and smoke began rolling up from the tank part. Obviously it was on fire. I hopped into a jeep and was immediately on my way to take pictures of what was going on. On arrival I shot my first picture of the fire at the rear of the tank. Someone said, "The drivers still in there!"

Sure enough as I moved out to the side I could see the driver struggling with his seat belt. Apparently it wouldn't release and he was held fast in the seat. Some brave soul raced forward to help him. He had only gone a few steps when the tank ruptured and the entire truck was engulfed in flames. There was nothing we could do but stand there and watch through the flames as the driver made his last effort to free himself from the seat belt.

The seat belt must have burned through as the driver, now quite dead, slid from the truck and landed in the gasoline which had puddled around the cab. It looked as if he was still trying to crawl out of the fire. The fire was so hot no one could get anywhere near close enough to even try to help the man.

One of the men in our group muttered, "What an awful way to die." I looked around and saw there wasn't a dry eye in the lot, mine included. I'm quite sure each and every man in the group still has nightmares about it, I know I do.

Then there was the time when the maintenance people were testing out the radar controlled gun system on a B-36. There were no bullets in the guns but they were set to track anything moving toward the plane.

Some poor guy in a weapons carrier was headed out onto the tarmac. He must have looked out the window at the B-36 and found every gun on it tracking him as he moved. I don't think the truck had even stopped before the poor guy was on his feet making a mad dash away from it.

It was just about this time when I got my first and only Dear John letter. This is a letter your girl friend writes to you when she finds someone who has managed to avoid the draft and stay home. They usually start off, "Dear Bob, I have found someone else so I don't need you any more. good - bye forever."

I already knew my girl friend was leaving me, this just made it official. This little place, pictured on the right, near Kadena seemed like a great place to start the serious business of getting quite drunk.

Getting one of these things when your far from home, in a strange situation and not in the best of spirits to begin with, kind of makes your day. I did just what all my fellow Air Force buddies did, when they got a Dear John letter. I went out and got plastered.

Whisky was selling for $.25 for a one ounce glass of the stuff. I had $20.00 in my pocket and I drank it all up. Returning to the barracks I signed myself in and fumbled my way through three combination locks. Then I couldn't get my shirt unbuttoned.

Figure 9 The Bar Where I Learned About Demon Rum.

60

Oddly enough I can remember a lot of this stuff. I remember there was someone with me who took my empty wallet, put it into my locker and made sure everything was all buttoned up before he left. I think it was a fellow photographer from the base photo lab but I'm not at all sure.

I had darn near killed myself with the stuff. I awoke in a hospital and the doctor in the room with me said, "Welcome back to the land of the living. We thought for a while we had lost you." The man was dead serious about what he said. It took about a week for my stomach to heal and return to almost normal.

Somehow, I avoided any trouble over this but it did teach me a good lesson in survival. I guess the military thought I had paid a high enough price for my transgression. There are those among us who can drink hard liquor and there those of us who can't handle it. I'm one who had best walk on by the stuff.

I never drank hard liquor again. I have sampled it on rare occasions but never more than a taste or two. I still don't like the taste of the stuff and I sure don't like what it does to me.

There were only certain taxi cabs allowed on base. I was told later I had about six of them stopped and I couldn't find one with the correct license number even

Figure 10 An Okinawan Sign Painter

though several of them were just leaving the base.

I have often wondered as I look at this particular picture if my $20.00 helped pay for the painting of this sign. I guess after all these years, I'll never know.

You might note the sign painter isn't wearing any shoes. Most of the Okinawan's I saw during my stay didn't wear shoes. Their feet were so toughened by walking barefoot all the time and the constant warm weather, they didn't have to wear shoes.

I have always loved to plant things and watch them grow. To this end I had carefully carried an avocado seed all the way from the states with me. Once on Okinawa I planted the thing in a glass of water and settled back to wait for the roots to show. It took about two weeks but show they did. I was dead sure I would soon have a huge avocado tree to show for my efforts.

Figure 11 My Very Own Avocado Tree On Okinawa

The rest of the guys in the photo lab, were sure I had lost my mind as they watched me crawl around on the ground taking care of my new avocado tree. Someone had watered the thing during my stay with the Military Police. I never found out who so I could never thank them.

I suspect it was the officer who ran the Photo Lab. He looked like a nice enough person and he seemed to have a genuine interest in the avocado tree. Each morning he would stop by where I was working and ask about it.

After two weeks the little tree was on its own and doing nicely. Of course I watered it each day and it rewarded me with a long narrow shoot, it seemed to be quite hardy. It was about thirteen inches tall when the Typhoon hit. It seems avocados are not very salt tolerant.

So much for my dreams of being the first Okinawan avocado farmer. The day after the Typhoon my poor little tree was stone cold dead. I didn't have another seed so my effort was all in vain.

This little lady, made her living picking expended bullets and shell casings out of the dirt by the side of the road. She'll probably never make it into the ranks of the worlds

Figure 12 Looking For Salvage Brass.

63

richest people but she sure had a winning smile. I never found out what her name was but I have won several photo contests with the picture since then.

It had only been a few short years since the United States Army has wrested control of Okinawa from the Japanese. Of course, we all knew there had been one Hell of a fight for the island.

Everywhere you looked on Okinawa there was some kind of evidence there had been one heck of a fight there. The area I was in was one of the least contested areas on the whole island. The area to the North of Kadena and to the South were the really hot areas.

Figure 13 The Big Rock At The End Of Main Street Kadena.

Here is what "the big rock at the end of Main Street" looks like from the End of Main Street. I have walked past this rock on many occasions and never called it anything else but the Big Rock.

It was just past this rock and about a quarter mile to the right where I photographed the little lady picking up the shell casings and bullets.

This is another shot looking up Main Street. Aside from the bars and a few little shops, there wasn't a whole lot of interest. Kind of makes one wonder why we fought so hard to get it.

I never really understood how much of a fight there had been until a group of Engineers took on the job of clearing an acre or two to build some Quonset huts. Their first job was to remove all the unexploded ordinance from the ground they had to work on.

They called us out to photograph the stuff. There was a pile some twenty feet long and about three feet high of an incredible mixture of shells and bombs, some ours some Japanese. I looked at the pile for quite a while until it sunk in, this was only the unexploded stuff.

It made me

Figure 14 Looking Up Main Street Kadena.

Figure !5 Deliveries Okinawan Style.

very happy to think I didn't get there until after they stopped shooting at each other.

Some of the more modern of Okinawa's freight transportation system. As you can see, surplus army truck wheels found a good home on Okinawa. Although the sign in the background says Hotel, I don't think anyone ever spent the whole night in there.

Figure 16 Keeping The Dust Down.

This is how they controlled the dust on Main Street. This guy's job was to keep wetting down the street so it wouldn't blow away. As you will note, here again, Army surplus wheels found many good uses.

On Okinawa it was either too hot or too wet, we used to say, "Okinawa was the only place in the world where you could stand knee deep in mud on a sunny day and have dust blow in your eye only to have it washed out by a rain storm." Although I never found myself knee deep in mud, there were several times when dust did blow into my eyes.

Figure 17 Two Little Guys Playing In A Ditch.

    These two little fellows were sitting in the drainage ditch in front of their home playing. When I walked up with my camera, the one boy grabbed his brother and turned his head around so I could take this picture. Here again, I won some nice photographic contests with this print.
    Exactly why he was looking at the fellow with me instead of the camera is something I will never know. They were good little kids and I made a big blow up of the picture and delivered it to their home a few days later. It was well received.
    Let me introduce you to Judy. She is typical of the "hostesses" once found in the various bars in the town of Kadena.

As I remember, several of us chipped in and paid her three dollars to pose for us. Judging by the number of gold teeth in her mouth, she must have posed for a lot of pictures.

Figure 18 Judy

Judy was the older more experienced of the ladies working the bar and when she smiles the glitter of gold teeth was enough to blind you.

The other girl in the place refused our offer and would not pose for a picture no matter how hard we tried or how much we offered. This is me hard at work with a film pack in my back pocket at the ready in case she changed her mind.

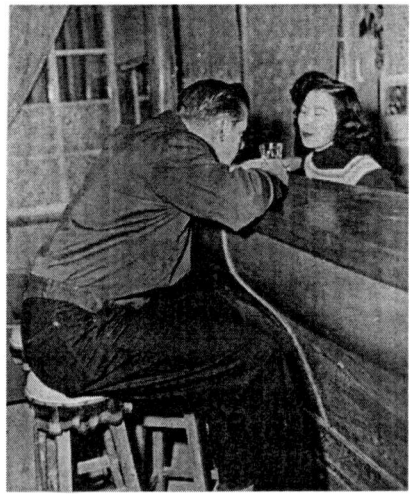

Figure 19 Negotiations.

I had several suites made over there and always with my job as photographer in mind. The pockets needed to be extra wide and deep to accommodate the film packs we used.

There were a number of fellows in our outfit who became so enamored with these little gals, they married them.

The story we were told by these gals was, they had been sold as young women to the woman who owned the bar. Until she could be reimbursed for her expense in buying the young girl, the girl was expected to preform as a hostess (prostitute).

This is an Okinawan Civilian Guard. He stands at his duty station. To a man, these guys were tough soldiers. From their ranks grew the new Japanese Army. These poor guys had to walk into the most hostile situations without weapons other than their night stick and bare hands. They rarely lost in one of these altercations.

I consider myself fortunate to have known several of them on Okinawa and in Japan.

Figure 20 Okinawan Civilian Guard.

Although there was always a certain amount of language barrier between us, we were always able to make ourselves understood and the result was a friendly association with them.

I never tried to argue with any of them. Big as I was, I had learned from taking Karate classes, I was too big to cover myself from an attack by a smaller man.

Figure 21 An Okinawan Grocery Store.

Here we have the Okinawan idea of the Corner Grocery Store. Aside from dealing directly with the farmer at the open market, this is it. Note the little walkway around the outside. This is so the customer can get up out of the mud while they shop. The items inside were limited to dry and canned goods.

A little later I had an opportunity to visit a place they called "The Cave Of The Virgins" it was a large cave on the North end of the island where a large number of children and Catholic Nuns had fled during the invasion. They were terrified and none of them spoke any English. When the Marines arrived they saw movement in the cave and demanded the inhabitants of the cave surrender.

There was no sound or further movement inside the cave. I

guess the Marines were concerned there was a bunch of Japanese soldiers in there. They got some drums of gasoline and rolled them into the entrance of the cave. Then with grenades, exploded the drums.

No one survived inside the cave. This part of the story of our invasion of Okinawa is not generally known. As I understand it, the cave is still only visited by large numbers on Americans. No one goes there alone. Even after all this time, the Okinawans are still angry about it.

It was an unfortunate situation but who can say the right or wrong of it? The Marines had no idea who was in there and the residents of the cave didn't understand they were being asked to come out. It's one of those extra horrible things which happen in any war.

I should have taken some shots of an average Okinawan home. They were interesting to look at. The walls were all made from a wooden frame work covered with rice paper. In looking at the home, you'd thing there was no way it would survive a Typhoon. I found out later on in my travels how it was done.

When the home owner hears of a Typhoon approaching he gathers his family together and buys a "Typhoon Jug" of Saki. Together the family takes the walls of the house and stores them, along with all their belongings, under the house. Then they all crawl under the house to wait the storm out. It is during this time the Typhoon Jug is drained of it's contents.

Whether this is done to numb the pain if the home is destroyed or to have

Figure 22 Farm Land.

71

something to do while the storm rages around them is something I guess I'll never know.

Farming on Okinawa was still done the time tested way as modern agricultural practice has not yet been introduced.

The little mounds surrounding the fields retain water at a given level. Too deep, the rice drowns, too shallow the rice dries out and dies. Some things will never change.

Figure 23 Farming Is Still Done The Old Way.

Even when plowing a field the old time tested method was still employed. I guess they figured they could kill two birds with one stone, tilling the soil and fertilization at the same time.

As you can see from the telephone pole, there was telephone and electrical service even out in the "boondocks".

The man holding the plow wears an old Japanese army uniform left over from the War. The practice was discouraged but not stopped. In a way it was sad. The uniform must have reminded them of how hard they had fought and how many were killed defending their home island.

On the other hand, things are a lot better since the Americans took the island than they ever were under Japanese rule.

Here we have an Okinawan movie theater. There are four features playing none of which were in English, nor were we in any way invited to attend. This place was strictly for the Okinawan civilian population.

Figure 24 An Okinawan Movie Theater With Three Features.

Note the dirt road and how the surface has been hardened by the constant traffic and water wetting. The dirt is made up of a lot of crushed Corel and it almost fuses together under pressure into a solid surface.

Here, Okinawan children play outside their school house. Note the window shutters which ride on a rail system just over the window under the little secondary roof. During a storm these window shutters are rolled out to cover the openings and bolted in place from

Figure 25 Okinawan Kids At Play

the inside. The thing to the right of the shutters is the part which covers the doorway.

Somehow, no matter how hard times have become, the kids will always find a way to play. They have no shoes and no sporty gym outfits but it hasn't slowed them down in the least. They were happy healthy little kids who did their kid thing every chance they got.

Figure 26 The Same Group Hamming It Up A Bit

This is the same group with a little better shot of the school house. The door with the windows in it is the inner door which is covered during storms.

No matter where you find them, kids are kids even if they don't speak the language. They didn't have very much but they were happy with what they had.

Although you can't see it, the fellow standing in the shadows at the right is grinning like a Cheshire Cat. He's pleased as punch to have me take this picture of him, his store and his family on the Main Street in Kadena Village. Even on war torn Okinawa there is a certain pride in having a healthy family and a home. Here the man has not only a home and family but a business he operates right out of his front door.

Figure 27 The Man And His Family Live Behind The Store Front.

This is typical of the Shinto shrines found in both Japan and Okinawa. This particular shrine is a bit more spread out than their Japanese counterpart because there is a lot more room per person per square foot of land on Okinawa than there is In Japan.

The Japanese Shrine is a bit larger and more intensely landscaped. There are usually pebble walkways up to the shrine with ornamental shrubby placed around them. The atmosphere is a good bit more relaxing.

The idea here is to approach the shrine, throw a coin into the collection dish, clap your hands together three times and make a wish. If the Gods are pleased with your offering, your wish will be granted.

Figure 28 A Shinto Shrine On Okinawa.

Sorry about the finger prints. It was hot on the day I processed the film. The sweat on my hand made the thumb print on the negative.

Nopo San

Chapter 10

The F-86

I know it will come as a great surprise to most of you, but during my entire four year stay in the U.S. Air Force, I had very little to do with aircraft of any kind. When I did get close to one, it was usually to photograph what was left of it.

The first time I ever got close to a Fighter Plane, it was an F-86, and it was about twelve feet underground. Do you believe this? It was underground!

I had only been on Okinawa about six weeks and I was still kind of new at the job, although I was learning fast. It was my habit and still is, to get to work a little early in the morning. I like being there when the doors open or better yet, open the doors myself.

Another guy, who's name I don't remember, and I were standing around outside the Photo Lab. We were waiting for our C.O. to show up and let us in so we could go to work. It was hot on Okinawa and the only cool place on the base we could get into, was the Photo Lab where we worked.

A flight of four F-86 fighter planes was just going overhead on their final landing approach run. We were standing there watching them go by. It always gave me great pride in the Air Force to watch those planes go by. I knew in my heart they were the best in the world and I was a part of it. A small part maybe, but none the less a part.

Suddenly, the outboard plane, the one on the far Left outside of the turn soared straight up, then did a complete turnabout and headed straight in toward the ground. While still about five hundred feet in the air the pilot cut in the after-burners. Judging by the noise, he must have also pushed the throttle all the way home. It had to be deliberate. I was told later, some of the noise and shock wave was the plane breaking the sound barrier on its way to the ground. These are things only a few officers at the top of the command chain really knew.

When the plane hit the ground it felt like an earthquake, even as far away as the Base Photo Lab. We were at least a quarter of a mile away. There was a plume of smoke and fire which shot straight up in the air many hundred-feet, but there were no bits and pieces flying about.

In the movies when something blows up, there was always lots of junk flying about. Not here, there was just smoke and fire, no junk. It gave me an odd feeling to stand there and watch. I was involved, yet detached somehow.

Our C.O. got to the Photo Lab a few minutes later. The Air Police got there a few minutes after the C.O. had arrived. I was standing at the door, camera in hand, ready to go. No one said much of anything. I guess we all knew what to do and there was nothing which could be said to help the situation one way or another.

When we arrived at the crash site, I was shocked to learn the plane had only missed the barracks I lived in, by about ninety feet. Somewhere around sixty men lived in the building. Had the plane hit the building, it would have been an awful mess.

The plane had apparently gone straight into the ground. I mean straight in. All you could see was a crater. No parts of the plane were visible, just a hole in the ground. The rescue team had to dig into the bottom of the crater which was already five or six feet deep. After digging another six feet they found the first part of the plane.

The pilot who had weighed 180 pounds, according to the records, was never found. Air Rescue found only about 18 pounds of what they thought was the pilot. I had the unpleasant job of photographing what they found. First in the hole, where and when the parts were found. Again outside the hole, all lined up in the order in which they had been found. Lastly at the morgue to be sure all the parts found made it to the morgue.

The biggest problem at wrecks like this was keeping dogs away from the remains. Man's best friend became our worst nightmare as they sneaked in to carry off whatever they could find in the way of meat.

I guess if it had looked like a body it might have bothered me but it didn't. It looked more like the meat counter at your favorite Butcher Shop. They never bothered to dig the plane out of the hole. When they had found as much of the pilot as they thought they were going to find, they simply filled the hole up with dirt and walked away. It was the first time I'd ever seen anyone get killed and the cavalier way they just walked away from the filled hole left me with a very strange feeling.

When it was all done they took what was left of the pilot away in a bushel basket. It seemed strange to me after all the gore. All I could think about was what made him do it. From where we had stood, outside the Photo Lab, the pilot had done this deliberately. Why? I never found out.

The second mess we worked on was another F-86 which had apparently had a flame-out. The pilot had tried to make the runway with no power. He didn't make it. The plane hit the top of a hill at the end of the runway. It flipped upside down and came to rest at the bottom of the hill with its nose pointed up the hill. It then burst into flame and was still burning when we got there to photograph the mess.

The whole thing looked just like it might look in the movies, this time. There was the plane upside down at the base of the hill. A huge pall of black smoke rising from the bright red flames and people running around trying to put the fire out.

There was a whole bunch of us standing up there on the top of the hill looking down at the plane when the fire got to the armament. Suddenly, the air was full of fifty caliber bullets flying every which way. We didn't know which way to jump.

By the time it was all over, we had five more people to photograph. The people on either side of me were dead. I was too scared to even be sick. Once again, I had to ask myself, "Why me?"

The pilot had tried to eject from the plane but he was too close to the ground. The parachute never opened. He landed in a rice paddy and bounced out, leaving a crater about ten feet across. There was so much mud all over the place, it took over an hour to find the poor guy.

When we did finally find him, it was by accident. One of the other fellows was about to climb up on what he thought was a mud covered rock, when it moved. The pilot was still alive.

Every bone in his body must have been broken, but the guy was still alive. The medics on the scene tried their best to help the poor guy but there was really no hope. He died on the way to the hospital. I don't even like to think about the pain he must have felt.

The last mess I had to photograph on Okinawa was when a Constellation with a full load of Korean Vets came in to land. The pilot forgot to put his landing gear down. The plane hit the end of the runway, broke in two, then burst into flame. There were no survivors.

There were bits and pieces of wreckage and people mixed together strewn down almost the entire length of the runway.

It took three photographers and about fifty pounds of film to photograph all of it. There seemed to be no end to it. I clearly remember looking up the runway at what seemed like an endless line of total destruction.

Oddly enough here again, it was man's best friend which gave us the most trouble. There were an endless number of dogs, both wild and domestic running all over the runway with chunks of the dead. It was all we could do to get the pieces away from them to photograph.

For gross shock value, I think the worst was seeing the Air Police shoot one big dog trying to run away with someone's head in it's mouth. The dog was trying to find a way through the fence when it was shot.

It seems there was a green light which indicated when the planes landing gear was up and a red light next to it to tell if the landing gear was down. The green light was so bright it bothered the pilots. They had a bad habit of putting a small can over the two lights and forgetting it was there.

It was a fatal habit for ninety-seven people and a good crew. I have often wondered since then, why they didn't just change the light. I saw this happen once again in Tokyo at a later date. The little green light claimed one more life in an all to similar situation.

These were the times it was not a whole lot of fun being a photographer. However, the rest of the time we had a ball. There were a lot of mundane things to do like presentations and the officers wives sewing club, but we took it all in stride. After all, someone had to do it and after a while you kind of become hardened to it.

For me, the fun part was taking my camera off base and just taking pictures of people, doing people things. I would then make an enlargement of the picture and take it back to where I shot it. I would then try to find the person in the picture and give them a print of it to hang on their wall. I liked taking pictures of kids best of all, they weren't afraid to ham it up a little.

Nopo San

Chapter 11

The Base Alert

All went well for the next few weeks, and then we had a Base Alert. On Okinawa, a Base Alert was a test of our security. Some worthy soul was set upon the base with a picture of a monkey on his I.D. card instead of his own. He carried with him a brief case. If he was able to get into your building and place the brief case on your counter he said, "Bang! Your all dead."

Here's my friend Walter, all dressed up in his war suit. As you can see he's anxious to get started. I think we all had similar feelings about these alerts.

The assumption was he was a spy and the brief case was full of high explosives. To catch him, all you had to do was ask to see his I.D. Card. On seeing the moneky's picture one need say only, "You're caught." or something else of equal importance.

I think in all, he hit six different places and not once was he asked for his I.D. Card. Even our photo lab was amongst the destroyed. One of our people on seeing the man offered to carry the case for him. We knew how to take pictures. Security was definitely not our bag.

Figure 29 All Ready For Mock Combat.

Fortunately, I was not part of all this. When the Base Alert first came into being I was sent out to guard a "Quonset Hut". The Quonset Hut was way out in a place, far, far away from civilization. This was fine with me but it was also quite far from my barracks and the nearest chow hall.

I was told not to let anyone near the building unless I asked for their I.D. Card. Even then, no one was to enter the building without orders. Boy! Did I ever feel important. They even gave me a carbine to play with. No bullets mind you, but I had the carbine and a bayonet to wave around if anyone came by.

Time dragged on and no one came to relieve me. I was getting hungry. I had been told never to desert my post unless relieved by "The Corporal of the Guard" and this is what I made up my mind to do. I was going to stay right there and guard this place until someone I recognized to have authority, came by and told me to do something else.

This was the military way and, being a good little Airman, this is exactly what I was going to do. We didn't get to play soldier very often. Here I was given another chance to play soldier and I sure wasn't going to waste it.

By evening time hunger was starting to become a primary motivation and I was getting desperate. Through the dusty window of the building, I could see at least one of the boxes inside contained "C" rations. This meant **food**, or something reasonably close to it. At this point, even C Ration, sounded good to me.

Being careful not to damage the door, I forced the lock with my trusty bayonet and went into the building. Not only was there lots of C Ration in there but there was also a little stove to heat it on. I was home at last.

"C" Ration wasn't at all bad, I had no problem with it whatsoever. Some of the stuff was a little pasty but what do you expect to come out of a can, pheasant under glass? I ate my fill and enjoyed every bite. Not only was I playing soldier but I actually had a soldier type food to eat and a soldier type job to do.

At night, I fixed a bunk for myself out of a pile of

cardboard boxes. I rigged a trap at the door to wake me if someone tried to sneak in on me. Then I went to sleep.

No one came by. Planes didn't even fly over this place. There were no light at night, no sounds of civilization or anything else to let me know the rest of the world was still there.

Three days later found me fat, happy, and quite ignorant of what was going on around me. I had just finished lunch when I heard a jeep coming. I assumed my best guard posture and yelled, "**Halt!**" at the approaching jeep.

I pointed my carbine in their direction and the jeep screeched to a halt. I yelled again, just like they say to in the Air Force Hand Book, "**Advance and be recognized!**" Boy! Was I ever proud. I was doing soldier stuff just like it said to do in the book.

Two men, round eyed with fear, stepped out of the jeep saying, "**For God's sake! Don't shoot!**"

I said again, "**Advance and be recognized!**"

Both men stepped forward quickly and produced I.D. Cards. I looked the cards over carefully. They were not going to put one over on Herbst, not today at any rate. Satisfied neither card had a monkey on it, I asked what they were doing way out here.

They looked startled and both spoke at once, "Never mind us! What the heck are you doing out here?"

As one of the men was an officer, it meant I had to be nice to him. I explained I had been posted way out here to guard this building for the duration of the Base Alert. Once again, both men spoke at once, "But the Base Alert has been over for three days."

"**A-hah!**" I said back, "This is what you tell me now. I don't know you guys from Adam. Get the officer who put me out here to tell me, and I'll quit the post. Short of this, no one gets in this building without orders." I pointed my empty gun at then again. After all, only I knew there were no bullets in it. The two men looked at me again as if I were crazy. I, of course, looked back as if I wasn't.

They got into their jeep and drove off without another word

showering me with dust form the rear wheels. Somehow I got the idea they were not pleased with finding me out there. They seemed even less happy about the fact I was armed.

A little while later two Air Policemen drove up and asked for my weapon. Like the others, I asked for I.D. Cards. But, unlike the other two men, these guys pulled their guns. It was also quite obvious, unlike myself these guys had real bullets in their guns.

Undaunted by good common sense, I held my ground. I had been put out here to guard this building and guard it I would, until relieved.

Unfortunately for me, the Air Police had their orders also. They didn't know I didn't have any bullets and there was in their mind a kind of "Mexican Stand Off" in progress. Fortunately for me, they also realized I was rather confused by this turn of events.

Just as things were getting really tense, my C.O. from the Photo Lab showed up. "What the heck is going on here, where have you been all this time?" He was looking right at me as he talked.

"You put me out here to guard this building yourself, don't you remember?" I asked.

He looked at the ground a moment then, lifting his eyes to the sky, he said, "**Great Galloping Gobs of Goop!** You're right. I forgot all about you're being out here."

I found out later he had charged me with three day AWOL and stealing a weapon. With my kind of luck, had I been caught under any other conditions, I would have been shot on the spot.

When I got back to the barracks, I got the surprise of my life. There in the hallway was Billy Howard. How he ever made it all the way to Okinawa was something I will never understand. He hadn't changed at all, although it appeared he might have learned to wash himself. We talked a few moments and he went on his way. I found out a few months later, he had finally been discharged on a section eight.

Howard is out there somewhere, plodding along through life like the rest of us. I wish him well. He wasn't a bad sort, a little mixed up maybe, but not a bad sort at all. I was happy to hear he was out of the service. If ever there was a person who didn't belong in the Armed Forces it was Billy Howard.

Okinawa was the place where I learned all about demon rum. I went out one night to see just how drunk a body could get on twenty dollars. I had just received a "Dear John Letter" from my high school sweetheart and it just seemed to be the right thing to do at the time. I had known she was through with me and this was only an official notification but it was the last thing I wanted in my life at the time.

Whiskey was selling at twenty-five cents for a one ounce shot, at the time. I spent every cent of the twenty dollars I had, proving just how little respect I had for my stomach, or for all the rest of my body.

When I got back to the barracks, I managed to sign in and fumble my way through three combination locks. The one on the door to the room, the foot locker and my clothing locker. But then, I couldn't unbutton my shirt. Everything else worked fine, but those buttons just would not come loose, so I tore the shirt off.

It was kind of funny, in a way. I have such a clear recollection of all this and then there are parts of the thing I just can't place. I don't remember how I got back to the Barracks.

The next day, I was told I had volunteered for a cleanup detail. I guessed as a punishment for the night before. As I leaned over to pick up the first paper, something brown ran out of me and I fell headfirst into it.

When I woke up again, there was a doctor standing along side me. He smiled at me and said, "Welcome back to the land of the living. We thought we had lost you for a while there." Those words made a lasting impression on me and I never took another drink of whiskey or any other mixed drink. I was fully cured, I might drink some beer now and again but never whiskey.

I was asked once, why it was these things keep happening to me. I answered, "I guess I'm just lucky." In truth, I never really went out of my way to have any of these strange things to happen to me, they just happened. Except maybe, the fire cracker at Lowery A.F.B.

My first and, fortunately my last, Typhoon on Okinawa came ashore in September. I had to report to the Photo Lab for storm duty. Somehow, I had volunteered to work during the storm and occupy the Lab. This meant another fellow and myself were to stay in the Photo Lab to be sure no one broke into it during the storm.

Figure 30 Classified Trash.

Naturally, during the storm, we had lots of unsupervised time to play around with the equipment. As you can see from the picture, I got well soaked from my field jacket on down just walking over to the photo lab. We never missed an opportunity to play with all the expensive stuff we could get our sticky little claws on.

Since this time, I have often wondered just who would be

crazy enough to try to break into a place like the photo lab during a Typhoon. Most people are busy enough just trying to stay alive. But I guess there is some kind of screwball for every occasion.

The wind was howling and the rain was driving at me, as I walked to the lab. I can clearly remember the rain tasted salty. During a letup in the wind and rain, I walked out of the lab for some fresh air and for the first time saw the roads and lawns were littered with seaweed and little fish, most of which were still quite lively.

They didn't last long in the hot sun, but it was one of those unique experiences which lasts you all through life. It seems the wind got so strong it picked up a few inches of water off the tops of waves and blew it inland. The fish and seaweed were mixed in with the water.

Nopo San

Chapter 12

The Trip Over

It is said, into each life a little rain must fall, why then does it always seem to fall so long and hard on mine? I arrived in Tokyo, Japan, only because I was the one person in the Photo Lab on Okinawa who did not step forward for a change of duty assignment.

I liked Okinawa, it was warm and to my way of thinking, a tropical paradise. When the officer asked if there were any volunteers to be reassigned to Tokyo, I held fast while everyone else eagerly took one step forward. Guess who got reassigned? It just wasn't fair!

The trip to Tokyo was a joy which will live in my heart forever. For the first time in my military career, I was to go by air. I was told I could take everything I could carry and this suited me just fine.

I didn't want to go in the first place, now they told me I had to hand carry everything I owned. Even on Okinawa, one can accumulate one heck of a lot of stuff, in a relatively short period of time. In short, I showed up at the flight line laden with about 225 pounds of personal property.

When I went to check in for the flight, I was told the maximum I could take with me was 60 pounds. Now this was a kick in the teeth. I began to wonder just how I could get rid of all this extra stuff, when a friendly voice in the background came through, "He's Air Force, let him go and mark it down as 60 pounds."

The voice came from a man a little further down the counter, As I moved down to thank him, the man who was in line behind me moved up to be checked in. He was a Marine and was 6 ounces over the limit. They made him throw away a pair of socks.

To this day, I live in fear the Marine will somehow find me and exact a fearsome revenge.

The flight itself was uneventful. We had plenty of room as we flew in the cargo hold of a C-124. Do you have any idea what it's like to be plucked from a warm tropical paradise, placed in an unheated cargo hold, and then brought up to an altitude where warmth is only a dim memory?

To make matters worse, all my heavy winter type clothing was at the very bottom of one of my two duffel bags - and I didn't know which one it was.

Figure 31 A C-124 With Cargo Doors Wide Open.

This is the thing we flew to Japan in, a C-124. It was huge. There was some talk about the wings on the thing being too small to support it in normal flight. This did little to quell my fear of flying as this monster lumbered down the runway.

The flight did have its bright side. The Marine, who was forced to give up the pair of socks, was so cold he forgot all about me for the duration of the flight. I was glad about this because he and his buddies had threatened to make me fly on the outside of the plane.

Figure 32 Ready For Take Off.

As you can see, there would have been plenty of room out there for me. Still, I'm glad they never got the chance to put me out outside.

I had been told my new duty station would be Tokyo International Airport. As luck would have it, this is exactly where we landed. I reported to the duty officer on the base for orders and guess what? There were no orders for me.

There is no way I can describe to a civilian, the feeling one gets when he hears the ominous phrase, "You have no orders". It means your out there in limbo somewhere. Lost in a stormy sea where nobody wants you or cares about you except maybe, the Air Police.

You know your orders are out there somewhere and there is

someone somewhere looking around saying, "Where is this guy? He should have been here by now." The problem is, this person is usually saying this into a phone connected to Military Police Headquarters.

I was told, by the duty officer, my orders had not yet arrived so I produced the copies I had hand carried. Unfortunately, there were no matching orders on file at the base. The duty officer told me I should get on the bus and go to the Air Force Headquarters at Tachikawa and get some new orders.

Having no idea where Tachikawa was or how to get there, I had the officer sign my orders with the time, date, and reason he had sent me to Tachikawa. Then I went looking for a bus.

The bus trip to Tachikawa was four hours long. For me it was four hours of pain and aggravation. The bus had to be at least two-hundred years old, the heater didn't work and it was cold. I had to stuff my six-foot four-inch frame into a seat designed for a person no taller than six-feet two-inches. Add to this, the fact I was toting over two hundred pounds of stuff and you can begin to see the problem.

At Tachikawa I again, reported to the duty officer and explained my problem. He searched the files and, again, came up empty. There were no orders here either. I did manage to get him to give me a Transient Chow Pass so I could get something to eat, but this is all he would do for me.

And so it went. I got a first hand tour of every Air Force installation in Japan, by bus. I could not eat in a military chow hall because I had no orders, so I floated from base to base by bus for four days. Sleep on the bus was next to impossible and all I could get to eat were candy bars and an occasional sandwich.

At long last, I wound up back at Japan International Airport where I was promptly arrested for being three days AWOL My orders had arrived shortly after I had left for Tachikawa by bus. I was so tired I didn't care. I just handed over my copy of my orders and fell asleep on the bench at the Air Police Headquarters.

The only thing that saved my skin, was I had asked

someone to sign my orders at each base I had gone to. It proved I had been hard at work trying to find my duty assignment. The AWOL charges were dropped.

At long last, I had arrived at my new home, such as it were. It was too dark to see very much as I had arrived late at night. The Air Police drove me, and my stuff, to what looked like an old aircraft assembly hanger and brought me inside. My new life at Japan International Airport had begun.

Nopo San

Chapter 13

A Whole New Way Of Life

I had arrived at Japan International Airport in the wee hours of the morning and, in my condition, any place with a bed would have been heaven. I was taken in hand by a sympathetic Air Policeman, led over to a huge building and shown to a bed onto which I flopped without even making it up.

The next morning, I unpacked my stuff and settled in for the duration. It was during this time the full horror of where I was, and the conditions under which I was expected to live, settled in on me.

Figure 33 A Picture Of Our Beloved Base.

The barracks at Japan International Airport was a beauty. Just the corner of it is visible to the right of the peak of the hanger roof. On a clear day Fuji Yama was visible just about where the three smoke stacks are.

The outside was painted, or "dirted" as the case may be, a dirty grey which kind of blended in with the dirty grey overcast which seemed to hang over the base most of the time. At one time, the building must have been a kind of yellow but the color, as was the color on most of the base, was covered by thick grey grit.

The only good thing about the barracks was it was located just around the corner from the chow hall. As a matter of fact the back of our barracks almost connected to the back of the chow hall but in the infinite wisdom of the military mind, you had to walk about four blocks to get out of the barracks into the chow hall.

Figure 34 The "Kuso Gawa" In Front Of Our Chow Hall.

From the front door of the chow hall I had to walk a block to the left. Then two blocks toward the runway. At the main road through the base I turned to the Left again and walked about two more blocks past the craft shop and the base movie theater. It was not a pleasant looking place and I longed for the clean white sand of Okinawa. There was nothing white on the base.

There was a canal which ran past the front of the Chow hall. We called it the Kuso Gawa. The name certainly seemed appropriate. Kuso, meaning human excrement used as fertilizer and from the smell of it, the Gawa was appropriately named.

Across the canal was the Oki Steel Works and it belched smoke and soot, day and night. There was always something going on across the river. The Oki Steel Works never slept.

The Chow Hall was probably the only bright spot in my life on this base. It, like the one on Okinawa, was completely staffed with Japanese civilian workers. The Japanese seemed to be a lot more friendly than their Okinawan counterpart. It was a pleasure to go to the Chow Hall here.

To be very honest with you, there were lots of other guys there with me and we all managed to get along. In the end, we all survived the experience and had a good time of it. I guess you could say to yourself, "The grass is always greener on the other side of the fence." Every one else in the Far East envied us because we were only minutes from Tokyo.

In the background was Mt. Fuji, shrouded in smog from the Oki Steel Works. It was the same smog which seemed to cover the base and make everything a dirty grey color. It was so bad at times it was hard to tell where the road stopped and building began. Likewise, it was just as hard to tell where the roof stopped and the smog began.

Looking at the situation as I saw it, I often wondered just how the bombers found their way through the stuff to bomb Tokyo? Better yet, how in the world did they ever know if they had hit the target?

The inside of the barracks was every bit as terrible as the outside of the building led one to believe. The only partition in the whole place was the floor separating the first floor from the second floor, and it was home to about 500 people.

Everything was painted grey, battleship grey, this paint could only have come form the Navy. The Navy must have truly hated the Air force to have done this to us. The only relief I got from the perpetual grey was to go into the darkroom, at the Photo Lab, and turn on the red light for a little color. Even though I was color blind, it helped to know there was some color other than grey left in the world.

There were two bathrooms, one up and one down, located in the middle of each floor. The bunks seemed to stretch out forever in neat rows with standing lockers along side each one with the ever present foot locker at the foot of every bunk.

The only hint of deviation was some poor soul had tied a red ribbon to the head of his bunk, probably so he could find it in this veritable sea of identical bunks.

There were some windows scattered about but there was so much dirt on the outside no amount of cleaning helped. They did let a bit of daylight in but not enough to do much good. If one woke up, there was just enough light to see if it was day or night outside.

If a pin were to be dropped at one end of the room it could be heard at the other end. There was nothing in this place to obstruct sound or light. As luck would have it, my bunk was located about ten rows from the bathroom. Or should I say bath area, so I was privy to everything which went on in there, day or night.

The base was so grey the fellows in the radio shop used to look into boxes of color coded radio parts to get their daily color fix. It really wasn't so bad for me, I am color blind, so everything looked grey to me anyhow. It must have been hell for those people who knew what color was and were now experiencing a total lack of it.

The first thing I did after settling in, was to find a place off base in which to sleep and call home. Life in The Goldfish Bowl was just not for me. I would maintain a bunk in the barracks for inspection, with a full compliment of military clothing in the locker, complete with polished shoes under the bunk, but I was determined to live off base. I hired a Japanese civilian to maintain the bunk for me. It wasn't expensive because this same young man maintained about a dozen bunks like mine.

For about the first week or so, I slept on the floor of the Photo Lab in the dark room, but this would never do for the long haul. I just hated the living conditions in the Gold Fish Bowl. I have never liked sleeping in the same room with other people and I have avoided it whenever possible.

Figure 35 Our Beloved Base Photo Lab.

The Photo Lab was only a few blocks from the barracks. It was part of the Signal Corp on this base and we were right next door to the Radio Repair Shop.

It was just behind the little picket fence to the left of the door where I buried my little dog Goofy Bopolo.

I have just got to tell you about the bathroom we had at the Photo Lab. It was an outbuilding we shared with the Japanese Civilian Guard, the Signal Corp, and the general public. It was half Japanese and half American.

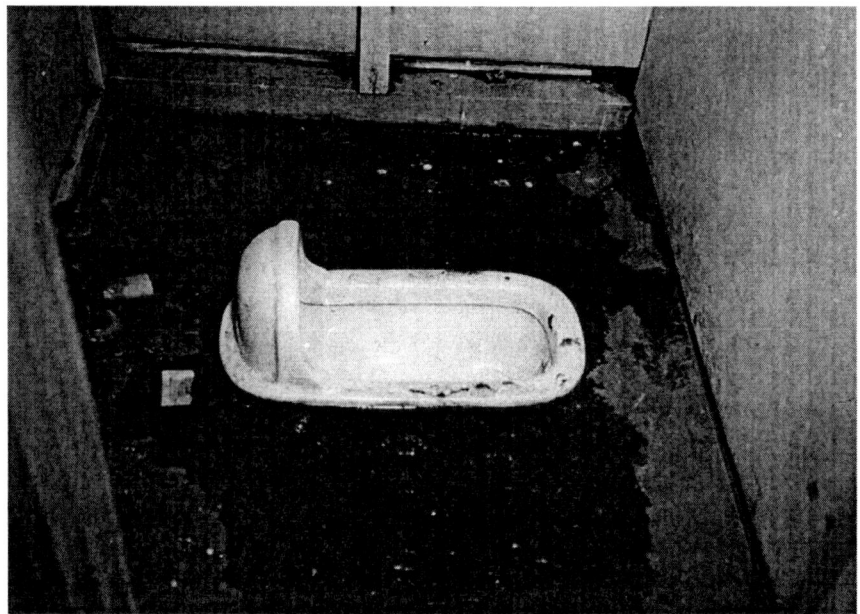

Figure 36 A Japanese Benjo or Gofugio.

This might seem a little gross, but it must be told. The Japanese half had a typical Japanese toilet in it. It was a ceramic thing which looked a lot like a urinal but it was flat on the ground. One straddled the thing, but did not sit down. When finished, one flushed it just like a regular toilet.

Naturally, since we got there, things have changed a great deal but you're still going to find this kind of plumbing in the outback.

We had a group of school kids come through one day and, of course, there were the predictable calls of nature. When we went to the latrine later to use it ourselves. It was obvious at least, one of the kids had never used an American style toilet before.

The evidence was piled on the back of the wooden toilet seat, and there were two muddy footprints on the seat with the evidence. The seat just wasn't long enough for the poor kid to get the job done right and there was obviously no time to wait for the facilities the poor kid was supposed to use.

This is all that's left of the Mitsubishi Fighter Plane manufacturing plant. It's what's known as a "Tori", (gate way or chicken roost). How the bombers missed the thing is a mystery. Even the road leading through the Tori was destroyed.

Way off to the right you can just make out the bombed out building. The man standing under the Tori is about 5 feet 8 inches tall.

Figure 37 All There Was Left Of The Mitsubishi Fighter Manufacturing Plant

Inside, the buildings were a complete bombed out shambles. The devastation was total and complete. There wasn't a usable part in the whole place.

Americans were discouraged from going there because there were some Japanese who once worked there still living in the area and they were a bit bitter and resentful about the destruction.

I guess you can't really blame them. Their whole way of life was destroyed in a flash. There was absolutely nothing left to fall back on. It must have been a bitter pill to have to swallow.

For some reason nothing was done with the area. This was strange because of its proximity to the airport.

I don't know who this fellow was but his moustache certainly identifies him as someone important. This style originated before WWII.

The ends of the moustache were tied behind his head to maintain their shape when he slept or was at ease in his home.

It was typical of the style before the Second World War and the influence of the American occupation.

Figure 38 Now This You Could Call A Moustache.

The statue was in front of the Fuji View Hotel where a bunch of us went on a three day pass. It was in every way a beautiful place to enjoy nature.

A bunch of us Base

Figure 39 The Fuji View Hotel.

Photographers went there with our cameras on a three day pass. It was a beautiful place with a large lake and very well maintained gardens every where. The rooms were clean and neat as a pin.

Even tree care at the hotel was a fine art. This man's job was to maintain every tree on the property and nothing more. He controlled every aspect of the trees growth meticulously. The Grounds of the Fuji View Hotel were about thirty acres and he took care of every tree on the acreage.

The ladder he uses is a triangular affair with three legs. This is so he won't have to lean the ladder against a tree possibly damaging it. As I remember it, he stepped from the ladder onto one of the larger limbs next to the main trunk in order to get at the very top of the tree.

Figure 40 Tree Care Is A Fine Art.

Also typical of life in Japan is the electric fence used to keep people out of the grounds. The Japanese tended to be rather possessive of their properties. Stone or cement walls were usually topped with broken bottles or something similar. It did tend to discourage the armature trespasser quite nicely.

From our window on the second floor of the hotel we

looked down on their gardens. Like the trees on the property the gardens were the subject of intense maintenance.

As Americans, we were not accustomed to this kind of intensity in maintenance. However after seeing someone follow us around fixing what we moved, we became quite conscious of their efforts to pick up after us. From then on we tried best to comply with them and started picking up after ourselves.

Figure 41 A View From My Window At The Fuji View.

In the background is a large lake and we were welcomed to take pictures of it and the grounds any time we liked. There were also boats to rent but the Japanese oar system was a mystery to us. They used only one oar and made a sweeping motion with it behind the boat. Try as we might none of us ever got the hang of it.

The front of the Fuji View Hotel was every bit as beautiful as the gardens at the rear of it. During the whole time we were there we had only one complaint. There was no place on the grounds or inside the hotel from which you could see Mount Fuji.

No trip to Japan would be complete without paying your respects to the Kamakura DiButsu. Did you know he is hollow and the Japanese priests used to climb up inside the statue and speak to the crowds through the eye slits.

Figure 42 This Is The Kamakura DiButsu I'm to the Right Walking Towards It.

This is truly an impressive statue and one does get a feeling of reverence in its presents. This is me on the right walking toward the statue to pay my respects.

On this particular day we had the park pretty much to ourselves. We got to poke around a lot more than if we had been with a tour group. It was a wonderful place to visit and a photographers dream come true.

Due to the size and weight of the Speed Graphic Camera,

we usually only carried one with us. There was also a secondary consideration, there were only two cameras on our base. If we took both, the feathers would surly have hit the fan.

If you look closely at this photo, there is a slight ridge along the bottom of the statue. The ridge breaks on the right hand side and you can just barely make out the cleverly concealed doorway to the inside of the statue. The windows speak for themselves. Although you have seen many pictures of the front of this remarkable sculpture, I'll bet this is the first time you've seen the back of it.

Figure 43 the DiButsu Is Hollow

You might note how well the grounds behind the statue are maintained. There isn't a scrap of litter anywhere in sight.

The large stones are for visitors to sit on. They were not at all comfortable to sit on for any length of time but it was a lot better than standing on your feet the whole time. We spent about a day poking around in this park. It was well worth every minute of the time we spent there.

During my stay in Japan I was fortunate enough to visit with an old friend of my fathers. Mr. T. Sakata. This is Mr. Sakata's place of business in Yokohama.

Figure 44 Sakata Seeds In Yokohama Japan.

Note the circular well in the foreground. At one point the Korean slaves imported before W.W.II revolted and poisoned the water supply in many of Japan's larger cities. Until the poison could be flushed out of the system people relied on wells like this one for clean water to drink and cook with

Sakata Seeds was the first business to get going again after the war. They imported several thousand pounds of onion seed from our family business, Herbst Brothers Seedsmen, Inc. Mr. Sakata was awarded a medal personally by the Emperor of Japan for this service to his country.

Herbst Brothers Seedsmen, Inc. Had an unbroken contract with Sakata Seeds from 1924 to 1974. It was one of the few contracts to survive the Second World War.

Here Mr. Sakata, His wife and Mr. Masuno stand in the company garden. Mr. Masuno took over the company when Mr. Sakata retired.

Figure 45 Mr. Sakata, Mrs. Sakata and Mr. Masuno.

Mr. Masuno was born in New Jersey before the war and went over to help Mr. Sakata build his business up again. You might note, Mrs. Sakata wears Eastern style shoes while the woman on the sidewalk wears the traditional Japanese Geta (shoe) and a traditional Japanese outfit.

Take a look at the interesting box around the electrical wires on the pole at the far Right of the picture. I have no idea what the box was for except it might be a safety feature to keep the wires from dropping into the road if they were broken.

The street is a main road leading up from the Yokohama train station. Is was still in pretty rough shape but there were working trolley car tracks in the center of it.

T. Sakata & company was recognized the world over as the world's leader in the introduction and production of Hi-Bred flower and vegetable seeds. Sakata gave us flowering cabbage and kale to name only a few. Here he is with his wife and Mr. Masuno in one of his experimental greenhouses.

Figure 46 The Inside Of One Of Sakata's Greenhouses.

My father, Fred P. Herbst Sr. Introduced many of Sakata's creations into the United States. Flower growers were especially pleased to be able to buy seeds of a flower and have the entire field produce the same color flowers.

The Seedless Watermelon was one of Sakata's ideas and was introduced here in the early 60's.

Most of the experimental work was done by hand pollinating the various flowers with small camel hair brushes. This was back breaking tedious labor and it went on for hours. Then the seed is hand picked and grown in special greenhouses.

Working conditions in Sakata's office were not the best but this was fairly typical all over Japan at the time. Note the ever present tea pot for the making of Green Tea. Water had to be boiled and those who did drink from the faucet paid dearly for their stupidity.

Figure 47 Working Conditions In the Office Were Not The Best.

He did have the first Kanji Typewriter I have ever seen. It was a huge affair in a room by itself. The walls of the room were stacked high with trays of Kanji characters. When you typed with it, you selected the tray in which the character was located. You then loaded the tray into the machine and printed the character. After printing the character the tray was replaced in the spot it was found and the next tray was brought out.

My father took these pictures on his trip to Japan to visit with Mr. Sakata around 1924. Unfortunately he did not date the pictures nor did he indicate what the ladies names are.

As you will see in other pictures in this text, there has been little change since then in lady's fashion over there. The lady's hair is done in a typical style for the time period.

My father took these pictures in 1924 when he visited Japan to see Mr. Sakata's operation.

It's a shame my dear old dad wasn't a bit better about marking his pictures as to content. I have absolutely no idea where these pictures were taken or who the ladies are.

Please excuse the fuzzy picture at the far right. These

pictures are almost 80 years old and they deserve to be a bit fuzzy.

The more modern Japanese woman, the Japanese I saw when there use a wig instead of trying to maintain a hair style like these lady's have.

Figure 54 Three Ladies In A Typical Japanese Room.

There is a tea set in the lower Left hand corner and a rice paper door center Right. The floor is usually covered with a one inch thick rice straw mat called a "Tatami". Under the Tatami is a more or less standard hard wood floor.

The round window would be considered exotic and only found it the better Japanese homes. I would have to suspect the pictures were taken in or around Sakata's home. However I'm not at all sure about this.

One thing which surprises me is the quality of the pictures he took over there. They are pretty darn good considering the kind of cameras they had to work with back then.

Here is the last of my fathers pictures from 1924, you will note in the pictures he took,

Figure 55 I Sure Wish Dad Had Marked These Pictures With Names And Dates.

there is an interesting mixture of traditional women's fashions.

The pine trees in the background would indicate this picture was shot in the early Spring.

The picture may have been taken near the Sea because of the type of tree and the stunted growth pattern.

The ladies all wear the traditional clothing of the 1924 period including the Geta which you can just see above the grass.

The sock worn with the Geta has a stitched pocket for the big toe. This is made so the toes can be used to hold the Geta in place when walking.

Figure 56 The World's Only Three Roofed Bogota.

This is, or was, the worlds only three roofed Bogota. It was located in a beautiful park near the center of Tokyo. Almost every other Bogota in the world has five roofs.

It's hard to describe the serenity one feels in these perfectly maintained parks. It's kind of as if you have stepped into another world. A world without the everyday noise and pressure of

Figure 57 A Tea House In The Park

business. There's no traffic and large crowds are kept to a minimum. I spent hours just wandering around taking pictures of everything I could find of interest.

I found this very nice little Tea House where for only a few cents you could stop and refresh yourself. When the tea is served you also get a hot wet towel to wipe your face and hands with. As you can see the water in the pond is absolutely still. There is nothing to disturb the serenity of the place.

This Tea House drew a bit larger crowd but was none the less beautiful to just sit and look at. As you can see, at this time there was still a fairly good mix of traditional ladies wear represented.

Figure 58 Another Little Tea House In The Park

Unlike the American point of attraction, the Japanese woman used the back of her neck instead of the more frontal approach used by American and European counterparts.

It was a bit hard to get used to. You walk up to a lady to start a conversation and she immediately turns her back on you. It kind of takes the starch out of your sails until you realize she is trying to show you her best side.

In this park you find a good mixing of both Eastern and Western fashions. Most of the time while I was there, the lady is expected to wear the traditional Japanese dress when appearing in public on formal occasions. For general everyday wear, the traditional outfit was way too time consuming to get into.

This park was only a few blocks from the very center of downtown Tokyo but there was no traffic noise and it was very

Figure 59 I Never Did Find Out What This Was Used For.

peaceful.

I never did find out what this thing was. It isn't a bridge and it isn't a wall of any sort. It was only one roadway width wide

115

but there was nothing on the other side of it. The only thing I could think of was, it was some sort of ammunition bunker left over from the war. The thing is probably long since demolished and built over but I'll always wonder just what its purpose was.

Nopo San

Chapter 14

The First May Day

I was lucky enough to find a room in the house of a Japanese fisherman and his family. The man spoke no English, and my mastery of the Japanese language left much to be desired.

In the beginning, we conversed more by guess-work than anything else. He spoke and I had to guess what he was talking about, then I would speak and I had to assume he was guessing at what I was saying. At least, on this one point, we were equal. Soon, a friendship developed between us which was to endure until the day I left Japan and, I hope, long after.

As a gesture of good will and friendship, I would go to the B. X. (Base Exchange) and buy my Cigarette ration and the two bottles of booze I was allowed per month. Then, as I neither drank hard booze nor smoked, I would give these things to the fisherman and his wife. I really thought I was doing them a favor.

The fisherman would trade the cigarettes on the black market and drink the booze. In turn, they would have me over to dinner a few times a week and I thought everything was going very nicely.

Then one day, the Fisherman's wife, who spoke no English whatsoever, stopped me. Through an interpreter, she asked me to please stop bringing the gifts to her house. The fisherman, when drunk, became quite abusive and used to beat his wife.

Naturally, I stopped on the spot and life, once again, returned to normal in the fisherman's home. I bring this up to point out the Japanese have basically the same problems we do, they just have a little different way of handling them.

I like kids in general, I like to think of them as small people and actually this is quite true. Kids have it all, over us, they learn faster, they develop faster, and they are quicker on the up take than their older counterparts. Because I like kids, I began taking the fisherman's kids to the movies on Saturday.

As time went by, the kids multiplied. Soon all the kids in the neighborhood were tagging along just to sit in the movie theater and watch Nopo San, as I was called, do his thing. Nopo San meant Mr. Giant in plain English.

In Japanese legend, Nopo San was a friendly giant who helped people and liked kids. I fit right in to the description and I laughed right along with the rest, whenever someone called me by the name Nopo San. In short, I had a ball with this mob, even though I had no idea what they were saying about me. Whatever it was, it seemed to be along the lines of good natured fun.

The fisherman's wife had a bed made specially for me and when it arrived it was the talk of the neighborhood, no one had ever seen a bed so big before in their life. I guess she was kind of paying me back for not bringing any more whiskey around. Then, more as a joke I suppose, the fisherman had a pair of Japanese Wooden Shoes made for me.

These things were at least fourteen inches long, six inches wide and three inches thick. They were cut from, what looked, a four by six plank. The things looked very much like the Shower Clogs, which are so popular today, but with two by two cleats located on the front and back. The cleats ran from one side to the other of the "Geta," as it was called, about two inches from the toe and about an inch from the heel. They were huge and clunked along on the road advertising to one and all Nopo San was coming.

As my hulking form became more widely known, I heard my name called out more and more from the local Saki houses, or bars in English. I would go in, have a few drinks with the locals and invariably learn a word or two more of Japanese.

We would sing songs and give the traditional **Banzai** salute for the Emperor in Tokyo. I tried my best to follow the custom of these friendly people and they responded by trying to teach me as much Japanese as they could, as fast as they could.

Towards the end of April, I began to notice there were

preparations for some kind of festival going on. It was not like my new found friends to exclude me and I felt a little hurt. I mentioned my feelings to one of my new friends, who spoke a little English and he made sure I was included from then on.

It was to be a **May Day Celebration** and I could remember, in school, reading about the children dancing around the May Pole with ribbons. It seemed, to me at least, this was going to be a real ball. I pitched in with both arms right up to my shoulders and helped decorate the boats with banners and slogans, all in Japanese, and helped load the gallons of Saki and beer which was to be consumed, during the upcoming festivities.

Finally, on the last day of April, all was in readiness. I was handed a blue headband which would identify me as one who had helped make the party a success, and a wild bash was thrown at a local Sake House.

The next morning, I found myself on a boat, like the boats on the right, headed out into Tokyo Bay with about ten other people. In the background is the Kana Gawa Bridge where so many ended it all on January one.

Figure 60 The Fishing Fleet

It seems, all Japanese debt comes due on the first of

January each year. If you are unable to pay or renegotiate the debt for another year you are expected to do the honorable thing. The bridge over the Kana Gawa was a popular place for this to happen. It was either done by ones self or with the help of those you owed money to.

We were all, myself no exception, drunk as lords. We were singing songs, I didn't understand or know the words to, at the top of our voices. Somehow, when you have a snoot full, words have little meaning.

We joined, what seemed like, hundreds of other boats, all filled to the brim with equally drunk merry makers. I can remember thinking to myself this was going to be the kind of party I would be able to tell my kids about, when and if, I ever had any.

The Flotilla sailed out of the mouth of the Kana Gawa River and into Tokyo Bay just at sunrise. As I looked over toward the base, I could see the shore was lined with my comrades and I waved to them. They seemed to be waving back what could be more natural than this. Frankly, I was a bit hung-over and after waving a moment I went looking for a Saki bottle. I needed a bit of the hair of the dog that bit me.

A huge banner was unfurled and one of the poles was thrust into my hands. I never got a chance to read the banner. It was strung between three boats and I was hanging on to the trailing end of the thing for dear life as the wind pulled at it.

The trick was to keep it taut between the boats, as they bounced around on the small waves out in Tokyo Bay. I had to concentrate on keeping the banner steady, rather than what was going on around me for the moment. There seemed to be no agreement whatsoever as to which direction we were going, and I was pulled first this way, then the other way, as the boats went in different directions.

Finally, about noon, I had to let go of my end of the banner or be pulled over the side. Everyone laughed and we sang another song. We finished off the last of the Saki and beer, before we headed in for the evening. For some reason, I seemed to be the hit of the party, although the details of why were a little fuzzy.

We hit the shore and moved inland like a Marine landing practice. Aimed, of course, at occupying the nearest Saki House. I missed this last party, as duty called the next morning and I wanted a clear head. I went back to my room at the fisherman's house and collapsed.

The next morning, as I walked towards the base, everyone seemed unusually glad to see me. I had no idea why, but I was flattered by the attention. Once on the base, however, I was greeted with a totally different reception. People scowled at me and muttered unpleasant things in my direction.

I had never met a Supreme Commander before, however, this situation changed abruptly. I was ordered to appear before his mightiness, **at once!** I suppose under ordinary circumstances the man might have been considered friendly looking.

For some strange reason, this was not the case on this day. His face was beet red from the collar up, fire belched from his flame red nostrils threatening to ignite the papers on his desk. His mouth moved but no sound came out, just smoke which smelled alarmingly like sulphur and brimstone. It almost looked like small button horns were trying to push their way out through the hair on top of his head.

At last, regaining some measure of control, he looked right at me through red-rimmed and bloodshot eyes. "**Where were you yesterday?**" he screamed. "**Is this you in these pictures?**" and he thrust a newspaper in my face.

Sure enough, there I was right on the front page of an all Japanese newsletter. I nodded my head to indicate yes and I pulled the blue headband out of my pocket to show them I still had the proof.

A look of total disbelief flooded the Supreme Commander's face, he seemed to pale and collapse back into his chair. "**Good God!**" he said, "**It's true!**" he paused for a moment as if to get control, then he looked at me again and asked, "Do you have any idea what you have done? Look carefully at these pictures."

I followed the line of his pointing, but still shaking, finger to the center picture on the front page. There I was firmly attached to one end of a huge banner. This time I could see, for the first time, what was written on the banner. It said, "**Yankee Go Home!**"

Now, also for the first time, I noticed the other people in the boat with me were not waving, they were shaking their fists.

Only now did it occur to me the May Day celebration I had attended was not the benign celebration I had remembered from school, but in reality, this was the **Communist May Day Celebration.**

My friends off base were glad I had not been killed by the communists and this was why they had greeted me with such enthusiasm.

My former friends, on base, were sorry I hadn't been killed, and this is why they greeted me with scowls and mumbled oaths.

Somehow, I had an awful time getting it through my head, these people I had been having such a good time with might just have killed me for political reasons. I had known they were communists and it hadn't made the slightest difference to me. It was like a Republican drinking with a Democrat, you just didn't discuss politics.

For the first time, I got the feeling I was in Big Trouble! I looked slowly around the room, all eyes were focused on me. There wasn't a friendly face among the lot and there was enough brass represented in the room to sink a good sized boat.

The officer who had taken my blue headband made a loop of it and slowly pulled it through his fist. He made a hissing sound through clenched teeth as he did so. Somehow, I got the idea he was not going to be my friend.

It took over an hour for me to convince these worthy men I was not a communist or a subversive of any kind. I don't think they will ever believe, all I did was attend a party and get myself totally smashed.

In the end, I was allowed to go back to the Photo Lab but

only after being made aware big brother would be watching every step I made, from then on. I was also told the officer who still had my blue headband would be in charge of watching me. I debated with myself about asking for the headband back but in the end I opted for silence.

Figure 61 Japanese Fire Fighters Show Their Stuff

Shortly thereafter there was a fire on the runway and the Japanese Fire Department showed up to help us fight it. Like their Civilian Guard counterpart, they were tough and well schooled in their job. After what they had to contend with during the bombing of Tokyo, they could probably have taught us a few things.

They had their part of the fire under control in short order. Their method of fire fighting was a bit different from ours. They relied more on the individual fireman running up to the blaze with the hose rather than fighting the fire from the comparative comfort of an enclosed truck.

Their head gear was every bit as good as ours and possibly

a bit more protective. Unfortunately, their equipment was a bit dated and some of it was even left over from the War.

Figure 62 Telling The Stick To Remain Still And Not Fall.

    I thought this fellow was worthy of two shots. He was demonstrating his mastery over the natural elements.. In the first picture, he tells the stick with the stone tied to it to remain still and not to move.

    He then proceeds to threaten the stick with all sorts os screams and attacks with the stick he brandishes. Note the WWII boots and trousers he wears. He is obviously a "retired" officer from the Japanese Army.

    He managed to draw quite a crowd but I don't know how much of what he said they believed.. At the end of his performance he passed the hat and nearly everyone gave him something.. In the foreground of the bottom picture is a stick held between two posts by paper strips. Using the stick he brandishes at the rock, he smashed the suspended stick without breaking the two paper strips.

Now, this was a good trick.

I'm sure you can see a lot of what he did was determined by his ability to balance the rock and stick perfectly. The other trick was determined by the two little sticks holding the paper ribbons swiveling at just the right moment and releasing the paper.

Figure 63 No Threat Moved The Stick

After the war there was little left standing. Every effort was directing at rebuilding Japan from the ashes of defeat. Any entertainment of any kind was immediately seized on by anyone within ear shot.

He had the added advantage of being positive entertainment. This man was showing the others there capable of being more than just re-builders. They could still enjoy the simple things in life like a little magic or what have you.

You can see most of the people in the crowd wore dark

outfits. This coupled with an almost total lack of street lighting makes night driving a tricky proposition. Now you have to also take into account the schools are open 24 hours a day and the children attend in three shifts. They also wear dark colored uniforms like the boys and girls in the front row.

The Japanese Civilian Guard also wore dark uniforms but you didn't mess with these guys if you knew what was good for you.

Figure 64 Japanese Civilian Guard

Nopo San

Chapter 15

Fatso

I had made lots of new friends both on and off base. I was anxious to share my off base friends with the other fellows back on base. Among these other fellows was a supply clerk, whose name I have long since forgotten. All the rest of us called him "Fatso." He was only about five-feet six-inches but he must have weighed well over three-hundred pounds. He was not the most pleasant person I had ever met, but he kind of went with the territory.

One night a few of the boys from the Photo Lab and myself, decided to party it up at one of the local Saki/Geisha Houses. Nothing would do, but what we just had to take Fatso with us. After all, he wasn't a bad a guy. Besides, he had access to all sorts of neat things, we needed.

Figure 65 Geisha Girls Doing Their Stuff

By the way, just for the record, these girls are not prostitutes. They are high priced entertainers and this is all they are.

It was through Fatso we got our, much needed, replacement

enlarger. We had asked for a standard four by five enlarger to replace the worn out enlarger we were trying to use in the darkroom. We knew there was a freeze on resupply because the base was due to be handed back to the Japanese in the near future. Still the enlarger was on its last legs and had to be replaced if we were to continue functioning as a photo lab.

The enlarger we got turned out to be a **huge** eight by eight aerial roll film enlarger which would not fit in our dark room. It was in almost as bad a shape as the enlarger it was to have replaced. We had to keep it out in the parking lot and only use it on dark nights.

Even so, it was fun to have. We used it to project pictures up against the sides of building and then develop them out in the parking lot with mops and buckets. We did some great stuff with the old relic. It was the policy of the men at the Photo Lab, nothing should ever go to waste. We even managed to jury-rig the old enlarger to continue in use for a little longer.

It was Fatso who cut the order and got the replacement order through for us. We owed him one. Like the not wasting bit, we had another policy, **we always paid our debts**.

The place we went to was just off base so it was within easy walking distance. With practiced skill, we invaded the place and set about drinking all the Saki and Beer they had in stock. The other fellows drank the local "Ocean Whiskey," but having learned my lesson on Okinawa, I stuck to the Beer and Saki. It wasn't long before none of us were feeling any pain.

Then the imponderable happened. It all started with a simple question; "Where is the bathroom?" Fatso had a call of nature. These things do happen when one drinks a lot of beer.

There was, however, one thing you should all keep in mind. As I explained to you earlier about the Japanese toilet, you must add to your knowledge, the Japanese used Cesspools.

These cesspools are located directly under the floor of the bathroom. Naturally the cesspool produces a lot of moisture, this tends to rot the floorboards in the bathroom at a rapid rate.

The Japanese people tend to be slightly built and a good bit smaller than their American counterpart. The floorboards lasted a good bit longer with their use than they did for us. Now, however, it was our very own Fatso who was going to test the strength of the Benjo floor.

Figure 66 The Honey Bucket Man. By Fred P. Herbst Sr. 1924.

The product of these Cesspools was sold to the "Honey Bucket Man" to be used as fertilizer, by the farmers outside of town. The Honey Bucket Man would come by once or twice a month and bail out the Cesspool.

He used his "Honey Bucket, to bail the stuff from the Cesspool into his "Honey Bucket Wagon." Then the stuff would be hauled out to the country, by the Honey Bucket Man, in his Honey Bucket Wagon, and used to fertilize the crops.

About the only thing changed since my father took this picture in 1924 is the cart is now motorized instead of horse drawn.

These Cesspools were located under the floor of the house, bar, etc. Every building in Haneda had one, it was like our indoor plumbing. The flooring over the Cesspool had a hole cut in it so the Cesspool could be refilled by whom ever chose to use the facility, and for whatever reason.

It's only logical to assume the flooring of this one having been subjected to the ravages of constant moisture, had become weakened in time. Of course, **no one** thought of this at the time Fatso asked where the bathroom was.

Timing had been essential, we had watched the Honey Bucket Man for weeks as he made his rounds. He was due at this place the next day. This meant the cesspool was full to the brim with all kinds of goodies. We were a devious lot. When we put a scam together, it was a study in flawless perfection. "Mission Impossible" couldn't have put it together better than we did.

We all watched Fatso waddle his way back through the building toward the "Benjo," as it was called in Japanese, without saying a word.

As one, we held our breath. Shortly, from the rear of the building, came a crash --- followed by a scream of fright --- followed by a resounding splash --- followed by a strange blubbering noise. Not one of us could even guess what was going on in the back of the building. We were all too busy laughing so hard we couldn't stand up without help.

Moments later, however, we all raced to rescue Fatso. It was a sight I will never forget. There was Fatso standing neck deep in liquid --- fertilizer. A piece of toilet paper was draped from the back of his head, down over his face and he was trying his best to scream for help without opening his mouth.

Somehow we managed not to laugh as we stood there looking down at this poor unfortunate individual, but I mean to tell you this was hard to do.

We got a length of rope from a nearby merchant and hauled him out of the Cesspool. Then, keeping up-wind and a goodly distance away, we led poor Fatso back to the base.

We brought him out to the end of one of the runways and hosed him down with a fire hose. Then, we had him throw his clothing out into Tokyo Bay and made him walk back to the barracks naked.

Although we tried many times after this to include Fatso in our drinking plans, we could never get him to leave the base with us again. Fortunately, we never needed anything from Supply again before I left Japan. I could just imagine what the Photo Lab's priority would have been. I wonder if the military has a priority lower than last?

Nopo San

Chapter 16

Osoba

"Osoba" is a type of noodle soup which was quite popular in Japan, back in the days when I was there. I see now, it is also quite popular here. It isn't called Osoba here, it goes under many different names. You can recognize it by the noodles. They come from the package pressed in a block. There is also a little packet of soup flavoring, inside the package with the noodles.

Figure 67 Osoba At The Japan International Terminal

It's great stuff and you should try it. In the States, it comes in four flavors, beef, chicken, pork, and oriental. In Japan, there were many more flavors than there are here in the States. Here,

Sgt. Henderson and I enjoy Osoba at the international Terminal Restaurant.

I found Osoba in a little Osoba Shop just off base. Hey! Just what else would you expect to find in an Osoba Shop? I had wandered in out of the rain, one day, and decided to try the stuff. It smelled so good, as it was being cooked, in the back room.

Here again, my knowledge of Japanese hampered my ordering from a menu, so I just pointed to something on the, all Japanese, menu and hoped for the best.

Within moments, a steaming bowl of noodle soup was set before me. Floating on the surface were several pieces of brightly colored Soy Cakes and some small pieces of meat. I guess they were more of a decoration than anything else because, they didn't seem to have any taste at all. Still, they were in the bowl, so I ate them.

There was only one other time when this business of eating everything in the bowl presented a problem. I was at a very formal restaurant with Kiyoko. When the food arrived, it was garnished with what looked like some kind of leaf. Naturally, I thought like the soy cakes, they were to be eaten. It was only much later Kiyoko told me they were plastic, a good grade of plastic, but none the less plastic. Funny, they hadn't tasted bad at all. A little chewy maybe, but not bad.

There had been many times, when I had eaten something and had absolutely no idea what it was. Most of the time, when this happened I was quite drunk. I am sure if any of the stuff I had eaten was still alive, the alcohol in my system would have killed it for sure. The proof of this outlook was, during my entire stay in Japan, I was never sick with more than a light cold and my ever present bronchitis.

The noodles and the clear broth were great and there were even bits of meat floating about in it. It tasted kind of like chicken and I learned later the soup was also flavored with a type of dried seaweed. Flavored as it was the broth was called DashiMoto. It all combined to produce a soup so good it was almost habit forming. I just had to bring my friends from the base out to this great little Osoba Shop I had found.

It wasn't long before Osoba was a household word on the base. There were lots of little Osoba Shops in Haneda. Each one seemed to have its own specialty or best dish. We made the rounds and tried them all.

My favorite remained the first one I tried. There didn't seem to be a name on the place I could read, so I just called it "The Osoba Shop." Every one knew what I was talking about so it made very little difference. If, for instance, Roger mentioned, The Osoba Shop. It did not necessarily mean he was talking about the same Osoba Shop, I was talking about. Each of us had his own favorite place and to each of us it was, The Osoba Shop?

I was pleased as punch to think, I had a first hand part in the making of a popular item with the base personnel at good old Tokyo International Airport. I would drag anyone who showed even the slightest interest to my Very Own Osoba Shop at the drop of a hat. I think after a while, it got so my friends on base, hated to see me coming.

It went on like this for several months. Then I met Kiyoko. I tried my best to get her to go to my Osoba Shop but she resisted my every effort. I tried for weeks to get her to go out with me and sample this great fare I had found. Her excuses ranged from, "I must go somewhere else, right now!" to, "NO! I won't go!" the latter seemed to be quite final. For some reason, she just would not go to my Osoba Shop, and she wouldn't explain why.

We went to lots of other places, during this time, and always had lots of fun together, yet, it bothered me to no end, she would not share my favorite place with me. I could have taken the thing in stride if only she would explain her reason.

No matter, I was a regular patron of my favorite place and no one was going to talk me out of it. Even if they wouldn't say a word about it.

Then one day, my travels took me up the side street which went by the cook shack part of my favorite place. I had never been up this road before, during the daytime, I was looking everything over with great interest.

As I walked past the door to the cook shack, I could see the cook, busy at work in the kitchen. I paused for a moment to watch, after all this was my very own favorite place. It was close to the base, and cheap. A bowl of Osoba cost only ten yen or about 3.6 cents American at the time I was there.

The cook seemed to be cutting up meat to put in a large soup kettle. There was a whole pile of multi-colored skins heaped on a table near him and I couldn't help wondering what kind of domestic animal came in so many different colors.

The cook looked over his shoulder and saw me standing there. He recognized me as a regular customer. He bowed and flashed his best toothy grin at me. He had been in the process of reaching for something in a cage when he had spied me watching him. Now, momentarily distracted, what he had been reaching for got away.

With a wild screech, the thing bounded over the cook's head and flew out the door. It was a large red and white cat. It had made its dash for freedom and was headed up the street with the cook, cleaver in hand, in hot pursuit.

Suddenly, alone on the street and the door to the cook shack open, I looked in. There hanging in a neat row were about a dozen cats, all skinned out and ready to be cut up for the soup kettle. There was also a medium sized dog and several large rats. I stood rooted to the spot long enough for the cook to return holding a headless cat by the tail.

Knowing my understanding of Japanese was limited the cook held the cat up, pointed at it, and said, "Osoba!" as if I couldn't have guessed. He flashed me another toothy grin and went back to work.

I wandered about in the streets of Haneda for several hours, until the shock wore off. Gradually, I began to realize I had been eating this stuff for months now and I was still alive. It hadn't hurt me in the least, in fact I liked the Osoba.

A few days later, when I saw Kiyoko again, I asked her why she hadn't told me what was in the Osoba. She told me she knew I liked it and I also liked cats. It would be wrong to hurt my feelings by telling me what it was I had been eating.

Later, after Kiyoko taught me a little bit more about Japanese, I was able to read the menu. There is all kinds of Osoba, cat, dog, rat, chicken, pork, horse, and on into the night. It didn't change my eating habits one little bit. In fact, it broadened my outlook and I was able to try other great dishes. Sushi, Yak Tori, Sukiyaki, Tempura, and so on.

There were, of course, things I didn't like but I was determined to try them all. Now, years later, I see where many of the things I liked so much in Japan are sweeping this country in popularity.

Among the things I didn't like was something the kids, who I took to the movies, introduced me to. It was some kind of bean cake, which looked like a blob of uncooked dough. I think it was reddish-grey in color, although I will never be sure. Inside the blob was some kind of cooked bean which was laced with sweet stuff, like our baked beans without the spices. To my western taste, it was enough to gag a maggot.

The kids looked on this stuff as a special treat and gobbled it up as fast as I could buy it for them. I just wished I could have given them mine. However, in the interest of good relations I waited until I was out of sight, then I dropped mine into one of the many open sewerage ditches.

No matter where you were in Japan, in those days, you were never far from one of those open sewerage ditches. They laced back and forth all through the town of Haneda and every other town. Back in the States if I had put something tasting as bad as this, I would have been arrested as a polluter.

During my stay in Japan, I met a very nice Japanese couple. They invited me to their home for dinner one evening. Knowing of my German lineage they made a special treat for me, German Potato Soup, in my honor. It was horrible, the stuff tasted like old dish water. No! Old used dish water would have tasted better than this stuff did

Still, I was a guest in their home and I just couldn't hurt their feelings. I finished a full bowl of the ghastly stuff. I even choked down a second bowl. It was hard but I did it in the name of good Japanese American relations.

If only the President had known what a sacrifice I had made for my country, I am sure there would have been a Medal of Honor in it for me. However, once again I survived.

Nopo San

Chapter 17

Culture Shock

Do you know what Culture Shock is? It's a hard thing to explain. An expression associated with Culture Shock is, When in Rome, do as the Romans do. Ever hear this one? I think I can best sum this thing up by an example. Remember when you were a teenager? Always hungry, right? Remember your first girl friend? Remember the day her whole family got together and invited you to the house for dinner?

You're in High School, you have this great girl friend you're madly in love with. She is Catholic (or what ever) and you're a Protestant (again, what ever, so long as it isn't Catholic. The idea is you don't go to the same church.), so what, no problem.

It's Thanksgiving (Christmas, or some other meaningful holiday to your girl friend's family.) and your girl friend's family has a get-together. Her whole family turns out for this thing just so they can meet you for the very first time.

You really put on the dog, as they say. Fancy suit, hair cut, white shirt, the whole works, Boy! You look great.

You arrive at their front door and make a grand entrance, it seems like everyone in the whole house likes you. Even their cousin the Priest, (Monk, Rabbi, High Lama. again whatever.) likes you. You've made the grade, you're the hit of the party.

Then dinner is served, being a teen and perpetually on the verge of starvation, you just can't wait to sink your teeth into a big juicy piece of turkey (or whatever). Following the rules of protocol, you carefully seat your girl friend and take your place by her side at the table.

A plate full of great looking stuff to eat is placed in front of you. You begin to drool, but you resist the temptation to dive in until you are sure your girl friend and her family are all served.

Then, without further adieu, you dive in.

The stuff tastes great! You're in a feeding frenzy! You gorge yourself with food! You're only half finished with your first helping and you're beginning to eye the serving dish for another heaping plate full of goodies.

Suddenly, you notice everyone else at the table seems to be looking straight at you. Something is wrong! You look at your girl friend, her mouth is hanging open, her eyes round with horror. You freeze, then you look around the table again! Suddenly you hear those ominous words, "Father, would you say **Grace** for us and bless this meal?"

You have just experienced, culture shock!

For me it was a little different, but not much. I had been assigned to take some action shots of a Basketball game between the Army and the Air Force at Japan International. I took a whole gang of great pictures and headed for the Photo Lab to process them. They had to be at the office of the Far East Armed Forces Newspaper, no later than midnight. I had to print the photos from a wet negative, but this was nothing new, we did it all the time when there was a rush job.

As the pictures rolled out of the print dryer, I put them in an envelope and headed for the motor pool. I was supposed to meet a driver there who would take me to Tokyo so I could drop off the pictures at the Newspaper office.

It was just my luck, the driver who was supposed to take me was sick. This meant I was going to have to drive myself. There was no time to round up a replacement driver and the pictures had to be there on time or miss the printing of the paper.

Things were still a little hot in parts of the Tokyo area so, I was issued a sidearm. **Wow!** A real gun and it was all mine, for the evening. I was even given real bullets to go in the thing.

I was told I would be driving through parts of Tokyo where the news about the Japanese losing the Second World War still hadn't been accepted. It was kind of like being a Yankee and having to drive through parts of Georgia wearing a Union Suite. It was still open season on the Hated Yankee Devil and there had been cases where American personnel went there and never came out again.

The man at the Motor Pool asked if I knew how to drive a car. Obviously, the man wasn't so sure he should be letting me take the jeep without the regular driver. He was just as sure he didn't want to face the Supreme Commander if the pictures didn't make it to the Army Newspaper on time. "Sure!" I said, "I've been driving since I was fourteen."

With a resigned shrug of his shoulders, he motioned for me to take the jeep and go. Almost as an after thought he handed me a road map which was carefully marked with the streets I needed to take.

I jumped into the jeep, jammed it into gear and popped the clutch. The jeep lurched forward and nearly threw me over the seat backwards. Someone had left it in four-wheel-drive-low-range.

The man at the motor pool nearly fell over laughing at me. Once I sorted out the gears and got the thing going again, I was off to the wilds of Tokyo.

This was great fun, it was my first time behind the wheel of a jeep and I was going to enjoy every minute of it. I roared down the road by the Kuso Gawa, screeched around the corner to the bridge and sailed flat out past the Civilian Guard at the Military Gate.

I looked in the rear view mirror and had to laugh to myself as I spied the Civilian Guard standing in the middle of the street waving his fist frantically at me. I nailed the gas peddle to the floor and just let the jeep do its thing.

I had a big sign on the side of my jeep which proclaimed to one and all, I was an Official Military Courier, as such I could not be delayed by anything short of an act of Congress. I had more rights on the road than the U. S. Mail did!

I had speed, mobility, a sidearm, and impunity. In short, I could be considered quite dangerous. As I raced headlong down the street, people were diving for cover in all directions. This was more fun than Bumper Cars at the Fun Park.

The Japanese had a very dangerous habit of wearing dark, or black robes, at night as they walked about on their unlit streets. It made them hard, if not impossible, to see with jeep headlights. No matter though, I was sure they could hear me coming. The jeep however, was pretty quiet, quieter than I had thought it was. This made for several near misses.

As I raced toward them, the people in my way were forced to dive for the scant shelter provided by the roadside. Some of the people, forced to dive for cover were winding up in the open ditches full of good old stinky, you know what.

Somehow they weren't too awful happy about this. I guess I was about half way to Tokyo, before I realized the reason all these people were diving headlong into whatever cover they could find, was because I was driving on the wrong side of the road.

It would have been the right side of the road if I had been in the States, but I was in Japan, and this made all the difference in the world. To my credit, without a white line painted down the middle of the road, I took my half of the road out of the middle. However, I was an Official Military Courier and this alone gave the right-of-way.

Finding the Army Newspaper office was a breeze, I made my delivery and headed back towards Japan International Airport. Somehow, on my way back I got lost in Beautiful Downtown Tokyo. I wound up at the Imperial Palace.

It was a huge place with a wall, a moat, and a four lane highway all the way around it. It was this highway, which was giving me all the trouble. I couldn't get off the thing. I was riding around and around the Imperial Palace, but I couldn't seem to find the sign which pointed me back to Japan International.

I guess I was on my third time around when I realized the signs were on the wrong corner from where I was used to looking. At last, I found what I was looking for but I had run by my turn off and was a little too far past to make a proper turn. No matter, there was no traffic at the moment so I decided to take a chance.

I pulled a sharp left and gunned the engine. I was headed up the far right hand lane of what looked like an eight lane road way. There were also two train or trolley tracks in the middle of it.

There were two lanes where I was, then a set of trolley tracks protected by some kind of short guard rail to keep cars off the tracks, then two more lanes of traffic, a center island with hedges, two more lanes of traffic, another set of trolley tracks, and two more lanes for cars.

At each intersection there were little islands for people to stand on who were waiting for the trolley. Once again, I was on the wrong side of the road, in the wrong lane and I was going like a bat out of Hell.

Suddenly, before me there were four lanes of oncoming traffic and a trolley. It looked like a wall of headlights advancing on me like a herd of rampaging elephants. For a moment I was dumfounded. What does one do in a situation like this? Where does one go? To the right was a sidewalk, protected by a pipe fence. To the left, were two more lanes, a center island with hedges on it, and then safety.

I made the dash for safety. Cranking the jeep hard to the left I floored it. People were diving for the comparative safety of the open road in front of the oncoming traffic as I bounced over the trolley island. The oncoming traffic passed only inches behind me as I bashed my way through the hedge separating the two sides of the highway.

Now to my left I heard the toot of horns. There was four lanes of traffic coming at me from the left now. I had only one chance, I had to go on straight across the remaining two lanes, the trolley tracks and another trolley island to get to the far right hand lane. It was the only lane which didn't seem to have any traffic in it at the moment. At the moment, it was also the only lane I could make a right hand turn into at the speed I was moving.

Once again, there was panic as my jeep bounced across the other trolley island. I made my turn to the right to early and hit the gas again, only to find myself in the trolley lane and held there by

142

little guard rails which were supposed to keep cars out. The rails were slick and kept throwing the jeep back and forth across the trolley lane, until I got to the next intersection. There I was able to escape from the trolley tracks hang a sharp right hand turn, terrify two more lanes of oncoming traffic, and head back to Base.

Once again I had just experienced, culture shock!

The next day, I heard the poor driver who was supposed to have driven me to Tokyo, had been called out on the carpet by the Supreme Commander. He was given one heck of a dressing down for having caused, **"Massive turmoil in the Downtown Tokyo Traffic system around the Imperial Place, and complete disruption of the Commuter Trolley Service in the whole Tokyo Area!"**

I don't know how I did, it but somehow I got by Scott free

Figure 68 A Samuri Shrine.

on this one. I never heard another word about it. The driver who was supposed to driven me was transferred to another base. He was told it was done to protect him from the Japanese who were on the road when I bashed my way across the streets. I think they sent him to some obscure base in Greenland.

This is typical of Japanese art work. It was the Samurai Shrine I had ever seen and it was a beauty. It stood right in the entrance of the Karate School I attended in Tokyo.

I was too darn big to get very far in the school but at the time I was there it was still taught by the old masters who firmly believed your opponent should never reach the floor at your feet alive. This is exactly the way they taught us. It was all self defense but very terminal in nature.

I was sure luckier than the group who got drunk, swiped a Japanese subway train, threw the operator out and drove the thing at full speed from one end of the line to the other without stopping. A quick thinking subway official had the Air Police waiting for my friends at the end of the line.

Then there was another lot who hit a power pole with their car and knocked out the electricity to all of Tokyo for several hours. It's no wonder there were groups in Tokyo who thought the war was still on. All of these worthy souls were made to face the ire of an enraged Japanese population. Fortunately they were rescued to the comparative safety of the Air Force Stockade where they remained for some considerable time.

Although I had nothing whatsoever to do with these last two incidents, I was again viewed with considerable suspicion by the Supreme Commander. The poor man just couldn't believe something like this could have happened without my direct participation.

This part isn't as nice as the foregoing bit and there may be some among you who will not want to read the next few paragraphs. Be forewarned.

At the North end of one of the runways, there was this neat little dock. It was the place the tanker barges tied up to pump off the fuel they were delivering to the base and to the civilian

Airports. It had one other reputation which wasn't so nice.

In Japan, at the time I was there, all debts come due on January First. If you couldn't pay you were expected to make other arrangements or do the honorable thing. In Japan, the honorable thing was to end it all. This was done by leaping from tall buildings in beautiful downtown Tokyo or jumping off the nearby bridge over the Kana Gawa. Gawa, means river in Japanese. I never found out what Kana meant.

The unfortunate debtor, suitably weighted would sink to the bottom of the river and be carried out into Tokyo Bay by the current or tide, as the case may be. It was odd to see two people commit suicide by tying themselves together with heavy wire, back to back, then attaching themselves to a heavy weight. The weight would then go over the side with them.

So long as the water was cold there was no problem, but in April, Tokyo Bay began to warm up. All those nice people, who had given of their bodies to feed the crab population of Tokyo Bay all winter, now bloated with gas and floated to the surface. Poor crabs, no more yum yum.

The current and the wind now pushed the bodies like little sail boats right up to the barge dock at the end of our runway. It then became the job, no matter how unpleasant, of the Base Photo Lab to photograph these things for the record.

Once photographed, the bodies were turned over to the Japanese for disposal. I never asked how they got rid of the bodies, nor do I ever want to know. I can guess and this was bad enough. The Japanese Police would show up in a boat with a boat hook on a long pole. They would drive the boat hook into the body, then hook the other end of the pole onto their boat and away they would go back up the river.

The only reason I mention the above is to give you an idea of just how different our cultures were. Here in the States, a dead body is treated with almost reverence. Maybe because of the war and all the death they had to look at for all those years, over there a dead body was just so much garbage and it had to be disposed of,

Culture Shock again.

Nopo San

Chapter 18

Kiyoko

In all of my life, I have always had a difficult time relating to the ladies in any respect. I guess it was due in part, to the fact, since I was twelve I had been hard at work building my own little world around me. By thirteen, I had formed the largest paper route in Westchester County. It was a seven day a week job. So, while the other guys were out getting acquainted with the ladies, I was hauling newspapers. I never had a chance to practice the social graces.

It didn't stop there either. In High School I worked after school, in a gas station, pumping gas and learning to be a mechanic. As time went on, I became a darn good mechanic, again after school.

I never even made it to my own Senior Prom Dance, instead I was hard at work putting the finishing touches on my first hot rod. After I finished school, I spent the summer with the family out on Long Island and then in September of 1954 I joined, over the objections of my father, the Air Force.

As you can see, I never really had a chance to get to know girls like my peers did. I was always too busy doing other things. The one girl friend I did have during my last year of High School and who I almost married, sent me a Dear John Letter shortly after I arrived in Okinawa.

It wasn't until I reached Tokyo and had a chance to settle in, before I finally met a second girl who took a shine to me. Lord only know why, but this little girl liked me.

Her name was Kiyoko and she stood a towering 4 feet 10 inches tall, while Nopo San stood 6 feet 4 inches tall. She even called me Nopo San. We were sure an odd couple.

Kiyoko was a nice little girl and we would meet on the weekends at the U.S.O. club to dance together and drink soda. We never really got serious about each other, but she was just a fun person to be with and this made it all worthwhile.

I guess I might say this girl was responsible for educating me in the ways of the native Japanese. She corrected my grammar and taught me how to read and write the, Hetogana, Katagana, and Kangi styles of the Japanese language. Then latter being the script understood by both the Japanese and the Chinese.

There are only about 50,000 different Kangi characters, so I never really got a good handle on it. I was told when I left Japan I had the reading and writing ability of a 5 year old school boy. This isn't at all bad when you remember I was only there for a little less than two years.

The other two, Hetogana, Katagana, were the true Japanese language and like our printing and script, had an alphabet of fifty two sounds or letters. In time, I was able to read a menu and price tags in the shops.

Towards the end of my stay in Japan, I even got to the point where I was able to read parts of the newspaper and everyone would stare at me. Americans simply were not supposed to be able to read Japanese.

The reading if price tags, however, was lots of fun. In general, the prices marked in English were about three to four times higher than the prices marked in Japanese, on the same item.

For instance, a cigarette lighter marked at 500 yen, would have a second price tag on it in Japanese. The second price in Japanese was 100 yen. I could read both tags, thanks to Kiyoko, and this led to some very interesting situations.

I had wanted to send my mother a Japanese painting and I asked Kiyoko to help me pick one out. We visited several art dealers before I found something which appealed to my Western taste.

The man behind the counter smiled broadly and told me the price was ten-thousand yen. Out of the corner of my eye, I say Kiyoko shake her head. I haggled, a moment or so, as I looked the painting over for another price tag. Sure as heck, there it was on the lower back corner, three thousand yen written in Japanese.

When I pointed this out to him, the shop keeper was furious. He raged at me, "You're not supposed to be able to read Japanese!" I assured him I was quite capable of reading Japanese, and began pointing out several other instances of double pricing in his shop. This was not a big deal, as just about everything in his shop was double priced.

A crowd was gathering, as I went on pointing out these minor differences. They were mostly American Service Men and they were all very interested in this double price system. I pointed to one thing after another, describing in detail just what to look for.

Finally, in desperation, the shop keeper handed me another painting and pointed me toward the door. "Take this and go away. **Please go away!**"

I couldn't understand the man's attitude, after all he was

about to sell everything in his shop, and at considerable savings to his customers. Outside the shop Kiyoko smiled up at me, saying, "You're learning."

We moved on to a very fancy restaurant and broke the price code there also. This was fun! It was my first free meal in a restaurant and did it ever taste good. We left the place in utter confusion, as dozens of other people insisted on paying the Japanese price rather than the inflated English price.

I always found it hard to understand why the shop keepers got so hostile when we pointed out they were completely wrong about the exchange rate.

We went from place to place on a wild spree of buying at phenomenal savings. There also many free gifts. All the time leaving behind us, the seeds of World War III. Kiyoko even showed me how to get into the Tokyo Zoo for about half price. This was a good trick as I was about twice as big as the average Japanese.

We went on like this for about two months. During which we hit about every resort area we could find, which didn't involve an overnight stay. I had to be back on the base by five-thirty in the afternoon or go back on day shift. This, I would never allow to happen. I was having too much fun.

As I have said before, all good things must come to an end sooner or later. Thus it was no surprise when early one morning, I was escorted to the Supreme Commander's office. Again by two armed Air Policemen. By this time, I knew them both by their names. They would just walk in the front door of the Photo Lab, point at me, crook their fingers a few times, and away we would go without a word.

The other fellows at the Lab would just look at me, then say to each other, "I wonder what he did this time?"

The Supreme Commander didn't even look up at me, he just kept looking at the, very proper looking, Japanese gentleman in the black suit sitting in his office. Pointing in my direction he said, "Is this the man?"

Jumping to his feet the man in the black suit pointed at me and screamed, "**Yankee Devil!**" He then sat down again, and resumed his rather stoic decorum. It was probably all the English the poor little guy knew, but he used it with a vengeance. Then again, maybe he just didn't realize how big I was until he jumped up.

The Supreme Commander gave me a frigid look and said, "I'll deal with you later." His words were hung with icicles. At this point, big as I am, I was picked up by my two escorts and dragged backwards out of the room.

The man in the black suit, it turned out to be the representative of a group of Tokyo businessmen who wanted me confined to the base, permanently, in chains if possible.

For the next hour I sat with my escort in an outer office while a yelling match went on in the Supreme Commander's office. I had visions of the Supreme Commander insisting I be sent to ground zero for the next atomic bomb test blast with the Japanese officials requesting I be confined to base, jailed or worse. I distinctly heard someone say, "Those two are a danger to the entire economic structure in Japan." Among other not so pleasant things.

At long last, the Supreme Commander came into the room where I was waiting. He gave me a long tired look and said, "I can't get mad at you. They were cheating us and you blew the whistle on them. I will, however, give you some advice. Don't go back to any of the places where you have been, wear a disguise, and for God's sake don't let them take you alive!" With this, I was released unharmed.

As I left the building, I heard the Supreme Commander say to my former escorts, "Why do I feel like I have just released '**Godzilla**' on Tokyo again?"

About two weeks later I got a letter from Kiyoko. She told me her whole family had been relocated to a remote corner of Japan and she would never see me again.

She signed the letter, "It was fun, Kiyoko."

Nopo San

Chapter 19

JP-40

It was one of those nights when you say to yourself, what else could go wrong, and something would go wrong just out of spite. It was cold and it had rained for three days straight. Everything was wet, even the film stuck together in the Photo Lab when we took it out of the refrigerator. The prints stuck to the drum of the big rotary dryer we used to dry our finished photographs.

As usual, I was doing the night alert thing, and in desperation for something to do, I was finishing up some work left over by the day crew. I didn't have to, but I tried to help out every time there was a job the day crew just couldn't get through with. It made for very good relations all around.

It was midnight, I was just wrapping up the work and was about to start the cleanup when there was a knock at the door. I had been this route so many times I didn't even look up. I just grabbed my big speed graphic, the film bag, and my rain gear, as I headed for the door. At least, at this time of night, it wouldn't be a contingent from the Supreme Commander's office looking for me again.

Outside was a new face, the guys I usually worked with must have been off doing something else. As I swung into the jeep, I asked the new man what was up. He told me he didn't know but there was a rumor about an aircraft accident.

Instantly, a vision of the horror I had to photograph on Okinawa exploded in my mind. A Constellation had come in for a landing on a clear night with 97 wounded Korean Vets on board. For some reason, the pilot had not put his landing gear down.

The plane impacted on the end of the runway and spread itself down the entire length. There had been pieces of 97 people spread along the runway mixed with the wreckage.

I was almost afraid to ask but in the end I had to know. Blood and guts on a night like this would be just a little too much. Even though, I had by this time, developed a somewhat hardened attitude about the whole thing. "Was any body hurt?" I asked.

The driver smiled at and said, "No. I don't think so. Rumor has it a truck ran into an aircraft on the runway. The truck driver was too drunk to get hurt and there was no one in the plane."

To myself, and under my breath, I muttered, "Thank God." and lapsed back into silence.

Upon reaching the runway, It was indeed a truck which had run into the wing of a parked F-86 fighter plane. Now an F-86 is a pretty big aircraft when compared to the little weapons carrier which hit it. It was as if the truck had deliberately run into the plane.

When I was much younger I can remember seeing on my way home from school, the tail end of a large car sticking out from the picture window of a home I walked past. I can remember how I had wondered at the time, just how the driver could have run his car into a house, now I know.

My duty, at this point, was to photograph everything about the accident could possibly make a difference in determining how much damage was done. Standing in front of and looking at the nose of the plane, the truck had run into the left hand wing and was partially wedged under it.

As I looked the situation over, I noticed I was out there by the accident all alone. The rest of the people had hung back and had formed a circle around the area. "How nice," I thought, "they are giving me lots of elbow room," and I went to work doing what the Air Force paid me to do, taking pictures.

It was still raining pretty hard and it made taking any long distance shots impossible. This was okay with me, I was ankle deep in water and my shoes were soaked through to my feet. There were not many pictures to take so I was done with the job in about thirty minutes. I sloshed around the plane one more time to be sure

I hadn't missed anything and headed back for the crowd.

As I approached the circle of people, one of them asked, "Aren't those the Japanese flash bulbs which explode every so often?"

With a great big smile on my face I said, "They sure are."

The man just stood there with a strange expression on his face. "They just didn't explode tonight for some reason," I went on, "We usually pop about every third one, on the average."

There was a dead silence in the group, it was almost a reverent silence, as all eyes seemed to be glued to me. I stood there a moment waiting to see if any one else was going to say anything. They just stood and stared at me. At last, I spotted my driver and motioned to him I was ready to go.

He wheeled the jeep around and I climbed aboard. As I sat down in the, more or less, enclosed cab of the jeep, I was suddenly aware of heavy, almost overpowering, smell of gasoline. I thought to mention it to the driver but before I had a chance to speak the driver turned to me and said, "You must have nerves of steel."

I was stopped short in my thought and asked, "Why do you say this?" After all, I didn't even know how to spell heroism much less be one.

He gave me a quick sideways glance and said, "Didn't you know? You were standing ankle deep in a mixture of gasoline and JP-40, Jet plane fuel. When the truck hit the plane it ruptured the trucks fuel tank and aircrafts fuel tank, the JP-40 ran out all over the place floating on the puddles of rain water. One little spark and **Whoosh!** You'd have been history."

I didn't say a word. I hardly dared breath as I looked down at my shoes. They were still full of JP-40, and my feet were in there with it. This would never do. Trying not to spill any of the stuff in the jeep, I slowly took off my shoes and dropped them in the road, as we drove along.

The new man, who's name I never did get, was good enough to drive me off base to my rented room where I had a second pair of shoes and from there to the barracks where I could take a shower and change my clothes.

I had to clean up a little and get all the gasoline off my body, before I got gasoline burns. Gasoline burns are caused by the gasoline removing all the oil from your skin. This causes it to become overly dried and it produces the same effect as a minor burn.

Anyhow, after getting the stuff off me, I went down to the Photo Lab and processed the pictures. They were nothing special. Just a collision between a small truck and an aircraft on the runway with nobody around it. Just for kicks, I took the last flash bulb out of my camera case, put it into the flash gun, and pressed the button. There was a loud bang, the tinkle of broken glass, and a shower of sparks hit the floor of the Photo Lab.

In the morning, the rest of the Photo Lab crew found me sitting at the desk with a hand full of photos. The job was complete. I had done it all. I handed the job over to the Sergeant and left without a word.

It was only a short walk to my little rented room and I was there within fifteen minutes or so. I hadn't even stopped at the chow hall for breakfast. I sat down at the little table in the center of the room and let go.

My hands began to shake and I was cold clean through to the bone. I just sat there for the better part of the day. Then along toward evening I went back to the base for dinner and to see what the world had in store for me during the coming night.

It was the first time, in my whole military career, my own people had sent me into a life threatening situation without telling me. I felt betrayed.

A few months later, the truck driver was stood up before a Court Martial for "Destroying Military Property." I was hauled into court to present the pictures I had taken. In the end, all my pictures were thrown out because the flash bulbs had not cast enough light to properly eliminate the overall scene.

As I left the courtroom, I couldn't help wondering, to myself, just how they would have felt about those pictures, if they

155

had been standing next to me when I took them.

Nopo San

Chapter 20

The Big Splash

Dawn was just breaking as I left the Chow Hall at JIA (Japan International Airport) and Mt. Fuji was looming over the Oki Steel Works in all it's glory. It was worth a shot, so I propped my big Speed Graphic camera up on my shoulder and started composing a picture.

Figure 71 The Open Front Of The Oki Steel Works

The steel works was loading a group of three barges which were tied up to the bulk head in front of the big open end of the building. I should qualify this, the plant worked round the clock but they only loaded barges during the daylight hours, because they had no lights out over the water to see what they were doing at night.

The open end of the huge building afforded an excellent view of what was going on inside. A crane was lowering a huge piece of steel onto the first barge and the barge owner's wife obviously had a problem with this. The barge was already low in the water, and this last piece of steel might just be, straw sunk the barge. Now, I don't know about you, but every once in a great while I get the urge to do something really off the wall.

As a photographer, I get lots of chances to photograph someone else's handy work, but I never get a chance to be really creative on my own. Now here before me was the opportunity of a lifetime. Unfortunately this picture does not show the barge going down. Those pictures and all the negatives were confiscated. You can see the way the heavy lift cranes extend out over the barges.

The air was crystal clear, thanks to a medium size typhoon which had roared through town a few days before and cleared the smog. Now Mt. Fuji, which was just visible most days, was a thing of beauty there in the distance. I had to have a shot of this, there was no telling when I would get another opportunity to see Mt. Fuji without the smog which usually hung over the base.

The shutter clicked and my shot was now a matter of record. At night, when I went on duty again, I would develop and print my work of art.

Suddenly my attention centered on the barge. Both the barge owner's wife and the crane operator were staring at me. With evil intent, I pointed the camera at the crane operator. I had noticed, when given the limelight, most people can't resist being a ham. This was going to be easy.

Having caught his eye, the crane operator flashed a toothy grin in my direction. I had his undivided attention. What more could I ask for?

The barge owner's wife was now jumping up and down on the stern of the barge just outside the entrance to the deck house, where she and her husband lived. She was screaming and yelling at the crane operator to attract his attention. It was like a scene from a comic opera, she began waving her arms in the air. She started throwing things, as the huge piece of metal got closer to the barge.

The noise of the crane drowned out her screams and she couldn't throw anything high enough to divert the crane operators attention from me.

The crane operators attention was focused on me with my camera and the proverbial straw was slowly descending on the ill-fated barge. I knew in my heart it was a selfish thing to do, but the devil was in me and had full control for the moment.

I raised the camera, again and again pointing it at the crane operator, who smiled his best toothy grin at me each time, in return. All the time, I was making sure the ill fated barge was well represented in the lower part of the picture.

I cursed, under my breath, at the slow single shot camera and wished fervently for a motion picture camera. I knew for sure these pictures would at least make honorable mention, in the archives of the worlds dirtiest tricks.

The barge owner's wife, now frantic, was running around the deck house banging on a large pot and screaming at the top of her lungs, in a vain effort to attract the attention of the crane operator. The operators attention was still focused firmly on me and my camera.

The noise from the crane still drowned out all other noise so he simply had no idea what was going on directly under him. I took picture, after picture, as the load began to settle on the already heavily laden barge.

The barge owner's wife, knowing full well what was about to happen and who had caused it, hurled the big pot in my direction. With a few well chosen words about my ancestry, or whatever, she abandoned ship.

I was a little too far away to hear exactly what it was she had said but I can guess. It must have been terribly difficult for the little lady as there are no profanities in the Japanese language. It must have been hell to be so mad and not be able to swear.

By this time, I was changing film a quick as I could, I

slipped the dark slide into the film holder and whipped it out of the camera. I dropped it carefully on my foot to break the fall, as I crammed fresh film into the camera, this was too good to miss. There was a nice little pile of film at my feet and it was growing by leaps and bounds. I hoped I had enough film to do justice to the scene being played out for me by circumstance and demonic direction.

I got one last perfect shot just as the water started over the bulkheads. My last shot caught the barge just as it disappeared from sight in the murky waters of the **Kuso Gawa**.

My last shot also showed the barge owner's wife thrashing about in the water and completely dismayed look on the face of the crane operator. Both of whom, I am sure, were ready to start World War II over again, on the spot.

The Kuso Gawa was what we, on the base, called the little river which separated us from the mainland. Literally translated, it means "River of Excrement" and indeed it was aptly named because it was the head water for all the open sewerage ditches in Haneda, the town we were separated from by the river, and it lived up to it's name.

My day had been made, there would be no sleep for me till I had made prints of these shots. Never before, to the best of my knowledge, had anyone caused so much commotion with a mere camera. I had made photographic history. And so it was, with a great smirk on my face, I picked up the film holders which were now littered about my feet and moved quietly away from the gathering crowd toward the Photo Lab.

I was supposed to be off duty because I had been on alert status all night. This only meant I had to be available for taking pictures at any time during the night. Not being tired I went straight to the dark room and began developing my classics. As they came out of the hypo, I studied each negative for flaws, there were none. It was a perfect job. By noon I had a great stack of prints going through the drier and each one was a work of art.

Suddenly and without warning, the Air Police arrived. Not

waiting for formal introductions, they grabbed me and my beautiful pictures. Within moments, I was once again facing the Supreme Commander.

The expression on his face indicated at once, he did not see the humor in what had happened. The large puddles of wet, vile smelling, liquid on the floor told me my visit had been preceded by a visit from a very irate little barge owners wife and a very unhappy crane operator.

Judging from the look on the Supreme Commander's face, water poured on his head would have boiled. There after new depth was added to my knowledge of the seamier side of the English language. I was told, in short, if there was ever a repeat of this sort of behavior on my part, I would be forced to drink the oil slick from off the top of the Kuso Gawa, and this was only the good part of what he had in mind for me.

Later, I found out I had created an international incident and nearly started World War II all over again. Hostilities were averted by the Supreme Commander telling the barge owner's wife I would be sent back to the United States tied to the outside of the plane with an open parachute around my neck.

My pictures were confiscated and it was only the fact it was government property, which saved my camera from being smashed. I was ordered to change my appearance before I went to Tokyo again, or even off base. If I was caught, I was told to tell them I was a Russian in disguise.

For the next month, we were treated to a real show. The Japanese had a diver, complete with hard hat and pressure suit, diving on the sunken barge to salvage the huge metal pieces and get the barge out of the way. I always wondered, as I watched them work, if they knew what part I had played in hclping the steel get to the bottom of the river.

Nopo San

Chapter 21

Typhoon

I awoke to the smell of punk in my little off base room at the fisherman's house. I can remember thinking to myself it might almost be better to let the insects bite me than to spend another bight breathing those foul fumes. Then again, the Japanese had been using this method for many years with no visible, ill effects.

One lights a stick of slow burning punk or incense at bed time, the smoke drives the bugs away and you can sleep through the night, without being sucked dry by the hungry hordes of insects which live in Japan.

The humidity was so thick, you could cut it with a knife. I have often wondered just how the air could hold so much moisture without raining. Then there was the heat. The heat was oppressive and it hung on my shoulders like a weight.

I rolled off of the Futon, (Japanese mattress) the fisherman's wife had been good enough to have made for me. There was nothing in the stores which would fit Nopo San so the thing had to be hand made.

Fumbling around for my clothing I tried not to move too fast for fear of breaking out in a killer sweat. There was no wash room at this house. If I needed a bath I had to go up the street to the public bath house.

Like most Americans I felt a little funny about bathing, naked, in the same tub with someone else's family. In fact, in all probability, there would be several families all bathing together in the same tub.

The idea was, first you took a shower and got all cleaned off, then you sat down in a hot tub and soaked. It was really a great way to do things and since I was in Japan, the hot tub thing has caught on in this country. Hot tubs are now available coast to coast.

The thing I had the problem with was everyone sat in the tub naked. There isn't anything wrong with this, it's just I had trouble getting used to it.

But anyhow, this was the day Bill and I were going to climb Mt. Fuji. We had planned this trip for weeks and nothing was going to stop us. Even the Typhoon was forecast was not considered a deterrent. I had some evil tiding about this trip. I had always believed, and still do, large storms feed on heat.

They will, almost without exception, move toward a hot area. Right at this moment, the Tokyo area was about as hot as it could get. I was dead certain the Typhoon was going to come ashore at Japan International.

Leaving the house, where I rented the room from the fisherman and his wife, I trudged through the early morning mist toward the chow hall. Unlike most of the other fellows, I still like the military food. It was good quality stuff and even here in Japan, there was no shortage of it. I have to admit on occasion the cooks did strange things to it, and it no longer resembled what it was supposed to be. I guess it was due, in part, to the fact there were many Japanese civilians hired as cooks in the Chow Hall, but I never got sick from it. This is more than I can say for many public restaurants I have been in.

The Japanese civilian cooks who worked in the Chow Hall must have had an awful time understanding the how's and why's of American cooking. Japanese cooking involves a lot of raw vegetables. These are kind of dropped into hot water but not really cooked in it. They also eat lots of raw fish. In truth, this is the best way to eat fish. Provided it's fresh.

The idea of cooking fish must have seemed, quite a waste to them. Cooked vegetables were another thing they had a problem with. We had been well schooled in just how the Japanese farmer fertilized his crops and insisted everything be cooked.

On this particular day, one of the eggs being cooked on the big griddle at the head of the chow line, had a partially developed chicken embryo in it. The poor Japanese cook must have been new at his job and thought this was the way we ate our eggs. He kept trying to pass it off on everyone who came through the line. Needless to say, darn few eggs were eaten for breakfast this morning. The poor Japanese cook must have thought he was doing an awfully bad job, because no one was eating what he was serving.

I usually tried to be one of the first in the chow line, so if there was something exceptionally good, I could go around again and get more. Today, there was nothing exceptional, so once was enough. Bill met me in the chow hall about halfway through my second cup of coffee.

He looked at me, wrinkled his nose and asked, "How do you drink this stuff?" This, coming from a man who kept a little hot plate in the Photo Lab and made instant coffee.

I considered the source and shrugged off the remark. I liked the coffee. But, then again, I was no coffee expert. I dealt in volume not quality. When you work nights you learn to drink lots of coffee.

The speaker system was blaring something about the base being in imminent danger of devastation by the approaching Typhoon, as we got up to leave. Bill said to me on the way out of the chow hall, "We had better get out of here quick or we are going to wind up on some detail holding a plane down on the ground or something." I agreed and we took off at a fast walk toward the civilian gate and ultimate freedom.

We took the local train from Haneda to Kana Gawa and from there the Tokyo Express. It was a long ride but worth every penny of the fare. The trip took us past many of the more scenic parts of suburban Japanese. Looking over the neat rows of paper and wood houses, it was easy to see how the bombers had done so much fire damage during the war. War is the pits, so many good people die on both sides, and for what? I still think ALL wars would be fought only by politicians who start them.

By ten o'clock, we were on another train out of Tokyo, and

well on our way toward Mt. Fuji. It was like an oven in the train. Fortunately, Bill and I were both tall enough so our heads stuck up above the tightly packed people on the train and the air was a little cooler, maybe not really cooler but at least it hadn't been used as much.

We arrived at the base of Mt. Fuji only to be greeted by a sign in Japanese, which was stretched across the gateway to the path leading up the mountain. Neither Bill nor I could read much Japanese at the time, so we walked around the gate and started up the mountain.

Had we bothered to look behind us we would have seen a large black cloud was building on the horizon. Unfortunately, we were headed up the mountain, the cloud was behind us, and for this reason, unnoticed.

Besides, neither of us had any idea what it would be like to weather a Typhoon on the dry land of a mountain side. To us it was just a big wind and nothing to be really concerned about. We had a lot to learn.

By two o'clock, we were several miles up the mountain and the wind was beginning to pick up. Bill looked at me over his shoulder saying, "Do you think we should have stayed on the base and helped hold down the aircraft?" Then, without waiting for a reply, he said, "**No Way!** Onward and upward!"

We reached the end of the trail about five in the afternoon, by this time the wind was really howling. There was a little way station back about a quarter of a mile, where an old man lived. He was obviously a caretaker and as we had passed by he had come out, looked at us in strange way, shook his head and said, "KichiGi-Yo!" In essence, this meant, You're crazy!

We looked right back at him, smiled politely, and replied, "Honto Des!" Which meant, You're right!

As we walked the last few hundred yards to the end of the tourist path, we could see the wind was now strong enough to move bottles and cans along the ground. Right at the end of the path, there was a large "Tori" or end of path marker. Bill thought if he grabbed onto one of the upright poles of the Tori the wind would hold him out like a flag. He was right. In fact, I took his picture as he fluttered in the breeze.

We fooled around for a few more minutes, until we noticed the wind was now picking up the cans and bottles, then dashing them on the rocks with such force they sounded like gun shots. We were on our hands and knees now, to prevent being dashed against the rocks ourselves.

It might have been a little too late, but I was beginning to wonder just what the two of us were doing on top of a mountain, with no place to hide during a major Typhoon. If we survived, and this seemed to be somewhat in question, I made up my mind to have a long talk with Bill about this.

Back down the path, we could see the little old man waving at us frantically. We crawled slowly back to the house, keeping as low a profile as possible. As we got to the front door of the way station, Bill looked over his shoulder at me and said, "I told you we should have listened to the storm warning."

I opened my mouth to object, but then thought, "What's the use?"

The little old man was indeed the caretaker and he invited the two of us to spend the night, at least, I think it's what he said. One way or another, it didn't take long for us to accept his kind offer. The wind outside had risen to a frenzy and the cans and bottles were hitting the walls of the house with considerable force.

We never found out what the old man's name was. About the time we were getting around to the pleasantries, a floor board came loose and began flapping in the breeze. The old man made a dive for it and began wedging it back into place in the floor. Using small pegs and his shoe, he drove the pegs into the crack between the wall and the floor to hold the board in place.

Other boards began to move, so Bill and I pitched in to help the old man hold his house together. On through the night, we were thus employed. As we worked, I could hear Bill muttering to himself, "I told the darn fool, we should have stayed on base and helped hold the aircraft down."

By morning, the worst of the storm was over. The old man, however, seemed full of life. He bounded to a cupboard and produced a two and one half gallon bottle of Saki. From another place, he came up with three cups. Even without a really good understanding of Japanese, there could be no mistake, it was party time. The rest of the morning was spent consuming the Saki. By the time this laudable task was done, it was time to head back down the mountain.

Sometimes, on dark and quiet nights, I can't help but wonder just what it was ever made us think we were in any kind of condition to try walking down a mountain. It had been hard enough getting up there sober. Now, here we were drunk as skunks, trying to get down the mountain.

The storm had expended itself trying to blow Fuji Yama away, and only a gentle rain and a light breeze remained. I don't remember much about the trip down the mountain. We slid on the muddy spots, fell on loose rocks, and tripped over each other, but we must have made it somehow.

Riding back to Haneda on the train was a nightmare I wish I could forget. Packed in a closed train car, with no ventilation and wall to wall people, while a hangover raged in my head and stomach, was not my idea of fun and games. But like the trip down the mountain we made it.

The next morning, in the chow hall, I happened to overhear Bill and a few of the other guys from the Photo Lab, Bill was saying, "Herbst is really nuts. He conned me into climbing Mt. Fuji the other day, during the Typhoon."

I can remember hearing one of the other fellows say, "Your both nuts!" I couldn't argue with the point, so I just sat there in silence.

Nopo San

Chapter 22

Dumb Luck

It had been a long, hot summer, quite frankly, I was ready for fall. The Typhoon season had just ended and it looked like my last winter in Japan was going to be a quiet one.

There was, however, always something to do at the Photo Lab. A plane had gone down, somewhere between Japan and Okinawa. A group of three of us from the Photo Lab volunteered to go up in a search plane to look for survivors. We searched for two days along the route the plane had taken, but found nothing.

We had hoped to at least find the spot where the plane had gone down but we couldn't even find an oil slick. Looking down on all the water I felt awful sorry for anyone might have survived. They sure would have been out there in the middle of a huge expanse of nothing.

There's a picture of one of our guys looking out of the planes window I took while searching. It was published in the newspaper. The picture is in the Chapter about Jane.

Ordinarily, this would not mean too much to the personnel at Japan International, except this plane had all or pay records on it. No one was going to get paid again, until the duplicate pay records were photostated by us and sent to Washington. We had hundreds of thousands of copies to make and if we wanted to remain in the top ten, popularity wise, we should get these copies made post-haste.

We had been promised, by the Supreme Commander, if the copies were not made up in good time, he would personally tell everyone in the Far East Air Command, it was the fault of the Base Photo Lab at Japan International, they were not being paid on time. With this kind of inspiration, we fairly flew to the task. We were turning out copies at a record rate.

On Base, we had a maintenance worker lock the safety switch out, on one of the "Ground Control" landing radar domes. He had wanted to make some repairs which could only be done while the door was closed and he was inside to watch the thing work.

The operator reported to work, and not knowing the maintenance worker was inside, turned the thing on. He Micro Waved the maintenance worker. Now this was a real mess to have to take pictures of. Parts of him, like a hot dogs of eggs in a microwave oven, had exploded.

It was almost as bad as the fellow who tried to stop the Tokyo Express Train by standing out in front of the train on the tracks with his hand up like Superman. Needless to say, the train didn't even slow up.

The poor guy was rolled head over heels under the train for almost seventy yards. People were just not meant to bend this way. Even the Japanese civilian helpers, we had working in the Lab, wouldn't process the film. They said it was,"TiHainYanakagi Desu!" (Way too ugly)

All of these things had, by now, become everyday occurrences. We had become hardened to what we had to take pictures of so it was nothing special. There was even one poor fellow who became hypnotized by an aircraft prop. He walked into it while the pilot was running it up one morning. This wasn't considered anything really special. In fact, this was thought to be an easy job, there was so little left to take pictures of.

Then one night, something really special happened. A Constellation, out of Korea, was coming in because of engine trouble. Nothing serious mind you, just a minor problem the pilot wanted to have fixed.

This pilot, like the one on Okinawa, had put a coffee can over his landing gear indicator light. He came in, making a letter perfect landing with ninety-six wounded Korean Vets. on board. Perfect in every detail but one. He didn't have his landing gear down.

Somehow, when he realized the gear was still up in the wells, he poured the coals to it and got the plane back up off the ground. A neater bit of flying you could not have wanted.

He flew around the pattern once again and put the plane back down on the runway, this time with the landing gear down.

I was working the night shift so I was the only one who got to take the pictures of the plane. There was a good eighteen inches missing from each blade of both inboard props and at least eight inches missing from each of the outboard props. The antenna protruding from the belly of the plane, it was ground off to within two or three inches of the body of the plane. Now this was something special!

The pilot had told us when he saw the inboard props chewing up the runway, he realized what had happened. He dropped the flaps and hit the throttle. By the grace of God, and not much else, he got the plane back up off the deck and back into the landing pattern. You can't get much closer than this guy got and still talk about it.

We drove out to the spot where the plane had first touched down. There were gashes in the runway from where the props chopped into it, as the plane flew in to land without the landing gear down. They seemed to go on for hundreds of feet. In another place, we found the long skid mark made by the antenna as it ground down to within inches of the plane itself. The pilot of this plane indeed led a charmed life.

Back at the terminal, the pilot looked a bit shaken but he was still on his feet. He wanted to see how close he had come to packing it in. I watched as an Air Police officer led him out onto the runway and began pointing out the things I had just taken pictures of.

At this point, the job, as far as I was concerned, was done. I packed up my gear and headed back to the Photo Lab. I heard later, when he saw how close he had come, his heart gave out and he died on the spot. Thank God he waited until he was on the ground.

Nopo San

Chapter 22

May Day Comes Again

A full year had now passed since my last May Day. This time I was a year older, by the grace of God, and a year wiser by pure experience. In preparation for the coming festivities, I had moved back onto the base and was once again sleeping on the floor of the Photo Lab, under the huge photostat machine in the entrance way to darkroom number two. Darkroom two was where we did our film developing, as it was more light tight than the other darkroom, where we did the printing.

Besides this, there was no evidence anything was any different except a few banners and wind socks which began appearing a few days in advance of May Day. No crowds or anything, just a few colorful streamers blowing in the wind. It might as well have been any other day.

In all my time in the service, I never really went out of my way to aggravate anyone. These things just seem to happen to me. I actually liked our Supreme Commander. He had a tough job to do and I guess having me around wasn't much help to him. Everything I did, just seemed to make him mad.

Everyone had been restricted to base and we were told it was for our safety this had been done. The communist's had become much stronger in Japan and American personnel had some reason to fear for their lives during the May Day 1957 celebration. I, for one, didn't understand all this because I had made so many good friends off base, but rather than incur the wrath of the Supreme Commander again, I had moved back on base for the duration.

In preparation for the coming festivities, we were to be trained in crowd control. This meant marching around in formations which were supposed to break up mobs. We were supposed to get carbines with bayonets on them. We were taught to hold them out in front of us as we did our thing, the idea being no one would intentionally impale themselves on a bayonet.

Figure 72 the Quiet Before The Storm

The guy who thought this one up, sure didn't know his history very well. During WWII the Japanese had intentionally impaled themselves on American bayonets to die for the Emperor.

In all reality, it was kind of fun. We were broken up into units of about thirty men and each of us was given carbines to play with for the day.

Ordinarily, Air Force personnel are not given weapons for fear they will shoot themselves. The big guys must have really been desperate to have handed us guns. Several of the men in my unit had saved a few live rounds from the firing range and vowed not to be taken alive if the Japanese stormed the Base.

If the Supreme Commander had known there were a few crazies out there with even a few live rounds, he never would have issued us real guns for us to play with. It was bad enough he had planned to issue sharp pointed bayonets to us.

Next, we were thoroughly trained in the use of a carbine as a tool of riot control. We were taught the wedge formation and a few other formations. I remember the wedge the best. I was the biggest guy in my unit, so I was to lead the wedge.

The rest of the unit kidded me without mercy, telling me they would be right behind me, and if I started to fall they would prop up my body on their bayonets. Assuming, of course, the higher ups decided to give us bayonets.

We trained for about two days, quitting only when it rained, or it got too hot, or we got tired. Which, for us, was most of the time. The training, involved a lot of sprawling about on the grass, waiting for the officers to get their act together. But only if the grass was dry enough to sprawl on.

The last day of training, we were taken to the areas we would be defending and we were put through our paces right out in plain sight. I guess this was done to scare the Japanese Communist's and make them think we were a well oiled fighting unit. **Thank God** we never had to prove it.

From where we stood, the intent might have been to cause the communists to laugh themselves sick and then we could simply sweep them out of the way, but the officers were deadly serious. The Air Force of my time, was never noted for its fighting skill. We could give them hell in the air, we could drop all kinds of bombs all over some one, but on the ground we weren't even particularly good at throwing rocks.

I remember one time when the Army came around with a big fifty caliber machine gun, they wanted us to get used to it and even to try to fire it. Usually they clip the belt and limit the number of bullets to five. For some unknown reason the belt had not been clipped and the gun had access to the full 250 rounds in the magazine.

The first man to try, was a big fat, black man from the motor pool. With the first shot he froze on the trigger elevated the barrel too much and over shot the back stop. He sank two fishing boats, almost five miles off shore, before the Army Firing-range Instructor could pry his fingers off the trigger.

By the time the gun was silenced, over 150 rounds had been fired and the gun barrel had turned red hot. Further firing of the fifty caliber machine gun was immediately suspended. As a matter of fact, there was no further training in weapons handling for any Air Force personnel other than the Air Police for the rest of my time in the service.

Later in the evening, a delegation of fishermen from Haneda arrived at the base under a white flag. They wanted to be sure we understood Japan had surrendered more than ten years ago. They also wanted us to understand , even during the war, the Japanese fishing fleet had never been any particular threat to the American Forces. If necessary, they were prepared to negotiate a separate peace treaty with us --- that very evening.

All the other bases had a few Marines attached to their staff and, according to the history books, a few Marines is all was ever needed. Japan International Airport was a civilian base and we had to keep a low profile. Therefore, there were no Marines only the Japanese Civilian Guard. In any kind of scrap, they were a force to be reckoned with. I had the utmost respect for this undermanned unit of the Japanese Civilian Guard. They were a tough fighting unit and were worthy of all due respect.

For our part, we were not a fighting unit, in fact there were not even enough carbines on the base to give each one of us a weapon. Even in the thick of the thing, the rear ranks would be unarmed. Then again, it could have been they were afraid to arm the rear rank for fear they might just injure the front rank by accident. I have no idea if the base had a supply of bullets to go in the carbines for any reason other than target practice.

The only people who did have ammunition were the Air Police. Having worked with this particular branch of the Air Force,

I knew in my heart they had no intention of sharing anything with the rest of us. In fact, the Air Police were skillfully deployed behind us. In the event anyone of us should decide to decline the invitation to the May Day Festivities, the Air Police were to re-invite us, by force if necessary.

Somehow, I got the notion they might just enjoy their work. We knew they were going to do their job with a little more enthusiasm than was called for. After all, if the communists got through us, the job of containment fell on the shoulders of the Air Police. Even the Air Police were going to have a minor problem if this happened.

Figure 73 The Military Bridge

After the Japanese Communists got through trampling us troops into the ground, they would go after the thin line of Air Police. They were not much better armed than we were. They had a few light guns but their idea of heavy weapons was a jeep with a radio in it and a .45cal. Pistol

The way this S.N.A.F.U. was set up was like this: There were two bridges connecting the Air Force Military Base and the Civilian International Airport to the mainland. We were to hold one bridge while another team held the other bridge. You can just make out the first bridge in this photo. At one point I had a room on the first floor in the second building on the right. I had the room until I left Japan.

If the situation got nasty, a back-hoe would come by and dig fox holes for us to hide in. I was never really sure why the Supreme Commander thought we might need fox holes. Maybe he thought it might be a handy place to put our flattened bodies when it was all over.

At this point, I feel it only fair to point out neither bridge was more than fifty yards long. We were then told if the sight of our ferocious formations didn't quell the frenzied mob, live ammunition would be handed out and we were to put up a last ditch fight to save the Military side of the base.

All of the above was to take place as three thousand or so radical fanatics were running across a fifty yard wide bridge. Quite frankly, the situation didn't look very good for our team. From where we stood, it was to be like a modern version of **Custer's Last Stand** with lots of Indians and no bullets in our guns.

Nopo San

Chapter 24

The Second May Day

All night, the few of us who dared to sleep, had wild dreams about being trampled to death by thousands of Japanese Communists bent on starting World War II over again. All this while the Supreme Commander marched around trying to hand out ammunition to flattened Air Force personnel, still in formation.

Figure74 Old Cast Iron Pete And His Boat

At four in the morning, we were marched to our respective areas and told to wait for something to happen. We stood around in small groups talking quietly and waited. Dawn broke and the quiet on the other side of the Kuso Gawa was deafening. Nothing moved.

The small groups broke up and we all lined up in a rough formation waiting for the **Call to Battle.** By nine o'clock, it was obvious either we were out there on the wrong day, or the May Day Celebration had been canceled due to lack of interest.

Everything was moving quite normally, perhaps a little slower than usual, but normal. Even old Cast Iron Pete, the scavenger, was out there doing his thing. He made his living picking up pieces of iron which fell off the barges delivering raw material to the Oki Steel Works. In fact, he had a big grin on his face. He waved to us, in a cheerful fashion, as we stood there waiting for the end to come.

I have to admit, we must have looked kind of silly standing there looking across the Kuso Gawa. However, like good little soldiers, we were going to stay there until we were told to leave. At last, a few hours late, the coffee came, no sugar, or milk, coffee only. It was better than nothing. We complained bitterly to the cook brought the coffee out to us but all we got in return was, "War is hell trooper, learn to suffer!"

It was obvious right from the start, sympathy was not on his menu. We even tried to get his attention by reminding him of what the Japanese would do to him if they got to the Chow Hall. His answer to was, "Let'um come, we saved some of this coffee for them." He was right, the coffee was awful, no one in their right mind would invade a place where coffee this bad was served.

At noon, an officer arrived and broke our unit into four parts and told us we would hold down the fort in shifts from moment on; Those not on Guard should go to their regular duty stations. I was off duty so I went to the Photo Lab and picked up my camera. I thought with a whole day to kill, I might as well have some fun.

I got the men, had been left, on guard to pose for me. They formed their formations and with fierce scowls on their faces, gestured with their bare bands as if they held weapons. It made for some pretty funny stuff.

As we played Army, a small group of Japanese gathered across the Kuso Gawa from us and flashed their best grins. They must have thought it was pretty funny also, because within minutes they were howling with laughter at our antics. My suspicions about getting the other side to laugh themselves sick were thus confirmed.

The next day was a tintype of the first of May. Nothing happened. We stood around and watched the normal life style go on across the water from us with little interest. Then about noon a, larger than normal, crowd began to form. An officer arrived at our position and ordered us to attention. We stood there watching the gathering crowd with great apprehension.

I could recognize a lot of my drinking buddies over there and it made my heart sad to think my one time good friends, might soon be tramping over my flattened body, as they charged across the bridge.

By two o'clock, there were what seemed like, about a thousand people over there on the other side of the bridge, milling about with no apparent purpose. No one could figure out what they were up to. They seemed to be having a heated discussion among themselves.

At last, the banners came out and we braced ourselves for the coming hostilities. A yell went up from the mob across the Kuso Gawa but it sounded a lot like, "Yankee Come Back!" The first banner unfurled, it said, "Yankee come back we miss you!"

The group, it turned out, was made up of local business men and representatives from many of Tokyo's bars, restaurants and other places of ill repute. They missed the money spent by the "Hated G.I." in their places of business and they wanted us to come back.

The mob across the bridge surged forward and our fearless officer told us to hold fast and stand our ground. Suddenly, the mob parted and a large wagon, all festooned with bright colored pieces of cloth and cheerful paint broke through, pulled by about ten or twelve brightly clad men. The wagon moved to the middle of the bridge and stopped.

It was obvious, at this point to one and all, if the Japanese had wanted to come across the bridge, there would have been little we could have done to stop them. A situation us troops had suspected right from the start.

Now, the entire mob began to move out onto the bridge, they stopped at the wagon and clustered around it. For a mob bent on tearing us limb from limb, they seemed unusually quite and almost friendly.

We could see they were getting something from the wagon, but from where we were, we couldn't tell what it was. It could have been weapons. We braced ourselves for the worst. Suddenly, the entire mob turned to us and with a single voice said, " **G. I. Come back.**" With that, they raised Saki cups and drank a toast to us.

What followed was a Saki party which will live in my memory forever. The wagon was loaded with Saki and it was on the house. So, while our fearless leaders fussed and fumed about not having orders to cover such a situation. Us **troops** helped pull the wagon the rest of the across the bridge.

The rest of the day was a blurred memory of wild party at which no one understood what the other guy was saying. The United Nations could not have done a better job of community relations if they had tried.

In the end, even our fearless leader joined in, and a good time was had by all.

Nopo San

Chapter 25

The Base Photo lab

    I think its about time to tell you a little bit about the Base Photo Lab. We had a staff of six Air Force people and two Japanese civilians working there. There were two Staff Sergeants, both from the Fifty-First State, Hawaii. I liked them both, even though you're not supposed to like the boss.
    These two guys were a pleasure to work with. I wish I had kept in touch with them but, here again, I didn't. What a shame. Maybe, if they read this, they will recognize themselves and drop me a line. There is, of course, the remote possibility my old Supreme Commander will read this and send a **hit man.**
    I liked to think of all of those people in the Photo Lab as my friends, even though when you put us side by side we were all quite different:
    Roger, was an ex-marine and a real likeable sort. He was almost as tall as I was and had type of go getter personality made us almost instant friends. He was a ladies man and his Irish background gave him a silver tongue, this I envied as long as I knew him. He could talk his way out of just about any given situation with ease. There were many times when he had to do just this.
    Stas, was a Polish immigrant he was kind of on the quiet side, but none the less a good friend. He lifted weights in his spare time and had a build on him was the envy of all the rest of us. His greatest fear in life was he would break a bone and not be able to loft weight any more. If happened his enormous appetite would turn him into a Hindenburgh look-a-like almost over night. He kept mostly to himself, it's too bad, he was good people and, I for one, liked the guy.
    John, was a boy from the sunny south. I never got to close

to him, he had other things on his mind and I never found out what they were. This, of course, was my loss. He was a good man to work with and a good friend.

Bob Peters, only wanted one thing in life, he wanted to get out of the service and become a Black Jack Dealer at a Las Vegas Night Club. I do hope he made it. He had kind of a wild streak in him matched my own. We went lots of places together and had a ball where ever we went.

The two Japanese civilians were lots of fun also. They were always going out of their way to do something nice for us. We, on the other hand, tried our best to return the favor.

It must have been **Hell On Wheels** for those two Staff Sergeants to be stuck with four crazies like us. On the bright side of this, I found myself in the midst of fellow conspirators.

I can remember on Halloween night, when we dressed Bob Peters up like Pancho Villa, complete with Mexican hat, and a huge wooden machine gun.

Figure 75 Pancho On The Loose.

Although he was of German extraction, he looked kind of

182

like the classic ethnic Mexican. His black hair and five o'clock shadow really made him look the part.

Figure 76 The Civilian Guard Weren't Quite Sure What To Do With Pancho. The Gun The CG Carried Was Loaded And Quite Real.

We had gone to the wood shop and made a reasonable representative of a Flexible Lewis Gun. We also made a pistol for him to carry and I let him use a cartridge belt I had made on Okinawa. The other belt was a standard military web belt.

Our friend Peters supplied the straw hat. He avoided shaving for a few days to get a really scruffy look and we were ready to go. We took this picture at the base photo lab and it was off to the Service Man's Club for the first step in our hi jinx.

First we went to the service mans club and took first prize in the costume contest. This guy really looked like a Mexican Bandito.

With first prize carefully tucked away we moved on in search of more trouble. Naturally we found it in short order.

The Japanese Civilian Guard didn't know it was a joke. They brought Pancho back to their Head Quarters at gun point. They failed to see the humor in what we had done.

The guy with the carbine was dead serious. Even the wooden guns Bob carried, were taken quite seriously.

We had to do some fast talking to get poor Bob out of this situation. The Civilian Guard really thought he'd caught some kind of bandit.

Figure 77 We Convinced Everyone It Was All A Joke. Everyone But The Officer Was Amused.

They weren't really sure just what to do with him, jail him or send him away to a rubber room. We let him stew at Civilian Guard Headquarters, for a while, before we went in and identified him. He wouldn't talk to any of us for weeks afterwards.

At long last we were able to talk our way out of the situation and from this moment on a good time was had by all. We got the Civilian Guard to pose for one more picture which we later blew up to a huge size and they hung it on the wall of their headquarters. Every time we went into their headquarters after this we had a good laugh over it.

They were a good lot and they had a "Ping Pong" table set up in their front room. We never failed to challenge them and never once won.

Figure 78 The Civilian Guard Shared Our Parking Lot With Us.

We shared the parking lot in front of the photo lab with the Japanese Civilian Guard. They were a good bunch of guys and we went to their headquarters on many occasions Somehow, I don't think the officer, front row center ever forgave us for the Pancho incident.

There were a good many of these fellows who not long ago

were ready to fight us to the death in defense of their homeland.

Then One day we had a big rush job. There was a Basket Ball game on base and we just had to get the pictures to the base newspaper in time to make it into the days print run. Having taken the pictures I raced into the photo lab to process the film. It was a flagrant breach of military protocol but I forgot to take my hat off as I dashed into the dark-room.

Having processed the film and made the prints I prepared to run over to the news paper office and deliver the finished product. At the door I stopped. I couldn't go outside unless I had my hat on. I searched the photo-lab from top to bottom. My hat was no where to be found. At last I asked around to borrow someone else's hat. Every one had an excuse why they just had to hang onto their hats. I was in big trouble again.

At long last one of the Sergeants came in and asked me what the heck I was so upset about. I told him about how I had lost my hat and couldn't deliver my prints until I found it. Without a word he snatched my hat from my head and handed it to me. His only comment was, "Now! You damn fool, deliver your prints!" To say I felt foolish would have been the understatement of the year.

Figure 79 A Nice Big Smile For The Camera.

One of the things we were charged with was to make a "36-93 portrait" of each officer on the Base, once a year for their files. Now on this base there were several female officers. I have mentioned earlier how I felt about female officers.

Fortunately, these gals were not a bad lot. Most of them worked in the base hospital and easy to work with. When they came in for their picture, they used a certain amount of good manners and common sense.

This is Peters, one half of the devious duo, ready to say, "A nice big smile for the camera please." Now, isn't this a face to instill confidence in a person?

The camera is the big 8"X10" we used for the really fine stuff like portraits.

There were also those, however, who did not. Those obnoxious people would come into our Photo Lab, demanding this or the other thing. They felt because they were female officers, they were due much more respect than anyone else. They demanded all kinds of special treatment, and we gave it to them.

We had a few boxes of good old high resolution film. This was the stuff they use for aerial photography, it brought out every little detail. The stuff was great, it cut right through makeup, it brought out every little blood vessel in the face and especially the eyes, zits became mountains of ugliness covered by a thin layer of white snow, it made the lips turn black, and last but not least, it partially cut through nylon.

The obnoxious female came out looking like a half dressed version of Dracula's Wife, after a three day drunk. The whole picture became a study in ugliness.

Needless to say, it only took one or two of these photos, making it through to their file, before the obnoxious ones got the idea, you just don't mess with the guys at the Photo Lab.

Many of these photos we kept in a special file in the back of the Photo Lab for emergency use. If one of these unfriendly gals happened to arrive at the Photo Lab screaming for vengeance, we would produce another copy of her picture and ask, politely, how would she would like for us to send a copy to her hometown newspaper.

As a matter of fact, by the time the end of my stay in Japan came along, we had amassed quite a collection of various photos. We had something on just about everyone on base. We never went out of our way to make trouble, but we were ready for it if it came out way.

We ran afoul of a Sergeant one day. The man insisted on making life difficult for us. This poor fellow got on our case about cleaning up around the Photo Lab. Well this was quite unnecessary, both of our Hawaiian Sergeants liked the Lab kept neat as a pin and would never have allowed it to become untidy. This fellow was way off base. Even so, he created a problem for us with the Supreme Commander, this we needed like a hole in the head.

It was about a month, after the problem he caused for us, he came to the Photo Lab for a favor. Obviously, he had forgotten all about the mess he had gotten us into, but we hadn't!

The Sergeant, had married a nurse from the base hospital and wanted to send a copy of the marriage certificate home to the town newspaper and his folks. He was being transferred to another part of the world and wanted to be sure his family and hometown newspaper knew about his marriage.

"Sure!" We said, "Just leave it with us and we will send it on for you." We made a copy all right, then we took the copy and altered it to read the guy had married a Japanese Street Walker with a long history of V.D. and an equally long arrest record.

We sent him back his original certificate and sent the altered copies to his family and hometown newspaper. In fact we sent copies to everybody we thought might be interested, like his new wife's parents, his hometown church, etc. We never heard from him again and he never thanked us for making copies for him.

The power we held was not an obvious power, it was very subtle but very effective. There was this one officer got mad at the Photo Lab, for some obscure reason, and began volunteering us for special duty over the head of our own officer.

He was so obnoxious he was given an award for what he was doing by the Supreme Commander. It became our duty to photograph the man being given his award. We took about six pictures in all. In one of the pictures there, was a huge roach crawling up the wall behind his head. Guess which picture made it to the newspaper.

He showed up at the Photo Lab the following day and asked for us to hand over the rest of the pictures we had taken. Somehow or another, they had been destroyed. He wanted a new picture taken to send to his hometown newspaper, naturally we obliged. We were always eager to help out a fellow man at arms.

We even offered to send them off for him if he would just give us some stamped self-addressed envelops. Some people, even after being told by others, never learn. We gave him his presentation all right, surrounded by Japanese prostitutes.

In yet another situation, a nurse came by the lab and wanted her medical record duplicated. She was on her way out of the service to a civilian job in a hospital near Denver, Colorado. About a month before this, she had refused to treat Roger, when he cut his hand on the edge of a film can. It was a bad cut and needed several stitches.

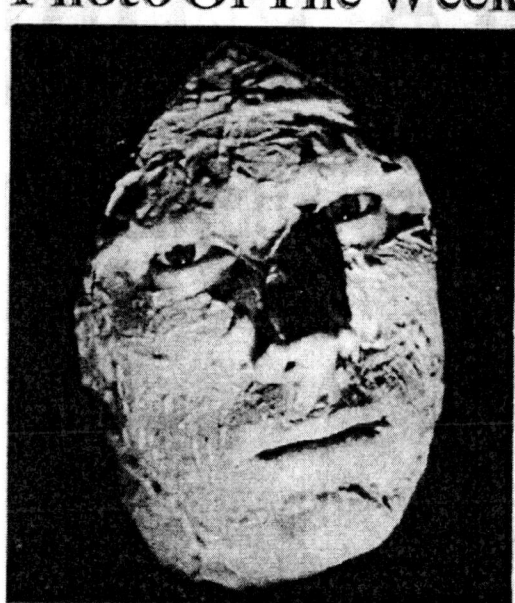

Figure 80 Spirit Face.

I guess Roger, in an effort to be light hearted about the thing, said something to her she didn't like. I had only known Roger for about three months when this happened, but I know he would never hurt anyone intentionally.

Now here this woman stood, asking favors. We fixed her up all right. When we got through with it, the woman was a walking plague carrier, on her record we put every form of V. D. we could think of, on record she became a real modern day version of Typhoid Mary. Once again, we never heard another word from her.

When there was nothing to do we had the time to become creative. This is what I looked like with wet toilet paper stuck all over my face.

The whole thing boiled down to this, as a general rule, the Base Photo Lab was one of the last people on the base to handle your records if there was anything to be duplicated. In those times, there were always some duplications needed, computers were still ten or twenty years away.

Once a person left the base it was virtually impossible for them to exact any sort of revenge. We had the absolute last word, and this made us very powerful.

A member of the USAF underground inspection team en route to his duty station, this denizen of the dirt pauses for a pose in front of the Base Photo Lab. Photo by Robert P. Herbst.

Figure 81 A Japanese Ant

We tried hard never to abuse this power and it was only for this reason we got away with what we were doing for so long.

How's this for a slow day. This is an ant being tempted with a small bit of sugar from the chow hall. It seemed there was always something to photograph no matter how mundane.

We knew it was a Japanese ant because we were in Japan and we were pretty sure no one had brought their ants from home.

However, once again I made it into the newspaper's photo contest. In the end, I was asked not to submit any more. I had taken the prize for several months running and it was time to give someone else a chance.

The prize, by the way, was the mention of my name at the bottom of the photo. Not exactly a get rich quick scheme.

Figure 82 the Personnel At The Enlisted Man's Club

When we couldn't find ants to take pictures of we resorted to things like this. These are the ladies and gentlemen of the Base

Enlisted Man's Club. It's kind of hard to remember there were a good many of these very ladies trained to defend the beaches of their homeland against us G.I.'s with nothing more than sharpened sticks. If you look closely, I think some of them wish they had those sharpened sticks right now.

All kidding aside, most of the Japanese I had dealings with both off and on base were just as friendly and polite as they could be.

I didn't spend very much time at the Enlisted Man's Club. I guess I was too busy getting myself in hot water both on and off base. There never seemed to be any shortage of trouble to get into.

This is Fuji Musume, the daughter of Mount Fuji. I sent the doll, in its case back to my mother to hold for me until I got out of the service

Later I gave it to my oldest daughter. The first thing she did with it was to take it out of the case and paint its face with lipstick. What a shame.

Just in case you didn't know, what to call it Mount Fuji Yama is redundant. Fuji Yama means Fuji Mountain. So it's either Mount Fuji or Fuji Yama but not both.

Figure 83 Fuji Musume

Nopo San

Chapter 26

The Shrine At Haneda

It was one of those hot sultry summer days when it's too hot to work, yet the only air conditioned place on the base was the Photo Lab. So, Hi-He, Hi-Ho, it's off to work we go. It was my time off but what the heck. I had volunteered for permanent night alert duty so my days were my own.

I had done this for two reasons:

One was I hated military protocol with a bitter passion. Shining shoes and wearing pressed uniforms was left strictly to someone else. I guess, when you come right down to it, I am a slob by Military Standards. Even today, I don't like to get dressed up. My idea of a Sunday-go-to-meeting outfit, is still clean blue-jeans and a clean white "T" Shirt.

Being on night duty meant I could sleep all day and no one would bother me. I was excused form most formations and I could wear civilian clothing more than my uniform. This suited me just fine.

And two: I found, quite by accident, being on night duty meant all I had to do was let the Air Police know where I was at all times, and I could go wherever I wanted to go, within reason. If they wanted me, they were quite happy to come and get me, where ever I was.

Most of the time I would take my big Speed Graphic camera and roam the streets of Haneda, the small village, town, whatever, just off base. If I was needed, I was so big, and Haneda was so small a town, it wasn't hard to find me. Anyhow everyone, but everyone, knew Nopo San.

If I was needed for a job all the Air Police had to do was go into Haneda and ask, "Nopo San, Doko Deska?" (Where is Nopo San?) and they would be guided right to where ever I happened to be.

Figure 84 Kids At An Accident.

    I just loved to take pictures of kids doing their thing. Kids are never reserved like their adult counterpart. These kids were looking at an accident. A jeep had slid off the road into an open sewerage ditch. They don't mind "Hamming it up" a bit for the camera. I got a lot of great shots of little kids, as they stood around watching whatever it was I was taking pictures of at the time.

    These kids went to school day and night. Their school never shut down. They went in three shifts. It was just like the shift work in any twenty-four hour outfit. This group was just coming home at midnight.

    This deal was fine with the Air Police and they were glad to have my cooperation when they needed a quick print of something or their picture taken to send home to the girl friend, the wife, or both, as the case may be. They knew where to find me and I could do as I pleased, everybody was happy and so it was for almost my entire stay in Japan.

Figure 85 An Impromptu Boxing Match.

As I said, my favorite thing was to take pictures of the people around the area, as they went about their daily life. I made large blowups of the pictures, and present the subject with a copy of his picture. This was just one more reason why every person in area knew who Nopo San was and where he was at any given moment.

It was during my late night wandering, I stumbled on this meat little Shinto Shrine on a back street near the border with the town of Kana Gawa. Kana Gawa was off limits to all Air Force personnel.

The place was largely communist and quite unfriendly towards us. At least this is what we were told to keep us out of there. For my part, I found all the Japanese people very friendly in spite of their political convictions. I really believe there is more hostility between Republicans and Democrats in the United States than there was between the Air Force at Haneda and the local Communists.

I went to Kana Gawa several times to test this theory, but it just didn't seem right to me. I had too many Japanese friends at Haneda, and there were supposed to be lots of Communists at Haneda also.

Anyhow, this shrine was a real beauty, with letter perfect maintenance, and lots of statuary along the little white, crushed stone path, led up to the shrine itself. I came back several times during the daytime to photograph the place but somehow the shots were flat. They were pictures of a Shrine. So what! I tried different angles, high shots, and low shots. But nothing really did justice to this beautiful piece of real estate. Next, I tried different lighting combinations but again some how I was missing the mark.

At long last, I gave up and asked for help from one of the other guys at the Lab. My friend, Roger agreed to take a look with me as soon as he got off work day. Together, we walked the mile or so to the Shrine and for a long time just stood there looking at it. In truth, it was a pleasure just to look at it. It gave you a feeling of peaceful order with its neatly done paths and plants.

Finally, Roger told me he had an idea, we would come back at night with every piece of flash equipment we could lay our hands on and do a high contrast, back light, night shot. Everything would be back lit with enough front lighting to give the detail of the statuary. It sounded great to me so we set about gathering the stuff we would need.

It was midnight by the time we found all the stuff we wanted. We had about twenty flash guns alone, along with a half a mile of wire to tie it all together. We figured if we tied the whole thing together we could get the camera to fire all the flash guns at one time.

If everything worked the way it was supposed to work, the effect would be spectacular. But only if it worked. We had fooled around in the Photo Lab on lots of occasions and played with different lighting combinations. This, however, was going to be a monumental effort.

There was no one about, at the late hour, when we started setting up for the shot. We were only going to get one shot at it because the removal of twenty flash bulbs from inventory left a gaping hole in the supply room was sure to be questioned the following day. But what the heck, you only live once.

Maybe we would have a spectacular picture to hang on the Supreme Commander's wall and all would be forgiven. Granted, it was a slim chance, but at least it was a chance and was better odds than I usually had. I felt, somehow, I was in some way responsible for making him angry. I really tried hard to stay on his better side but each time, I would wind up right in the thick of things.

Working in the semi-darkness, we place flash guns by each of the many statues at the shrine. In all, I think we set out all of the twenty flash guns. They had to be placed just so, or the light would be going in the wrong direction. It was to be a masterwork of lighting technology. By two-thirty, in the morning, we were finally set to shoot.

We made one last check of all the wires and connections, then we sat back and waited for a good big cloud to obscure the moon. It had to be pitch black for the shot to work.

At this point, I feel it necessary to tell you we were using Japanese Flash Bulbs. Now there was nothing wrong with the Japanese Flash Bulbs, except on the average, about every third one would explode.

It wasn't a really big bang but it did shower the area in front of the camera with broken glass and sparks of burning magnesium. We had checked the bulbs at the Lab to be sure we had good ones, but we really had no idea which one would explode or why, so we really didn't know what it was we were looking for, but we checked them anyhow.

At the time, all flash bulbs were a glass with a thin plastic coating over them. When they were used the glass fractured because of the heat generated by the burning magnesium but the plastic coating held it in place. We never found out whether it was a poor grade of plastic, too much air left inside the bulb, or the coating was too thin. All we knew for sure was about every third one exploded with a bang.

After only a short wait, a large cloud covered the moon, Roger and I looked at each other, held our breath, and with a nod of our heads Roger pressed the button. All twenty bulbs exploded at the same time, one bulb going bang wasn't bad, but twenty bulbs going bang all at the same time was something else again. It made a horrendous blast. When the bulbs went off, Roger and I both fell over backwards from the shock alone. We had never expected anything like this to happen. The entire area was covered with broken flash bulbs.

There were little fires everywhere caused by the burning magnesium scattered all over the place. Smoke was curling up from every statue. It was like a scene from hell.

Behind us, in the dark, there was a scream. Then something in Japanese I didn't understand, but it left little doubt in our minds we were in the thick of it again. Not bothering to be too careful about the equipment, we gathered up our flash guns and stuffed them all into two bags.

All the time, out of the dark came a mounting wave of noise. Lights were going on all around us and people were beginning to gather in the streets. For us, it was like old times, but the Japanese did not look like a happy lot. Somehow, they had failed to see the light side of what we had done. I had to admit, when I looked at the thing from the stand point of the Japanese, it would be to a Catholic, like someone setting a stink bomb off during Sunday Mass, at St. Peters Basilica in Rome.

We had not intentionally desecrated their shrine, we had only meant to honor it. Still, the road to hell is paved with good intentions and I had no intention of standing around and try to explain it to the growing mob. They didn't understand English anyhow. This was definitely a situation which called for a hasty retreat.

As we stuffed the last flash gun down into the bag with the camera, Roger looked at me and said, "Race you to the gate!"

I didn't think he really expected an answer as we took off together in a neck in neck dash for the, somewhat questionable, protection of the base. Behind us raged a storm, and we had no intention of allowing it to overtake us.

We fairly flew past the two Civilian Guards at the front gate. They didn't even try to stop us. They were too surprised to move. We must have been a strange sight. Running as fast as we could, trailing wires, flash guns, and other equipment behind us, as we sped past them, with what seemed like half the population of Haneda in hot pursuit. They just kind of stood there with their mouths hanging open and the strangest expressions on their faces.

The crowd stopped at the gate, but they could be heard clean over to the Photo Lab. Roger and I hid in there until daylight. Then, just at dawn we slipped back to the barracks for a change of clothing. Some where, Roger and I had both seen, in a book or movie, a change of clothing was a good disguise. It hadn't worked for us before and it sure didn't work this time.

By ten o'clock, we were standing, between armed escort, outside the Supreme Commander's office. We were listening to a rather heated discussion which was all in Japanese. Although my knowledge of Japanese was still limited, I could make out these people were from the Shrine in Haneda. They were convinced the United States Air Force had dropped a bomb on their Shrine during the night.

According to their story, they had shot the marauding plane out of the sky, with a divine missile, and had chased the pilot and copilot back to this base on foot. They were not asking for much. All they wanted was for the pilot and copilot, which was apparently us, to be handed over to them so they could be publicly stoned to death outside the Shrine.

In English I heard a voice, sounded a lot like our Supreme Commander say, "You know, I have a good mind to hand those two over to those people. I really think I would be doing the Air

Force a favor."

Shortly there after, the meeting broke up and, through another door in his office, the Japanese delegation left. We were ushered in, still between armed escort. The Supreme Commander, already not in the best of moods, seemed to be having trouble finding the right words.

He rose from his seat and, placing one set of knuckles on the edge of his desk, he leaned forward and pointed the finger of his other hand at us as he said,"**You! -You!**" At point we expected to see real fire, burst forth from his nostrils.

Figure 86 An Experiment In Lighting

Although this is not the picture we made that night it's close to what we did except on a much smaller scale. This was only one little shrine in a formal garden at a resort near Tokyo.

Roger was of Irish extraction. I have always wished I had

the gift of gab most of my Irish friends have had. Braving the devastation was about to be heaped on our bodies, Roger stepped forward and unrolled a print of the picture we had made of the Shrine.

He held it up in front of the Supreme Commander and said, "We made this great picture for you to hang on your wall."

The sight of the picture seemed to take the starch out of the man. The Supreme Commander slumped back in his chair and stared, first at the picture, and then at us. His eyes round with disbelief. Suddenly, he looked very tired.

Roger placed the picture on his desk in front of him so he could see it better. It was indeed a work of art. The glass from the bursting flashbulbs had shown up like snow, and really looked quite pretty. The sparks had not yet had a chance to ignite anything and the small puffs of smoke looked kind of like wisps of early morning mist.

After looking at the picture for a moment or so, he muttered something to our escorts and we were ushered form the office. Once outside, the Supreme Commander's office, we looked back to see why it was so quiet. He was just sitting there, staring at the picture, with a blank expression on his face.

None of us disliked the Supreme Commander, he was a reasonably nice person to get along with, under normal condition. I met him one day, as I was going to the Chow Hall, he was in civilian clothing. Recognizing him as the Supreme Commander, I saluted him. He stopped me and we had a few pleasant words.

Much to my surprise, I found he didn't dislike me. He seemed to realize these things were happening were not my direct fault. I got the idea he understood I was the victim of circumstances and I was not doing these things deliberately to antagonize him.

For me, it was a moment of profound relief to know the man was not really out to get me.

Still, he was responsible for the Base and everything on it, even me. It must have been terribly difficult for the man to explain to others, what was going on. What seems funny here on paper, must have been a nightmare for the Supreme Commander.

    The Supreme Commander had the picture framed and to the best of my knowledge the picture hung on his wall till the day he left the base. I would like to think he took it with him and has it on the wall of his of his favorite room today. However, a more realistic view would be he has a picture of Roger and I, and he's using it as a dart board.

Nopo San

Chapter 27

The Flight Over Korea

I was roused from a sound sleep around three o'clock in the morning. It was the lieutenant who had charge of The Signal Corp. He wasted no time in saying he needed a volunteer, and he looked straight at me.

At the time I was what was called the Alert Photographer and it was part of my job to be on call for any situation. The photo lab was part of the Signal Corp in the U.S.A.F. and this man was a lieutenant from this section so he had charge of the photo lab as well.

Don't get me wrong, he was as reasonable and likeable as an officer could be, we all liked him and we worked well together. If he had asked me to walk on the water, I would have tried my best. I didn't feel this way about many officers. Just this officer and, believe it or not, the Supreme Commander.

Now I had **volunteered** for God knows what. I was on my way to the flight line with two very silent, flight officers. They would only tell me everything I needed was already on the plane. I had no problem with the first part. But the plane part had me a little worried. I don't like flying. If God had wanted me to fly he would have put wings on my back and he sure as heck never would have made me as big as I am.

On our arrival at the flight-line, I was handed a wool-lined flight jacket and some wool-lined trousers by the jeep driver, who turned out to be the pilot as well. I made a silent prayer, on the spot, praying he could fly the plane better than he drove our jeep. The short trip to the flight-line had been an experience in white-knuckle terror.

Both the jacket and trousers provided, proved to be about four sizes too small in both sleeve length and leg length, but I wore them anyhow. It seemed to give the fly guys pleasure to see me stuffed into the tiny outfit. The person originally scheduled for this flight must have been a short, rather hefty chap.

As the plane roared down the runway, I was handed a pair of gloves that wouldn't fit, just to make the outfit complete. The flight engineer gave them to me when he came back into the cargo area to explain the mission to me.

The plane had two engines and the engineer called it a "Gooney Bird." We were off to Korea to fly a photo mission down between two mountains ranges to ascertain what the Chinese had on the slopes of the mountains facing what we had.

It was to be a simple mission, in and out, then back to JIA for dinner. Having the flight engineer refer to the plane as a gooney bird, a native of Australia which couldn't fly, did little to boost my already lagging confidence.

I was further assured the Chinese had no heavy stuff or anti-aircraft guns in the area. Actually, he went on to explain, we were technically not at war anyhow. All we wanted to do was make sure the Chinese were keeping their word.

There were two big aerial-roll-film cameras, one pointed out each side of the plane and slightly down. All I had to do was push a button to start them when the green light over my head went on. It was too easy for words. The engineer then handed me a Western novel to read and told me to enjoy the flight.

I was also directed to a pile of sandwiches. Unfortunately, I didn't feel much like eating. I was still kind of nervous about the piolet's ability to fly this crate. He had bounced the plane on the runway and now, here we were flying along at wave top levels toward some God forsaken place to take pictures of mountain sides. This was definitely not my idea of a good time.

The area where the cameras and I were, was an armored box-like affair with a steel floor and sides. It was obviously designed to protect the equipment and myself from small arms ground fire more than anti-aircraft fire. Other than these, the plane was unarmed.

Only the pilot carried a sidearm. I wondered silently just how one waved a white flag from an unarmed aircraft. It was my firm belief the pilot was the only hero type among us.

We flew down close to the deck all the way to Korea, which was not a long way anyhow, and then at the last moment, possibly for my benefit, the plane roared almost straight up to what I guessed was the proper altitude and headed inland over some mountains. At least, it seemed like we went straight up because every loose piece of equipment along with me wound up in great sprawling heap in the very tail of the craft.

As I extricated myself from the jumble of equipment the flight engineer poked his head into my area and yelled out how sorry he was. The big toothy grin on his face made me doubt his sincerity. It really didn't take my mind off the bone chilling cold that now flooded the plane because of the altitude.

The flight jacket only covered my arms to the elbows and the trousers only reached about half way from my knees to my ankles. The gloves covered my fingers but only half the palm of my hand and I had great trouble keeping them on. The seat had split out of the trousers the first time I sat down.

Now, with being bounced to the tail section without warning, the flight jacket had split up the back. Possibly, because I was now so well ventilated, I was slowly freezing to death, and no one but me seemed to care.

I was just in the process of trying to slip the gloves further down over my fingers, knowing there was no way I would get my thumb in there with them. When the red light flicked on over my head. This meant "Get Ready" so I moved over to my button, set my gaze on the red light and waited.

The green light went on and I hit the button just as a gust of ice cold air hit me in the face.

I was startled to see a large section of the fuselage was gone and other smaller sections of it were quickly vanishing without a trace. There was a little thud as each part vanished and louder thumps as things hit the armored section of the floor.

Someone was obviously shooting at us.

I couldn't help but find it funny, there was no loud sound. I had always thought there was a loud bang when this sort of thing happened. Then again my only previous experience had been in movie theaters.

I picked up the mike and told the fly guys their plane was falling apart. "Not so!" came the happy reply, "They're shooting at us."

We were being shot at, and these guys sounded happy about it. I couldn't believe it. But, then again, I guess anything is better than having to admit the plane fell apart. Somehow, I got the mental picture of the pilot, steering wheel in hand, with a big grin on his face, marching back to J. I. A., to tell my friends how I had gone down with the plane and the wheel was all there was left.

I yelled back over the roar of the engines, "I thought you told me the war was over?"

The voice in my earphone said, "I know it is. You know it is. I guess nobody told the Chinese! You want to try?"

All this and the plane gradually disappearing around me came as a great surprise. They had told me distinctly, there were no anti-aircraft guns in the area we were to fly over and, as far as I knew, the war had been over for almost a year.

What had gone wrong? Maybe the Supreme Commander had told them I would be flying overhead and this was some kind of welcome he had arranged with them for me. It just had to be some kind of major misunderstanding.

My friend, the flight engineer, popped his head in again and above the roar of the engines, which was now quite loud because more and more of the plane was disappearing, told me we had come down between the wrong two mountains. He went on to tell me the pilot was doing something about it right now.

I want to tell you, this really didn't make me feel a whole lot better about the situation. As I looked out of one of the larger holes in the side of the plane, smoke belched from the engine and the prop stopped turning. I was beginning to have a distinct feeling the end was near.

It suddenly got very quiet. The other engine had stopped. There volumes of smoke trailed past the holes in the plane along with sheets of flame. The only sound now was the rush of air past the holes. The funny crunching sounds that signified other parts of our plane were disappearing had stopped.

I asked into the mike, just what it was the pilot was doing about the situation, but they didn't answer. At this point, either the mike was dead or the fly guys just weren't answering me. There was also the unpleasant possibility they had already left the plane.

After this, I had a few quiet moments to wonder just what the pilot was going to do about our mutual problem and just what the Supreme Commander had to do with all this. Nobody has luck this bad without some kind of help from someone who cares.

Now with the crunching noises stopped, the flight engineer came back to tell me the plane has sustained some damage. I told him how glad I was it was only **some** damage.

After this, he assured me with his best professional smile, my worst fears were to be realized. **We were going to crash!** He said it was all right though, the pilot had spotted a rice paddy and planned to set us down in the mud. If this was supposed to make me feel real good about the situation, it didn't work.

I began thinking if I didn't make it through all this, someone somewhere was going to be very happy about it. The thought irked me and I resolved to ruin their day by surviving no matter what.

Now came the real ringer. I had one thousand feet of roll film on my hands and, I was told, if we were caught with it, it would mean instant firing squad. It was my job to get rid of it before we hit the ground or as quickly there after as I could manage it.

I yanked the back off the nearest camera, pulled the lead film off the spool and fed it through the nearest hole large enough to accommodate it. When the wind caught it, we had a nearly instant streamer tail, I did the same to the other camera and then sat back to pray the mud in the paddy was the soft gooey kind I had read about in books. The knee deep kind which smelled of good old manure.

Looking out the hole nearest me, I found to my horror the ground was almost up to us and closing fast. The flight engineer poked his head back into my section again and I was told to brace myself. This was a good trick, at this point, because there was darn little left to hang onto or brace against.

Moments later, we hit with a monumental splat! Thick gooey mud flew every where. It did indeed have a vile smell about it. God was smiling on me, the mud was everything I had hoped it would be.

The plane or what was left of it slid a few hundred feet, broke into several large pieces and came to rest at a grove of trees on the edge of the paddy. It was a perfect one point landing, the one point being the belly of the plane.

For myself, I was never so glad to get out of anything in my life. All my fears about flying had been reaffirmed. Once again on the ground, I confirmed my faith in **Terra-Firma**, the more **firma**, the less **terror**.

My friend the flight engineer, and I now used the term rather loosely, informed us we were about fifteen miles behind the lines -- **the wrong lines**! A quick look back along our skid path confirmed at least two thirds of the Chinese army had been roused from their nap. They were very cranky and put out with us. To make matters worse, they were all carrying guns and pointing them in our direction.

As yet, we were still out of range and none of us intended to let this particular situation change in the least. However this didn't stop the Chinese soldiers from trying their best to shoot us.

The navigator/co-pilot pointed out the direction in which we were to run and the four of us stood there staring at him for a second or so, I am dead sure the same question was on all our minds. We hoped to God he was better at direction finding than he was at navigation. It seemed like an eternity before he finally said,

"Yes! I'm sure 's the way, now let's go!"

The pilot, a real macho type, pulled out his forty-five and told us he would slow them down a bit. As he pulled the slide back he turned a chalky white. Turning to us and with a wide-eyed expression on his face he said, "**My God! I forgot to load it!**"

As I turned to start running, my only thought about this one was it seemed logical. All I could do was shake my head and think, **typical Air Force!** After all, everything else had gone wrong. Why not this?

At this point I was told by the pilot to go back into the part of the plane where the cameras were and destroy them. At first I thought he was joking but he repeated it and added, "That's an order!" I returned to the plane and smashed the cameras as ordered. On returning to the spot I had left the fly guys, I found I was all alone except for a huge mob of angry Chinese soldiers which was rapidly approaching.

Now I know for certain, in the two thirds of the Chinese Army which was chasing me, there must have been much faster runners than I was. However, I doubt if any of them had the same motivation I did.

Ordinarily, I would have found running half a mile would tax my endurance. Today, however, I had a reason to run. The thought of lots of pointy bayonets being thrust in my direction gave wings to my heels. The same thoughts must have occurred to the fly guys, because I never did catch up to them.

They had to have been jet propelled and judging from the stain on the seat of the copilots trousers as he disappeared over the far hill, he must have been running a little rich.

I topped the first hill without incident. By this, I mean I hadn't been killed yet. Now it occurred to me, I must go through the Chinese lines from the back to get to our own lines. I had no way of knowing where these lines were. All I knew was they were supposed to be somewhere in the general direction in which I had seen the flight crew go. At least according to our illustrious navigator, who's credibility now suffered greatly in my mind's eye.

I had long since lost sight of my more fleet footed fliers. Fliers they were called and fliers they were. If anyone got killed now it was going to be me and if the Chinese wanted to do this, they were going to have to catch me first.

Thus started an odyssey which I have tried these many years to forget. I had been abandoned somewhere behind the wrong lines. I had nothing but my bare hands and a miniature flight suit which had come apart and was rapidly falling off my body. Obviously the thing was leaving a trail of parts and I had to ditch the rest of it at the first opportunity.

I did this at a bend in the road I was running on and dove into the brush on the opposite side of the road for cover.

Fortunately for me, I had been smart enough to thrown the parts of the flight suite way off on the other side of the road and out into a field. The entire Chinese, army which converged on the spot, assumed I had gone off in this direction.

My luck held and they proceeded to fan out into the field. They left a small group on the road to make sure I didn't come back up onto it down the way a bit.

One of them was standing so close to me I could smell his feet. He hadn't washed in a while but I didn't dare move a muscle. I couldn't see how many there were but I could hear more than one voice. This alone would indicate the odds of my survival were heavily weighted against me if they found me.

I had to clench my teeth to keep my teeth from chattering and stiffen every muscle to keep from shivering. The man stood there for what seemed like an eternity. Why he didn't turn around and look down is still a mystery. I guess it just wasn't my time to go.

At long last he rejoined the rest of his group and the whole bunch moved off slowly down the road, keeping careful watch on their brethren out in the field.

When all was quiet and I could see no movement in any direction I slithered on my belly to the nearest bush and curled up under it to take stock of my situation. The words, **I'm in deep**

trouble, were the understatement of the year.

Nopo San

Chapter 28

The Horrors Of War

It was about noon and the sun was bright in the sky, I think it was the only reason I didn't freeze to death. I had to find shelter for the night or I was going to freeze for sure.

There was a small wood lot not far away and I made for not daring to let my belly leave the ground. Once in the wood lot I could move a bit faster but I was always conscious of the idea if I could see out, someone out there could see me.

I guess I had gone about two miles, moving slowly between trees and brush before I heard my first people. Unfortunately, they were not speaking English.

I was hungry and tired, quite frankly I debated giving myself up to this group no matter who they were. I had to think this out. I slid my back down the largest tree I could find and just sat there. I didn't know what to do. I had multiple bruises and small scratches and cuts all over my body. I had been bounced around pretty good when the plane landed.

Suddenly I was aware there was someone coming my way. I froze in place not daring to move. Out of the corner of my eye I could see a large man with a hand full of paper headed in my direction. He was looking back over his shoulder to see if anyone back there could see him. It was fairly obvious what he was up to.

Just on the other side of my tree he squatted down and proceeded to relieve himself. All he had to do was turn around and we would have been eyeball to eyeball. Under any other conditions this would have been funny. Unfortunately, at the moment I found very little to laugh about.

I was miserable in the cold. I ached in every bone. I was hungry. What right did this guy have to be so comfortable. The thought made me mad. Anger gave me strength. Moving very slowly I slid my belt off and stood up without a sound. The man finished his business and was pulling his trousers up when I dropped the looped belt over his head, turned my back to him and pulled on the belt with every ounce of strength in my body.

He didn't make a sound but he did kick and struggle to the point where I thought on several occasions I was going to lose him. As last he went limp. I waited and just hung onto him for a few moments to make sure. Then I placed him carefully on the ground. I had to move fast. I stripped him of everything I could think of I could use including his rifle, bayonet and ammunition.

Moving as quietly as I could, I moved off into the woods away from the sounds of the rest of his group. It was just getting dark when I stopped to take stock again. Things were looking up. I had a gun, some bullets and best of all, some warm clothing.

I pulled off my uniform and slid into the captured clothing. Then remembering prisoners out of uniform were shot. I put my G. I. uniform on over the purloined clothing. It didn't fit very well but at least it was warm. I had only gone a short distance before I realized I was not alone in this outfit. I had company.

The only thing I could think of was one bug saying to another bug, "Darn! American food, twenty minutes from now we'll be hungry again!" It was the first time I'd smiled since I was shoved onto darn plane back in Tokyo.

Now I had all night to find something to eat. This was going to be a problem. As I moved on the sky clouded over and night fell. There was a moonless darkness the likes of which I hadn't seen in many years. There was no light from any source but it made me a bit more confident because in this blackness, no one was going to see me.

Still moving slowly to prevent breaking twigs and the like I groped my way along heading in the direction I thought our lines were. I really had no idea were I was going but it made me feel a bit better to think I was headed home.

Every time I saw a campfire I moved away from it. During the night I had to change course several times because of campfires so by morning I was completely turned around and I had no idea which direction I was headed in. By this time I was so hungry my belt buckle was bumping into my back bone.

I had to find something to eat. I found some interesting smelling tree branches and using the Chinese bayonet as a knife I scraped the bark off some branches and chewed the stuff. It was awful tasting but it gave my stomach something to think about besides being so darn empty.

Then I got lucky. Just about the time it started to snow, I found a small cave behind a big bush and crawled inside bayonet first. I didn't want trouble but if there was anything else in cave ahead of me, I was going to make sure it was my cave in the end. It wasn't a big cave but I was alone in it. I didn't dare make a fire so I just curled up against the back wall and went to sleep. It had been almost two days of nonstop activity since my nice warm bed at JIA and I was ready for a bit of rest.

Morning came all to quickly and when I looked out side my eyes were treated to a sight I had hoped I would never see. There were about twenty Chinese solders out there in a line across the field I had crossed the night before. They were obviously looking for me. I silently thanked my lucky stars I hadn't tried to move on through the snow storm even as light as it was. I would have left a trail an amateur could have followed.

The line of Chinese moved off into the wood lot at the far side of the field and I lost sight of them. Now, I reasoned, I was behind them, things should be a bit easier this night. I waited until after dark before I moved out of my little cave and found the moon was giving me just enough light to see my way.

I made pretty good time during the night because I didn't see many campfires and I was moving in a fairly straight line judging by the position of the moon in the sky. Of course I still had no idea which direction I was supposed to be going in. Toward morning I remembered my Boy Scout training. I started looking for moss growing the trunk of the trees. I knew the moss grew only on the north side of the trees and found much to my horror I had been moving in the wrong direction.

It was time to find cover again and pass the day sleeping if possible. This was my third day with no food but some tree bark and I couldn't fool my stomach again with the same stuff. There were no caves around so I laid down between two old logs and pulled some leaves over me. During the day I moved a bit and one of the logs shifted with me. There under the log were a multitude of bugs they were dormant because of the cold.

I looked long and hard at my little room mates before I picked one up and touched it with my tongue. There was no taste so I swallowed the thing. The same fate awaited the rest of my room mates. I tried really hard not to look at what I was eating.

By nightfall I actually felt pretty good. The hills didn't seem so steep anymore and I felt I was making pretty good time in my effort to find the American lines.

I began to think about the man I had killed. Wasn't I supposed to feel all sorts of guilt and remorse? I didn't. He was the enemy and I desperately needed what he had. I had killed him and taken it. It was him or me and it was just simple.

Now I still had half the Chinese army looking for me and I had killed one of their brethren. I was without a single friend in the dark and quite lost.

I couldn't help but wonder what had become of those officers I had been with. Had they made it back and did they tell our guys I was still out there? Who knew, not me. All I wanted to do at this point was to stay alive.

Night fell as I topped a hill and I was greeted to a sight I hoped I'd never see. Before me was a campfire with several Chinese around it. They were eating their dinner while laughing and joking about something. Quietly I slid to the ground and watched for a while. One by one the solders got up and wandered down the far side of the hill away from me leaving only one man at the fire. He was apparently the cook because he started cleaning the pots and pans they had been cooking with. The smell of food came from the fire.

Slowly I inched forward until I was right behind him. One shout or noise of any kind and I was a dead man. With all the speed I could muster I grabbed him by the mouth, jammed my knee into his back and pulled back with all my might. A quick cut across the neck, then hang on until he went limp and I had all the food I could carry. There was no malice in the act, I didn't hate him, I just needed what he had and I had to kill him to get it. There was no other feeling of any kind.

I snatched all I could safely carry and lit out down the hill the way I had come. I didn't run but I moved carefully so as not to make any noise. As yet there was no sound from the camp site I had just left.

At the bottom of the hill I slowed my pace and turned to the left which should have pointed me to the West. I moved off in this general direction until morning forced me to hide for the day again.

During the day I looked over my newly requisitioned supplies. I had done well, some dried fish and a bag of rice. As I sat there looking at the stuff the thought went through my mind, "And for this I killed a man." I wondered how I could justify my actions later on. It just didn't seem right a man should die for a lousy bag of rice and a few dried fish.

The fish tasted awful and I was caused to wonder if they had been cleaned before they were dried. I put a hand full of rice in my mouth and washed it down with water from a nearby stream. Somehow I justified the act in my mind and went to sleep for the day in a large pile of branched next to a field.

That night, I turned once again to the South. It was dark again and there was a light rain but I made good time in spite of it. The rain made the twigs and leaves moist and pliable so they made no sound as I trod on them.

I avoided all contact again during the night and changed direction several times to avoid lights I saw in the distance. By morning I was once again confused about which direction I should be going in.

I found shelter in the wreckage of a farm house and slept through the day. Now an interesting thing happened to me. I couldn't for the life of me remember what day it was or exactly how long I had been hiding out in this God forsaken place.

It really didn't matter, the only thing that really mattered was I was still alive. Tired, hungry, hurt but still alive and on my own. It bothered me a great deal that I couldn't remember how long I had been sneaking around in those woods.

Once again it was evening, just about sun set. I deemed it safe to move out. It was still light but I had watched the woods all around for some time and nothing moved. I could save some time if I crossed the open field but it was taking a chance of being seen.

I had gone about a quarter of the way across when something metallic caught my eye in the grass. I leaned over for a closer look. It was about the size of a quarter and dark grey in color.

I was about to try to pick it up when something inside me said, "Don't do it!" Best darn advice I'd had in years. On closer examination I found it was connected to something buried in the ground. Being very careful to step only in the foot prints I had made on the way in I retraced my steps and made a solemn promise never to cross an open field ever again.

Now as I moved through the woods I had to start watching for bits of string strung between the trees along with everything else. Fortunately I didn't find any this night but my nerves had been dealt a severe blow. In the woods I was fairly safe from buried mines because of the of the tree roots. Booby traps were another story altogether. I now realized even walking through the woods was no longer safe.

It was morning once again and time to crawl into a hole to sleep for the day. I took a long hard look at the rifle I had been carrying. What earthly good was it. If I fired the thing I'd give my position away and if I continued carrying the thing there was always the danger it would get caught on a branch and make a noise.

Once again it was night, with my rifle still slung over my shoulder, I took to the woods again. This time I tried to control my pace to a slow motion walk with all my senses aimed at the ground in front of me. One mistake and I was history. The night was uneventful except for crossing a road where there was a military convoy going by. I had to wait and slip across between trucks. It was a scary proposition.

During the day sleep came hard and I took some time to reconsider my situation. With no survival training except what I had gotten as a Boy Scout in my home town under an ex ranger I had managed to elude capture for almost a week now.

Since fate cast me into this situation with nothing but my bare hands, I had managed to get warm clothing, a rifle, ammunition, a bayonet and food enough to eat. I wasn't in bad shape at all except I was so dirty I could probably be followed by smell alone.

As night came on, I chewed the last of my dried fish and washed down the last handful of dried rice. I was out of food again. The good side of this was I could eat just about anything I came across and raw to boot. I moved out into the darkness and picked my way South once again.

I had only gone about fifty feet when something touched my shin, it didn't feel right. I looked down to find a very thin string across the path. Thank God I had been doing the slow motion walk I had started a day or so before.

I followed the string and found one end tied to a hand grenade inside a small tin can. If I had walked into the thing, the string would have pulled the grenade out of the tin can and poof, I'm history.

Being somewhat of a prankster, I rerouted the string across the path in a different spot and went on my way. I can remember being rather disappointed because I didn't hear an explosion behind me during the night.

By morning I had reached the top of a big hill and I could see for quite a distance. I found a nice quiet spot under some branches and curled up for the day. I was too tired to even look out over the hill top. I couldn't even tell how many days I'd been on the go. All I knew was I had enough hair on my face to scare a bear and I was just too darn tired to care.

In the evening I slipped out of my little hiding place to take a look around before it got really dark. There on the valley floor was a sight made my heart jump for joy. There were two lines of concertina wire. I was nearly home. Unfortunately, from this point on I would be facing guns from both sides. I crawled back into my warren and spent the night gathering strength for the next day. There was no way I was going to try this in the dark.

Hunger was a real problem. I needed something to eat if I was going to try to run the gauntlet by day. It was about this time I found the rat. It was a good sized rat and it was curious about what, something as vile smelling as me, was doing in the same pile of branches it was living in. I had already eaten bugs, how much worse could rat be.

I tried hard not to think about it but it was just like I had been told in the Boy Scouts. You will eat almost anything if you get hungry enough. I was definitely hungry enough.

Next morning, while the mist was still rising from the ground I broke cover and stood up straight for the first time in a week. I had to do something to get rid of the cramps in my legs and back.

I took the bolt out of the rifle and dropped it in between some rocks. Then I broke the butt of the gun over another larger rock.

Suddenly from behind me there was a sharp splat and something whistled past me ear close enough I felt heat from it. The fat was in the fire for sure. I had been seen and there was only one thing for me to do. I dropped everything I didn't need to run with and got ready to run for my life.

Needless to say I didn't wait around for an introduction. I took off down the hill running as fast as my legs would carry me. As I ran down the hill it cut off the sight line of the person had taken pop shot at me. I was on my way home but I still had no idea whether or not I was going to make it.

About half way down the far side of the hill, I jumped to clear a bush. Much to my horror, I landed right in the middle of a game of chess, being played by two members of a Chinese machine gun crew.

Now these guys had no sense of humor at all, I know I had disturbed their game - and I know I should have stopped to apologize - but under the circumstances I was sure they would understand if I wrote a letter at a later date.

As I cleared the other side of their hole, I stepped on the barrel of their gun, upsetting it. This seemed to make them even madder. However, I was quite sure they would understand about this also, so I just kept going.

I was quite wrong concerning their understanding about the letter, because as soon as they were able to right their gun, they turned it loose in the direction I had gone. I was absolutely sure if I slowed down even a little bit, those bullets were going to start catching up with me.

Running down the hill was a breeze but I was now in the valley between the two hills, the going got a little tougher. I think maybe I had slid down most of the rest of the hill. There was lots of loose rock and sand all over the place. There seemed to be an awful lot of it still attached to me because I seemed to be getting heavier, it was either this or I was getting tired.

There was so much metal flying past me by this time I could have opened a scrap yard if I could have caught it. However, I reasoned it might be best to leave this job to others who had more time to spend on it.

By the time, I was about halfway across the valley, there were people in the direction I was running were shooting at whoever was shooting at me. The air was so full of stuff going both ways, you could cut it with a knife. There was someone way up ahead yelling for me to run faster.

Obviously, who ever it was, didn't know just how fast I was

already going. However, anything to please a friend.

If I live to be two hundred and fifty, I don't think I will ever know how I got through our wire, as well as the stuff put up by the Chinese, but I did and without a scratch.

Suddenly, a hand reached up out of the ground and grabbed my foot, I fell flat on my face, then I was dragged backwards into a fox hole. There were two other fellows in it who seemed to be as dirty as I was. Their clothing, however, fit them. They sat there staring at me for a moment or two, then they asked if I were a Marine.

When I told them I was not, they looked on me with great distaste. One of them said to the other, "He must be the Air Force guy we heard about, only the Air Force would send a man out to do a job dressed like that!"

Then they went back to shooting at something in the direction I had come from. It was great to be back with friends.

Nopo San

Chapter 28

Three Weeks With The Marines

As I lay there in the bottom of fox hole and tried to get up, one of the Marines stood on me and told me in no uncertain terms if I moved again he'd accidentally blow my head off. With an incentive like this it was easy to remain quiet. Besides, I was kind of tired and winded after my run across the open field.

When things quieted down I was allowed to get up and look around. Apparently no one got killed but it wasn't because no one was trying. Things were very quiet now and I was told to sit in the bottom of the hole and stay out of the way. Only not in those exact words. Their language left little doubt about their feelings toward me.

I asked, later in the day, about the three officers I had come in with. I was told they had been shipped right back to Tokyo. I told them I was also from Tokyo and I too had to get back.

No such luck, I was an enlisted man and as such, I was destined to spend the next three weeks as a guest of the Marine Corp. Or at least this is what they told me at the time.

Knowing the feeling of the Mud Marine toward the Air Force, I was, for a moment, tempted to go back over and stay with the Chinese. Then I remembered the game I had stepped on and how angry those fellows had gotten about it. I decided the Chinese had absolutely no sense of humor whatsoever. At least the Marines were shooting at something other than me for the moment, so I decided to stay.

I never would have believed anyone could get so mad over a simple chess game. Even the Marines, who's fox hole I now shared, were angry and claimed it was my fault things had gotten hot again. For a long time, the Marines shot intermittently at something out there. Something I couldn't see. I had remained at the bottom of the fox hole until my curiosity got the best of me. I just had to risk getting my fool head shot off.

The top of my head was just above the rim of the fox hole far enough for me to see when one of the Marines pulled me back down saying,"Keep your --- --- fool head down, or get it blown off!"

I asked, "Where are we?"

He looked me square in the eye. "Where the heck did you come from?" he asked. "Don't you fly guys have brains enough to stay up there where you belong?"

Words escaped me, I just sat there looking at him, hoping he would remember I was on his side. Things got suddenly quiet outside the fox hole, which for now was all in the world I wanted. The second Marine quit shooting and slid down in the fox hole across from me.

Now the two of them, silently stared at me as if they couldn't believe what they were looking at. It seemed like hours before one of the Marines turned to the other and said, "He **is** Air Force, isn't he? I just bet this is why things got hot again."

The second Marine, turning to his partner, asked quietly, "Can I kill him now?"

As dusk settled into darkness, a slight noise brought one of the Marines silently to his feet with his rifle pointed out the back of the fox hole. Just how one tells the front of a fox hole from the back, is still somewhat of a mystery to me. I guess the back of the fox hole, is where one looks to see where it went when it missed you.

Someone out there said something, the Marine answered and relaxed. He turned and pointed at me as he whispered, "You! Out! That way, on your belly and do it quietly. Keep your head and your butt down. Good luck." It was the first nice thing I had heard since the plane had hit the ground.

I quietly stood up and slid myself out of the fox hole as requested. Then, as an after thought, I turned back and, in a voice I felt was a whisper, said, "Hey! Thanks for the hospitality."

Then I flashed them my best toothy grin. Almost immediately, in the distance, there was a "**Pop!**" Seconds later, the sky lit up like daylight. Both Marines grabbed me at the same time and pulled me back into the fox hole just as all hell broke loose overhead again.

It seemed like hours before the light went out and quiet settled over us again. The two Marines, who had been sitting on me, got up and listened intently out of the back of the fox hole. A muffled voice came out of the darkness, "Ok! Send him out again. But this time gag him."

The Marine nearest me stuffed something, which had an odd taste to it, into my mouth and said in a tone could not be misinterpreted, "This had better still be in your mouth when you get back to H.Q. or the 'Sarge', back there, is going to make it a permanent part of your face." Under the circumstances, all I could do was nod in agreement.

Both Marines then grabbed me and shoved me, head first, out of the fox hole. They had shoved me so hard I slid along the ground for several feet. Ahead of me, there was only darkness and behind me was open hostility. Further back were the Chinese or North Koreans, whatever, and I knew none of them had any sense of humor whatsoever. In fact, since I had left the plane, no one seemed to be real anxious to have me around except the guys with the chess game and I knew what they wanted me for, target practice!

I opted to move forward into the darkness. At least this way I was headed back toward Tokyo, or so I thought. I still had no idea just where I was nor did I understand what was going on around me. All I knew for certain was it was dark, bitterly cold and I was surrounded by people who wanted me dead.

We were supposed to be at peace and the fighting was supposed to have stopped long ago. What ailed these people?

There was no way I could tell how far I had crawled before something grabbed me from out of the dark on my left. I was tempted to remove the thing from my mouth and yell for help. Just as I was about to reach up to remove it, a voice close to my ear said, "Make a sound and I'm going to shove the thing in your mouth all the way through!"

Somehow I felt sure I had found the Sarge and all at once I began to think being used as a target by the fellows with the chess game might just have its bright side.

Even so, I followed the instructions he gave me and after crawling for what seemed miles he turned to me and said it was okay to stand and walk, but I was warned to keep thing in my mouth **or else!**

At length, I was ushered into an underground bunker. There a red faced officer glared at me and asked, "What the heck are you? Some kind of new Chinese secret weapon? Sit down over there and keep thing in your mouth until I tell you to take it out."

There are times in life when it seems the most prudent thing to do, is to follow instructions to the letter.

The Sarge looked at me and said,"This one must have come in with those four officers who sailed through here last week. For the life of me, I can't figure out whether the Chinese are trying to get him back, or just trying to make sure there is no way he can sneak back!"

Then turning to the red faced officer he said, "I think your right, it is a new Chinese secret weapon! - **And it should be destroyed!**" Pointing directly at me, he went on, "Did you hear the fire fight back there? He did it!" Then with the most evil eye he could muster he went on, "You didn't kill anyone back there, did you?" I opened my uniform and showed him the padded Chinese shirt, then I held up two fingers.

The reaction was immediate and profound. "Here we sit, ordered not to shoot anyone no matter what. This guy drops in out of the blue and kills two of them!" The Sargent raged on, "What the Sam Hell are we supposed to do now?"

The officer looked at some papers on the table in front of him and asked, "You're Herbst, right? Those officers who came through here a while ago told us you were dead, killed at the crash site. What the hell are you doing here?"

I was tempted to ask if he wanted me to go back to the crash site and try again but, as I have said before, "Prudence is often the best part of valor." And I still had the thing in my mouth.

Looking straight at me, the red faced officer said, "Six weeks we have been here and not a shot was fired. Now you guys show up and the whole mess gets hot again. Take the stupid sock out of your mouth but don't utter a sound!"

He then proceeded to enhance my knowledge of the English language with some words and expressions he could only have learned in college.

Silently, I thought to myself there was a possibility these Marines knew, somehow, I had been responsible for one of their comrades losing a pair of socks, back in Okinawa, and this was their **revenge!**

I cowered in the corner, my eyes round with fear, as the two men heaped profound statements about my ancestry and of the three officers who had gone through before, on my head. Then they gradually got around to what they thought of the Air Force in general. As they ranted and raved, I began to sort out just what had happened.

The plane was supposed to fly down the valley we were in now and not the one on the other side of the hill. Half the Chinese Army was over there, but this I already knew.

Then we got to the meat of the problem, the Chinese didn't want us to know they were there. This gave rise to the theory the Chinese were going to do everything in their power to prevent this information from getting back to the intelligence boys in the rear and I was the only one left they could get their hands on.

Somehow, they also knew I was the one taking the pictures. This, in turn, meant they were going to do everything in their power to get me back or make every effort to make sure I'd never tell anyone what I had seen.

It was nice to be wanted. Unfortunately, it was the Chinese who wanted me and it was the Marines who wanted to make sure they got me.

The next morning, the Marines classified me as a non-combatant. Their exact words were, "This ------- guy is --- --- Air Force. What the ---- does he know about ------- fighting. If we give him a ------- gun he may just shoot one of us by mistake. Give him a ------- camera and let him earn his ------- keep doing something he ------- A well knows how to do."

With I was given some new clothing which, by the way fit me and a camera. I was then told to move out and sit in a deep trench about three hundred yards from the bunker. It was out by the edge of a grove of shrub brush. I was told to stay there until I had something to take a picture of.

They assigned a huge, burly looking, sergeant with a sub-machine gun to protect me if things got hot again.

The trench we were in wasn't far from the edge of a small patch of woods. The sergeant moved down the trench a ways and sat down staring at me without a word. He didn't look real happy about his assignment.

The Sargent told me to remain where I was and not make a sound until he got back. He then vanished into the inky black of awful night. I sat there looking off into the darkness after him and tried not to think. Eventually I closed my eyes and drifted off into an uneasy sleep.

I don't know exactly how long we had been there but the next thing I knew it had started to rain and it was pitch black. It had turned bitterly cold again and as I moved my fields jacket made a funny crinkling noise. Obviously my field jacket had frozen around me.

I guess I had been there in trench, sitting in a small puddle of water for about two hours, it was hard to tell as I couldn't see my watch in the dark. There was a thump and a shuffling noise from someplace down the trench. Figuring the Sargent might not remember exactly where I was, I whispered, "Hey Sarge. I'm over here."

There was more shuffling but no reply. I called out again a

little louder, "I'm right here in front of you."

Again no reply. I began to get nervous. I knew we were not far from the Chinese but the Sargent had assured me there was no danger. I called out again, "I'm right here where you left me."

There was no reply but what ever was making the noise was very close by now. I felt rather than saw what ever it was, was there, just beyond my reach. Now I was conscious of an odd smell from ahead of me. Things were not at all right. I didn't know what to do.

Slowly I raised my camera and held it in front of me. Just about this time there was a break in the clouds. The moon shown through revealing a young Chinese man with a rifle and a long pointy looking bayonet on the end of it. He was about to make a Shish-ka-bob out of me.

I did the only thing I could do. I took his picture. I guess the flash blinded him because he lunged forward impaling my camera on his bayonet. The force of the lunge carried the young man right up to me and spun me around 180 degrees.

I yanked the flash gun off the side of the camera and turned back to face him, I hit him in the head as hard as I could. The four D batteries flew in every direction from the flashgun but I was scared and in a complete panic. I hit him again and again until my arm felt like if I lifted it again it would fall off.

The young man stopped moving, there was no longer any reaction when I hit him. His head wasn't hard any more. It was kind of like hitting a bag of wet beans. I knew he was dead. My heart was still racing and my eyes were wide with the terror of the moment.

I fell back into the mud, closed me eyes, took a deep breath. I waited until morning. As daylight filled the trench I looked at my handiwork. He was a young man of about 14. Clean shaven, by the look of a small spot on the right hand side of his face had not been hit or covered with mud. He was five foot and about 4 inches tall and probably 130 pounds. He was wearing less than I had on, there was no jacket. His uniform was a greenish brown and somewhat wrinkled, but it had been clean recently. I couldn't see his shoes, his feet were covered with the same mud which covered mine.

By now the water in the trench had crept up over about half of the uniform staining it a much darker color and the blood from his head had run down his neck and stained his shirt to the belt line. There was a thin film of ice all over him as there was on me. His build was slight but wiry like all the rest of the Chinese I had seen. He must have been as cold as I was.

As the sun rose higher in the sky, I stayed there in that stinking trench with him for several hours just looking at him and wondering about his home life. I can remember thinking of how his family would feel when they heard what I had done. I felt sick.

Somehow, I doubted if either one of us really knew why we were there or why we were supposed to kill each other. I knew in my heart he was only following orders, just like me.

I reached into his pockets and found a wallet with identification papers in it. There was a picture of the man but there was no way anyone would ever recognize what lay in trench with me. I doubt if even a family member would have recognized him.

It must have been about noon before another Marine dropped into the trench with us. He took one look at the boy and whistled through his teeth. He turned to me and in a low slow voice said, "What you got there, Air Force? Whewe! We usually just killum." I left the young man and the Marine without a word. I couldn't shake the feeling there was something more I should have done.

When I got back to the Marine camp, I handed the wallet over to Graves Registration and set about developing the picture I had taken of young man. I carried picture in my wallet for years there after. I didn't show it to many people, I wasn't very proud of what I'd done. I had gone on living and he hadn't, but for what?

Even at this late date, some forty plus years after the fact, there are many times I will wake up in the middle of the night feeling I was again striking his head with the flash gun. The tears still run down my face after each incident. The picture in my mind of faceless boy crumpled up in stinking trench is still etched deep into my memory. I can almost still smell it.

This kid didn't look all different from the people back in Tokyo. I had friends there. I couldn't help but wonder if, under other circumstances, this kid could have also been a friend.

Someone was talking to me but I couldn't make it out. Quite frankly anything other than Chinese would have sounded friendly at this point. I was led back to the bunker and someone else had to do the talking, all I could do was sit in a corner and shake.

I found out later the Sargent had gone back to his tent, had some coffee with his friends and gone to sleep. In the morning he reported me killed in action and set out for reassignment in Japan. I caught up with the Sargent about three months later in a bar in Yokohama and settled the score. I made double darn sure he would never forget leaving me alone in trench.

I found a steel rod about four feet long and sat down in the ally next to the bar to wait. When he came out of the bar I swung the rod once with all my might and hit him square on the knee caps. It was over quickly and I didn't wait around to see how good a job I had done on him.

I did, however, have an opportunity to remind him it isn't nice to leave someone out in the dark, by themselves when they can't defend themselves. He got the message. I never heard anything more about it.

The next morning I was sent a little further toward the front and told to stay near a large bunker which, for the next few days would be my home. No one would tell me why I wasn't being sent back to Tokyo and whenever I asked I was told to shut up and do as I was told. No one wanted to be anywhere near me.

As night fell on the sixth day, I was told to move up to a machine gun post and be ready to take some night-time pictures of Marines in action. I dropped into a hole with four Marines and a light thirty caliber machine gun. To say they were not overjoyed to see me would be an under-statement. I was told to remain quiet and listen.

Hours past in the quiet of another pitch black night. At least it wasn't raining and in my book this was a plus. To the Marines it meant we would probably have visitors. They were right. There was a clanking noise out in front of the hole and we all froze like statues. Tin cans with small pebbles in them had been tied in the barbed wire a few hundred feet in front of the position. Something was moving the wire.

One of the Marines fired a flare, night was turned into day instantly. There was someone in the wire and the man behind the machine gun cut loose with several short bursts. The form in the wire stopped moving just as the flare went out and night descended on us again. The rest of the night was quiet. In fact, it was so quiet it put us all on edge.

The next morning we moved out to see what we has caught in the wire. The body hung in the wire was almost unrecognizable. Still one of the Marines recognized the body as the shoe-shine boy came by every so often to clean the boots of any Marine who had the price.

He must have lost his way and fallen against the wire in the dark. Just how anyone could recognize what was hung there in the wire is still a mystery to me. What was left looked like it had been through a meat grinder. I took its picture, it was my job.

That night, after a quiet day, I was told to move into the bunker. It would be my new home for a while. I still didn't understand why I was moving closer to the front rather than being moved back to a safer place.

For the next three days I was asked to photograph some pretty incredible things. I had never had any combat training except a little rifle practice in basic training, nothing to prepare me for what I had to look at and take pictures of.

The kid in the wire, the effectiveness of various types of anti-personal mines and other goodies. The effect on personnel hit by machine gun cross fire. What happens when you depress a quad fifty to horizontal and target individuals.

At this point the things I had to photographed were no longer gross, they were way beyond this. One becomes detached after a while and it's like working in a butcher shop. Still, some things bother me even today.

The idea I had to kill someone so some politician could sit in his office and send others out to get killed still bothered me. There was just something badly wrong with this concept.

The quad-fifty depressed to horizontal and used for anti personal was another one of those things bothered me. There was usually very little left to photograph. In one case just two feet, still in the shoes. The rest was simply gone. Of course there were pieces and parts spread over a wide area. No one knew what went with what.

One day a rumor spread through the area. We were about to come under heavy attack. We couldn't get additional help because it was only a rumor and there was nothing to support it but an eerie quiet from across no-man's-land. Every one was nervous as dark fell over us.

I didn't have long to worry about it. The bunker came under full attack shortly after dark. The Marines called repeatedly for support but none came, after all we were at peace. This was a policing action, there was no war going on.

We were pushed back until we were all in the one bunker. As the ammunition ran out I was pushed to the floor and people began falling on me. I heard grenades going off then someone screamed "Flame Thrower!"

It became difficult to breath for a few moments and then there was quiet. I tried to move but there was such a weight on me I couldn't. It was dark and the smell was terrible. Somehow, there is just nothing worse than the smell of burned flesh.

As time went by it began to get cold and the bodies heaped on me became ridged. The little mobility I had diminished. Awful stuff began to trickle past my face but there was no place to back away from it.

There was no way to measure the time I lay there under those poor brave men but I was sure it was several years. Then suddenly there was movement above me. A bright light flooded into my eyes.

I tightened my grip on the post I had grabbed on the way to the floor. Sheer terror gave me strength to clutch my post tighter as hands grabbed at me. Someone yelled out, "This one's still alive!"

More hands grabbed at me and I held on even tighter. I was told later it took four men to dislodge my grip on post and I had been buried under the pile for three whole days.

The doctor at the field hospital told me I had nearly died. It took two days for me to be able to get up and move away from my bed and even then I couldn't hold a cup of liquid in my hands because of the shaking.

The Chinese, however, had not forgotten me. Just about the time I was well enough to be moved out to another camp the field hospital was over-run. Hell had opened its doors to me once again.

As I ran out of the tent I was in, something exploded behind me. I felt myself flying through the air. Nothing worked, I just flew through the air with no sensation of pain. I landed upside down in a large bush with my eyes wide open.

They wouldn't shut no matter how hard I tried and I wanted to close my eyes, **Oh God** how I wanted to close my eyes. I couldn't move my arms or legs, it was difficult to breath.

I watched an upside down world gone crazy. Short people in what looked like Tennis Shoes were running around yelling and bayoneting anything moved. They ran right by me several times but I must have looked very dead or I'm sure I would have wound up being someone's shish-kabob.

In time there was a great deal of shooting and the Marines replaced the folks wearing the tennis shoes. They were doing the same thing the guys in the tennis shoes had done.

Once again hands grabbed at me and dragged me out of my bush. I was given a shot in the arm and everything went black again. The next thing I knew I was on an airplane headed for

Tokyo. There was a burning pain in my left leg from the hip down to the tips of my toes. I just had to look, the leg was still there. Six weeks had passed and I could only remember a small part of it. One must be thankful, even for the small things.

Obviously, I survived, although today I walk with a slight limp. A good thunder storm will cause me to get a little nervous. I don't like crowds. Places with low ceilings cause me to panic easily especially if there is a lot of noise and flashing lights.

All in all, my six weeks in Korea were memorable. My only regret is I could not share this memorable experience with my ex-wife or the politicians put me there.

Nopo San

Chapter 30

The Reason Why

In every case there is a reason why. It took a while but as I healed I began to put together the pieces of what had happened to me and why. This is extremely hard even at this late date. My memory of the events are still fragmented and for some reason I can't get the time line to fit in its proper order.

I guess it all had to start back at my home base. In short someone got very angry at me. Someone in a position to throw some weight around.

My job as Photographer, put me in many contentious situations. It was only natural to step on some toes as I did what I was supposed to do. I had always done my job in the best way I knew. If one can look objectively at the situation; my only crime was I did my job a little too well. This, I must assume, antagonized someone or I had taken pictures of something I should have overlooked.

At any rate someone had to select me for this mission. I was picked for the job even though there wasn't supposed to be any enlisted personnel on the flight.

It was supposed to have been an all officer mission so they could be sworn to secrecy if things went wrong. Well they went wrong and four officers wound up with a loose cannon on their hands.

After the plane went down, they didn't know what to do with me. They assumed I knew things I wasn't supposed to know. I had not been sworn to secrecy as they had. If the information I had was to fall into the wrong hands, it could have been detrimental to the peace accord going on at the thirty-eighth parallel.

Unfortunately, no one bothered to tell me all of this. Of course, if they had told me, I hardly think I would have laid down on the ground and died for them. I am by nature, a survivor. Much to someone's consternation, survive I did.

The easiest thing to have happen to me was for me become a casualty of war. Or in this case, a casualty of the Korean Peace? The officers must have decided this at the crash site.

They left me for the Chinese hoping I would be killed right there and this would put an end to it. I however, had other ideas and plans for the future.

When they saw I was still kicking, they must have left word with the Marines that I was to be their guest as long as I survived. The Marines had no love for me as I was not one of theirs. Add to this the fact I had stirred up a hornets nest and you have a fairly complicated picture.

The Marines were only following orders. They left me alone and unarmed in the trench knowing the Chinese patrolled the area every night. They had hoped this would end the problem they were stuck with. Fortunately for me, I wasn't the pushover they thought I was going to be.

The red faced officer had a real dilemma on his hands. He had his orders, I was not to be sent back to Tokyo alive, but just how does one do this without drawing attention to the act. Add to this, the Chinese were not at all happy with the situation and the stew gets even more sticky. The first night in the trench was supposed to have been the end of it but I fooled them.

When this didn't work I was placed on the front lines. I feel, however, it was never meant to go as far as it did. I think I was supposed to have been left outside the bunker but something went wrong again. I wound up inside the thing and under a whole pile of people who died trying to save my worthless butt.

Now I was wounded or at least rendered temporarily incapable of movement. The people who were in a position to know what the story on me was, had lost touch with me and the people directly connected to my situation were medics and dedicated to keeping me alive.

I was afloat in the system and listed as a medical casualty

of unknown origin. My credibility was in question because of the situation in which I had been found and my inability to speak coherently, made it all seem unreal.

At about this time, having finally been identified, I was sent back to my home base. The field hospital had been over-run and I now had a physical wound. The situation was now totally out of control.

Now the powers in charge had a real problem. It was no longer my word against theirs, I had physical proof. Of course, all written accounts of what had happened vanished into thin air. Not even dust remained.

On the plane back to Tokyo, I was informed I could make no mention of this incident whatsoever. There would be no record of the incident in my file and there would be no physical evidence of my wound.

During the next few months there were several operations, each removing a quantity of scar tissue. At last there was only a few small red spots to indicate where large openings had been. The only scar they left was the small bullet hole where I had been shot as a youngster while stealing watermelons one summer.

Today this was quite true, there is no scar to show where I was hit. They had done a great job of cover up. There is nothing in my military record to show it ever happened.

When I finally got back to my base there was nothing to indicate I had ever left. My absence was listed as an emergency leave for a family matter and even this soon disappeared from my record.

My stay in the hospital was listed as job fatigue because of my protracted assignment to night alert duty. I had volunteered for so now it was all my fault. This part remains on my record today.

On the plane I was also told of the scope of secrecy which shrouded the mistake made by the navigator on our plane. We were not supposed to have seen the Chinese buildup in the valley. I had become privy to information which should have been reserved for only the highest levels of the general staff.

The military knew all about it from high level reconnaissance but no one else was supposed to know anything about it. I was the only one not an officer and who could not be sworn to secrecy. The only one who had not volunteered for the mission and the only enlisted man involved. They had to shut me up somehow. So they simply made it all disappear.

There was to be no conversation about the incident under penalty of imprisonment or worse. It scared me so much it took over thirty years for me to get up the nerve to put it into writing.

Now, with so much time gone by, I don't think anyone really cares anymore. If there is someone out there who still cares, now I don't care.

If one were to look at my military record today they would find no mention of any time spent in Korea. The slight scars have long since faded and the small piece of metal left my left leg has rusted away. I am not bitter about this turn of events, certainly there are those of us who have paid a much higher price for our way of life.

I can understand some of the why's and wherefore's but wouldn't it be great if things could be done out in the open again.

Nopo San

Chapter 31

The Dark

At one time or another, I am sure all of us have had at least a little, fear of dark places. When I was little, I can remember being afraid to walk out in the woods after dark because of the stories I had been told, about the strange and fierce creatures which stalked the woods at night.

When I was really little a friend , I had been playing with, threw a hand full of quick lime in my face, thinking it was snow. The resulting burns blinded me for almost a year. During this whole time, I was naturally in total darkness.

I could not understand what had happened and I became frustrated. The stories I had been told about the things in the dark came to life in my mind. Having had sight at one time, I could picture them stalking me in the semi-darkness of my mind. It scared me half to death.

Later when, I was about ten, I found a cave out in the railroad bed of the, recently bankrupt, Boston and Westchester Railroad. It was just big enough for me to wriggle into. In the back of the cave was a large cavern I could sit up in and move about quite nicely. I played there for many happy hours all summer. It was cool and private in there, best of all my mother didn't know where my cave was.

During the winter, however, the cave was cold and wet so I left it alone until summer came again. The fact of life is little people get bigger, and so it was with me. Not realizing just how much I had grown, I headed for my cave as soon as it was warm enough to get by without a jacket. I was about half way back to the cavern when I became firmly wedged in the throat of the cave. Thus, I remained for the next six to eight hours.

This did little to help me get over my fear of the dark and it instilled in me an uneasiness about small tight places. In the Air Force there were few instances which called for me to subject myself to such an ordeal, until I got to Tokyo.

Both dark rooms at the base Photo Lab were small light tight places and out of necessity, dark. I guess the only saving graces were they had high ceilings and there was a red light which could be kept on most of the time.

The only time it bothered me in any way was when I had to work for long periods of time developing negatives alone in the dark. The room seemed to get smaller around me as I worked.

It wasn't really a problem yet because if things got a little tight I could always stop what I was doing and go out into the light in the front room for a few minutes. The moment I was in the light things settled down again.

I was fine in this situation until my stay in Korea. I won't bore you with the details again. However, to sum it all up I wound up in a small dark place only this time there were a bunch of angry people outside. They were indeed hostile and made the occupants of the bunker I was in, feel very unwelcome. I can't tell you how I got out of it, I don't remember --- or I won't remember. I was told later I was the only one who got out of it alive.

This little incident made a lasting impression on me. I didn't realize it at the time, but after my return to Tokyo, the walls of the dark room began a slow, steady pace of closing in on me.

In order to be fair I have to admit, by this time, I had almost a year of steady night duty behind me. Interrupted only by the Korea trip.

I rarely saw the light of day and when I did, it was going to or from the base photo lab. I slept all of the daylight hours away then, getting up at dusk, I would go back on "alert duty."

Now in the dark, I began to see the faces of the other fellows from bunker. It wasn't bad at first, kind of like a flash memory. It would flash into my head for a moment and then go away. As time went on, the moments began to last longer. They became more vivid in the dark of the darkroom.

Then I began to notice the door. Now the door was something else. I knew in my mind that at one time in my life there had been a lot of very hostile people on the other side of a door. The memories became stronger and more realistic. I even fancied I could hear the screams of those brave Marines who were killed and fell dead on top of me and saved my life.

Flash memories of the bunker began to remain longer than they should have and the door gained more and more significance as time went on. I began to have great reservations about reaching out for the door handle.

Even the curtain which hung over the door, to keep out light if the door were accidentally open, began to be a problem. I was cut off from the light source in the front room of the Photo Lab.

At last there came a time when I simply could not bring myself to reach out for the door handle. I was scared to death of what I might find if I opened the door. My worst nightmares came back to me in the dark. I realized I needed help. I grabbed the phone and called for my friends at the Base Air Police Unit.

At first they thought I was kidding when I told them I was afraid to open the dark room door. After trying for a few minutes to calm my fears, they sent someone around to break in the front door of the photo lab and get me out.

The doctors at Tokyo Army Hospital told me later I had a mild form of battle fatigue. Two weeks in the hospital and I was back at work. There would be, however, no more night duty for the rest of my time in the Air Force.

The doctors found it strange I had post traumatic stress syndrom with a record indicating I had never seen combat.

Somehow, I wasn't surprised to hear no one could figure out how I got battle fatigue while stationed in Tokyo.

My stay in the hospital was a memorable one. There were several people there worthy of mention. There were, of course, the usual lot of demented souls were there on hoaxed up acts of insanity trying to get out of the service on a Section 8. But there were also others.

There was a group of Turkish Veterans from Korea. They were fine friendly people all day long. They didn't know much English but they tried hard to be friendly anyhow. My first day there I couldn't for the life of me, figure out why such nice people were in a place like this.

Then at night, the rest of us were ushered into "private rooms" and the Turks were left alone on the ward.

It turned out the private rooms were for our protection. When the lights went out at 9 o'clock the Turks went bananas. By morning the entire ward was a disaster area. Apparently, like myself, they had seen a little too much night duty. Like mine, their horror was not imaginary. They were reliving what had happened to them every night. During the day they pitched in to help clean up the mess they had made during the night. But when the lights went out again, WOW!

There was a black man on the ward who was sure he was being followed everywhere by the ghost of a man he had abandoned in a fox hole near a place called K-14. He didn't talk to the rest of us very much, he just sat there casting furtive glances over his shoulder every so often. It was a sad case because when you could get the guy to talk, he was a real nice guy.

Enough about the horrors of war and it's aftermath. I had fun in the service but as you can see it wasn't all fun and games. There were times I wish I could forget. Like I said in the introduction, we can't change it so we might just as well look at the experience in the best light we can. The bright side.

Nopo San

Chapter 32

The Last Typhoon

It was Typhoon season again and, **Ho Hum**, another big one was expected to hit the base. The thrill, however, was gone. So what! It was getting close to the time when I would be going F.I.G.M.O. and the thought of another typhoon really didn't get any juices going.

For the edification of the unwashed neophyte, FIGMO is a state of mind more than a place to go. One goes FIGMO shortly after orders are received rotating the subject back to the states. My orders had just been received and this was the night of my big FIGMO party.

In theory, after tonight if I was given an order, I could invoke the FIGMO command by saying, "Forget it, I Got My Orders!", or words to effect. The military prison in Tokyo was full to the brim with unfortunates who did just this.

It was not my intention to join these screw-balls, but I did intend to have a party. Then, after the party, I would be given the little gold and blue ribbon from the neck of the whiskey bottle opened in my honor. I would then wear this ribbon for the rest of my stay in Japan.

There were only three of the original crew left in the Photo Lab, Roger, Stas, and Bill. They would be following me back to the states, shortly after I left. The base was to be turned over to the Japanese as soon as we were all sent home.

It was kind of sad in a way. I had a lot of fun in Japan and now all trace of my being there was going to be torn down and new buildings would rise from the ashes of the military section of Japan International Airport. An era was drawing to a close and I was part of it. I wondered if any of those little kids would remember their friend Nopo San.

The FIGMO party, however, was to be a thing which would live forever in infamy in the minds of the terrified people of Haneda. We selected a suitable Saki House and invited the local Communists. They, in spite of their political convictions, were great fun at a party. They knew all sorts of great songs to sing and the party somehow ended in a politically motivated brawl.

In short, we all had a great time and no one was badly hurt. A few bumps, scrapes and bruises were about the worst that happened, aside from the hang-over. The building fell down long before any one had a chance to get hurt.

It is said the Good Lord protects drunks and fools, I fit in there someplace. The Communists knew each time there was a FIGMO party another, **Hated Yankee Devil** went back home. Soon there would be so few Yankee's left they might just win a brawl or two, but not while Nopo San was still around. Deep in my heart I think even the Communists were going to miss us.

Tonight, however, was not to be the night the communists would win. This was going to be our night. And so to was. About three in the morning, drunk as lords, Roger and I left the smoldering ruin of the Saki House, and marched back toward the base. I had taken two captives. One I carried over my shoulder and the other I was kind of dragging along by his belt as we sang, "Heidy Heidy Heidy Ho! Where the Hell's the VO?"

I think somewhere along the way we had promised to take at least two of them back to the States with us. I was going to pack one of them up in one of my two duffel bags for the trip. Roger was supposed to pack the other one.

I wasn't really sure which ones it was I had promised to take. In any case, I had two of them and neither one of them was in any condition to object.

At the gate I was relieved of my captives and told to get to the barracks as quickly as possible. The storm was about to hit and all hands were restricted to base.

The guard at the gate pointed a long finger at me and said, "**You!** We got special orders about you. There will be no mountain climbing during this storm. We have orders from the Supreme Commander to shoot to kill if you try to leave the base tonight." As a general rule, I try never to antagonize an armed gate guard. So I agreed with everything he said and waved my FIGMO ribbon at him. He got the message. The FIGMO ribbon is worn in the top button hole of the shirt. The only button hole on the shirt is never used and the ribbon was to be worn both with the uniform and with the civilian clothing.

It had been months since I had slept in the barracks, but now I would have to because the Photo Lab was off limits to me at night. The barracks was all I had left. I had given up my little room at the fisherman's home and had begun getting rid of anything I didn't want to drag back to the States with me.

The Typhoon came ashore about four in the morning and shortly there after I, along with about thirty other guys, were herded into a truck without explanation. The wind was just howling and the rain seemed to be falling sideways, if this was possible. We were driven out to the point at which the two runways crossed and there we were told two planes had come in and as they landed the nose wheels had collapsed.

No one had been hurt but now the planes were stuck out on the runways and no other planes could get in or out until these planes had been moved.

Our job was to go into one of the planes one at a time. Then we were to walk to the back of the plane. When there was enough of us in there the tail would drop and a truck would be backed in under the collapsed nose wheel. It all sounded simple enough.

I assumed I would be among the first into the plane but some one stopped me and said, "No, you wait here until I tell you to go in." I never looked around to see who was talking, I just assumed it was someone with authority. No one else knew what we were doing out here in the first place.

I guess there were about fifteen or twenty people in the plane before I was told to go in. As I started toward the plane a voice in the dark said, "When you get in there, it will be your job to see no one gets scared and tries to run back out before the truck backs under the nose wheel. Do you understand?" I nodded yes and climbed up the ladder to the doorway.

Once inside the plane I moved down the aisle, kind of herding the others before me. Suddenly the tail of the plane dropped like a rock and landed on the ground with a monumental, **"Thump!" Instant panic!** The whole mob tried to rush back out of the plane. The only thing between them and the door was me. I yelled out over the howling wind, "My orders are to keep you guys in here until they get the truck under the nose wheel." Nobody was listening to me. As the mob surged forward, I grabbed the backs of the seats on either side of the aisle and hung on for dear life.

I don't know how long it was I held them there but I do know the longer they were held back the more they wanted to get out. Some of the people began crawling over the seats to my left and there wasn't a darn thing I could do about it. Just about the time I was convinced it was hopeless, a voice behind me said, "Okay. You can let go now. We got the truck in place."

Turning loose my grip, I instantly became part of the aisle floor, over which my comrades ran in their panic to get out. Picking myself up off the floor I checked for broken bones and the like. Finding I was still in one piece, I looked around for the source of the voice that had given the order to let go. It was the Supreme Commander, he was sitting there smiling at me.

For the first time in a year and a half the man seemed pleased by something I had done. Where had I gone wrong. He seemed to sense my consternation and his smile broadened. What else could I do, I smiled back and we both had a good laugh.

I asked him later why he had picked me to hold back the mob. He said, "Its been an education having you around. I learned one thing from it, if nothing else. You get things done. You don't always get them done the way others expect you to, but they get done. I knew if I put you in aisle and told you to hold those guys in the plane, they were going to stay right where I wanted them to stay until I told you to let them go. I was right."

Figure 87 The Typhoon Jug

    Had I obeyed my good common sense instead of orders I would have bought myself a Typhoon Jug and climbed in under the house with the fisherman and his wife even though I didn't live there any more.. Here is what a Typhoon Jug looks like.
    I made up my mind I would try to be more careful in the future. I really didn't want to give the Supreme Commander any more problems. There were only a few more weeks left of my stay in Japan, I was sure I could stay out of trouble for long.

Nopo San

Chapter 33

Jane

There have only been a few times in my life when I have had a chance to hob knob with the rich, and or famous. So when it was learned Jane Russell would be stopping over at Japan International Airport, we all looked forward to her arrival with anticipation and eagerness. She was on her way to do a show for the troops in Korea and her stop over in Tokyo would only be a short one.

I was double blessed as I was asked to get some photos of her on her way through for the base newspaper. The request for photos came from the Supreme Commander himself, so I was not really sure if I was being forgiven for past transgressions, or being set up for some new horror.

Anyhow, as the day approached, my buddy Roger and I began plotting just how we were going to get close enough to our target to get some good shots. And so it was on this fateful morning, as we sat there pondering our fate over coffee, this great idea struck me. From my wallet I produced my official U.S.A.F. Flight Line "Crash Pass".

Figure 88 My Crash Pass.

Roger, like wise, produced his and without another word a fiendish plot was hatched.

The big day arrived and Roger and I donned our best civilian outfits. We then moved on to the Photo Lab and made ready to get some great shots of a very famous and well liked lady.

The plane didn't land till about 8:30 and it was left a good way out from the buildings on the military side of Tokyo International Airport. I suppose it was for security reasons, and well they should. About half the photographers in Japan showed up with the same idea Roger and I had. But with one small difference, we had crash passes!

These passes, by the way, had been known to tear down some of the most stringent security barriers, on sight. After all, we were the Base Photographers. As such, we had to be able to take pictures of whatever was going on, on any part of the base, at any time of the day or night. It was absolutely forbidden to interfere with us for any reason, in the performance of our duty and we had the sole discretion of determining just what our job was.

Now these passes were in the hands of two devious, and completely unscrupulous, Air Force Photographers! These two photographers were about to fan the coals and, once again ignite the fires of World War II all over again.

Now at this point, one must step back and take a good look at the general overall picture; here was this plane about two hundred yards from any building. It was surrounded by a large number of Air Force Security Guards. It was dark and there was a light rain falling. To the left was a long line of barricades with another group of security guards. The barricades were about one hundred fifty yards away from the plane.

Behind these barricades stood several hundred of Japan's finest photographers. All of whom were waiting, not to patiently, for an opportunity photograph Jane Russell. Ms. Russell was I might add, still on the plane awaiting customs inspection before stepping off into the limelight.

Last, but not least, here were Roger and I, in civilian garb, trying desperately to hide our huge clumsy Speed Graphic cameras as we walked out to the plane with the customs officials.

To the Japanese, standing about one hundred fifty yards away, we must have looked just like civilians photographers. Our crash passes were pinned conspicuously to our shirt pockets, but from a distance, who could see them. It was a scene of unimaginable tension.

Roger and I, however, were not privy to the overall picture. We were part of it. All we knew was we were going to "scoop" the Japanese Photographers and have some fun doing it.

Mind you. We weren't mad at anyone. We had been told to get some pictures by our Supreme Commander and this is exactly what we were going to do. What's more, the Crash Passes gave us absolute control over the situation. We didn't even need our arm bands proclaiming we were the "PRESS". These passes also got us right in with Cardinal Spellman and The Brooklyn Dodgers when they came through. We did have some interesting times.

I know at this point it must seem like the Supreme Commander and I were completely at odds. Nothing could be further from the truth. Roger and I both liked the Supreme Commander. If the man had asked me to walk on water, I would have tried my best. He had asked us to get him some good pictures and this is what we were going to do, no matter what.

We went right on to the plane with the customs people and started taking pictures. As our flash bulbs winked on and off, we were conscious of a growing noise from outside the plane. The more flash bulbs we popped the louder the noise got.

Suddenly a red faced Air Force Security Sergeant ran up the ramp and told us it just wasn't safe for us to hang around any longer. He said, "For the sake of Japanese American Relations, you guys had better disappear quickly and completely. If you move fast enough, you might just live to see tomorrow."

Without argument, Roger and I bailed out. The sergeant couldn't order us to leave because of the crash passes but his suggestion made a lot of sense. The howling from the mob of our fellow photographers behind the barricades was still growing in volume.

As we hit the runway we looked over at the barricades. They were just now beginning to go over. A human wave of very irate photographers, screaming profanities in a language that had no profanities, was advancing out onto the field. I have often maintained it must be hell for those people to be as mad as they were and not be able to swear, no wonder they liked the English language so much.

Roger and I headed out onto the North-South runway and dove into a nice dark ditch where our equally dark clothing would give us some measure protection.

The human wave had stopped at the plane and the noise was deafening. I expected to hear "BANZAI!" and see bayonets flashing in the runway lights at any moment. In my heart there was a deep feeling of sympathy for those few Air Force Security Personnel. They were expected to maintain order and protect us from the chaos we had caused. There was also lots of thanks for the early warning. It got us off the plane and into this ditch, before the mob got there.

The confusion was simply unbelievable, an entire herd of full grown elephants could have evaded customs this night. There were people running every which way without the slightest measure of control.

As we lay there in ditch, we talked about what the Japanese Photographers would do to us if they were able to catch us. It firmed our resolve not to be taken alive.

The rain had stopped and as we moved about in the ditch our clothing began to dry out. However, as we took inventory we found we had a goodly amount of film left, and it would never do to waste it.

Carefully we slid out of hiding, and made our way over to the terminal. With all the confusion going on, no one noticed us as we moved across the runway.

Then with a bit of good luck, and by this time this is all we had going for us, we made it into the Military Terminal. The place was deserted, all those who had been inside had moved out onto the tarmac to watch the confusion as it ebbed and swelled about the plane Jane Russell had arrived on.

We slipped into the ladies lounge, where we were sure no one would look for us. It was, for the moment, deserted. Our luck was still holding.

Just then the door burst open and in walked Jane Russell herself, with her entourage, of course. There we stood face to face with a famous movie star. We were comparatively alone except for the entourage. Oh well, at least we had her undivided attention.

Roger asked if we could take some more pictures and permission was granted. We were absolutely sure the Supreme Commander was going to be very proud of us for this.

For the next half hour or so Roger and I had a ball taking pictures of Jane Russell. As it turned out Roger was from the same town as the famous lady and they talked a moment or so about home and all .

One thing always puzzled me, Jane Russell never talked directly to us, unless she had cleared what she wanted to say through another lady in her entourage. I guess, maybe she thought we were some sort of subversives from a rival movie company. I never quite figured it out.

Outside the window of the lounge, however, the human wave was beginning to build again. Still we
stayed on until all our film was used, we even had the gall to ask if she would hang around long enough for us to go back to the Photo Lab and get some more film.

We all stopped talking and listened for a moment to the mounting storm of rage and pent up hostility outside the window. The poor Japanese photographers were out there and could not figure out how to get at us with out breaking into the building. Breaking into the building would have been a breach in their code of ethics. This would have been unforgivable, so all they could do was sputter and fume as they made plans about what to do with our body parts after they dismembered us.

Finally Roger and I had taken enough time and obviously had worn out our welcome. We bowed out through a little used side door of the terminal led to an alley between two hangars. We made our way slowly back to the Photo Lab where we remained hidden for the rest of the night. This gave us lots of time to process our film and make a set of prints.

The next morning, we got one of the other fellows to get us some clothing from our lockers. We then borrowed a jeep and burned the clothing we had worn the night before out on the flight line. There was just no way we were going to take a chance on being recognized wearing those outfits.

About noon, Roger and I were cordially invited for visit with the Supreme Commander by two ARMED Air Policemen. As we were shoved through the door-way of the commander's office, it wasn't hard to recognize, the man was not in the best of humor. His face was so red it would probably have glowed in the dark. To this day I swear there was visible steam coming out of his ears. He looked right at us as he said, "I should have known it would be you!"

He pointed to a huge stack of letters on his desk and croaked in a unsteady voice, "These are letters of complaint received here today, through our embassy in Tokyo, they are from every news agency in Japan condemning the your actions and demanding an immediate apology!"

As he staggered to his feet his eyes glowed red and little button horns seemed to be trying to grow at his temples, "First the mess on May Day, then thing at the steel works, and now this! All I wanted was a few simple pictures." He groaned as he lifted his hands toward the ceiling and muttered, "Why me Lord?"

Roger and I looked at each other, we had no idea there was a religious bone in the Supreme Commander's body and now here he was calling for help from above.

Of course, there is always remote possibility he was calling for an air strike on us, but nothing happened. However, this was the Air Force and he was the Supreme Commander. There was always the remote possibility he might just be able to do something like call in an air strike. He was sure mad enough to try.

Gaining some measure of control, the Supreme Commander seated himself again, and through clenched teeth said, "Now I want every picture and every negative you two characters took the other night, and I want them five minutes ago!"

Peering out a window of a C-121 somewhere over the Pacific is A/2C Zbigniew S. Swiatek of the Base Photo Lab. Airman Swiatek was taking part in the great search for the missing C-97, which disappeared on the morning of March 22 about 250 miles out of Tokyo International Airport.

A/2C Jerome T. Sullivan, Base Photo Lab, talks with Hollywood star Jane Russell in the VIP Lounge of the MATS Terminal, Tokyo International Airport. Miss Russell is beginning a tour of Army installations in Korea, returning to Japan April 2. Photo by A/2C Robert P. Herbst.

Figure 89 Jane And Roger, Photo By Me.

Not wishing to incur any more of his wrath, Roger and I

headed for the Photo Lab. We gathered together our horde of great shots of Jane Russell. What a shame, all our work would be for nothing, but orders is orders.

We delivered all our hard work to the Supreme Commander's office a few moments later. All that is, but one. The one we saved is the one which we sent to the base news paper with a cover story.

If you look really close at the last line of the bit under the picture, it says, "Photo by A/2C Robert P. Herbst". It's blurred but what the heck do you want from 30 year old news print?

We had waited until just about the time Roger and I were transferred back to the states. In this particular situation, timing was essential. It would never do to have this bit hit the streets while we still within bomber range.

Later we heard from a friend, the Supreme Commander roamed the base for weeks after we left. We were told he had a gun and he was looking for some un-named persons from the Base Photo Lab. Roger and I both agreed it would not be wise, under the circumstances, to send our ex-commander a Christmas card with a return address on it.

Nopo San

Chapter 34

The Trip Home

It was over, the two years in Okinawa and Japan were over at last. I was going home. I still had more time to serve in the Armed Forces but at least I was on my way to a base near home. The orders told me to go to New York A.F.B. near Newburgh, New York. was only a short distance from my home in Pelham, New York, where my family had moved while I was overseas.

I packed all my photographic material which I had so carefully assembled over the two years I was there into a large foot locker and sent it on ahead of me to my family's home in Pelham, N. Y. It never got there.

I couldn't raise much of a fuss because it was all on military print paper and on military negatives. I hadn't swiped the stuff, it was dated and after a certain date we had to throw it away. Instead of throwing it away, I used it. It was gone now and what little I could do to find it, I did. It was lost somewhere between Japan and New York.

Roger and I threw a F.I.G.M.O. party will go down in military history. We got all of our off base friends together and tried our best to drink all the Saki and Beer in Haneda. We had plenty of help doing it. There were all sorts of addresses being exchanged. I later wrote to several of the people who's address I had taken but no one ever wrote back.

The next morning we were, "H.H. and on our way." (Happily Hung-over) The next stop was Tachikawa Air Base to get our final medical check up and then it was back to the States by plane, for a change.

While at Tachikawa I ran into one of the guys I went through basic training with. I had not liked the fellow very much during basic. But out here, in "never never land", he seemed a changed person. We had a few drinks together and exchanged war stories. We were going to different parts of the world again but who cares. Maybe I will run into him again someday and we will be able to exchange even more war stories.

Roger left for his new base and I never saw or heard from him again. I managed to lose his home address and I can only assume he managed to lose mine also. I never kept in touch with any of the fellows I knew in the service, sometimes I wish I had. We had some good times over there and it would sure be fun to sit down and hash them out again over a friendly glass of beer.

On the day before we were to board the plane we were confined to our barracks and each of us was given two small white pills. The official explanation was the pills were to remove any internal parasites we might have picked up while in Japan.

Most of the fellows threw theirs away. I took mine. It was like swallowing a can of drain cleaner. The little pills took everything out. I almost thought my Amoebic Dysentery had come back on me. **Wow!** I was a new man, I had to be, everything else got flushed through.

In retrospect, I think maybe they just gave us those pills to lighten the load on the aircraft. If this was the case, it had worked like a charm.

There was also some paper work had to be done. I sat down next to a desk in a large room as a clerk typed information on a form with my name on it. He had a huge pile of papers on his desk with all sorts of little red flags sticking out of it. I couldn't resist asking about. "I bet this guy has been in a lot of trouble, just look at all those red flags."

The clerk didn't say anything, he just looked at me for a moment in a kind of funny way, then he went back to typing. I went on, "Is this guy going back on the same plane I am?"

The clerk stopped typing and stared hard at me. "It's your file." He said, "You have apparently made a lot of people very angry at you. Now if you don't shut up and leave me alone, I'm going to **lose your orders**. Then you will be stuck here forever."

He leered at me as if to say, "And nothing would give me more pleasure." The man was obviously a Sadist and he was in a position to do just what he said he would do. Just to be on the safe side I didn't utter another sound until I was at least fifty feet from the building, even then it was in a whisper.

At last, the big day arrived. We filed out of the waiting room and boarding the plane. It was a beauty, one of the latest word in air travel.

At time the "Constellation" was the most modern transport plane the Air Force had with props. The new jets were still only in the civilian market and limited military use for passengers. Of course, there were all kinds of jet fighters and bombers but these planes didn't carry passengers.

The plane we came back on was a "Flying Leopard Line" plane under contract to the military. In its time it was a real beauty.

The hostess welcomed us on board and I just know we all thought, "How nice this is going to be." She was sure a cute little gal. Then I was introduced to a fiendish new form of torture. The engineer who designed the seating arrangements on this plane must have adhered strictly to the standard size limitations introduced by the Marques DeSade for all people over 6 feet 2 inches tall.

When designing things, the national standard maximum is six-feet-**two**-inches. I am six-feet-**four**-inches. These two inches difference made all the difference in the world to me.

I was assigned to the center seat of a three seat set. To all outward appearances this would be fine, except when I sat down I could not get my knees in front of me with my feet on the floor. My elbows protruded out into the seat area on either side of me causing my fellow passengers undue discomfort.

The two other guys were good about the situation and did not complain. I guess they realized just how hard I was trying not to bother them.

We were going to be stuck in this situation for the next thirty-six hours. I pulled my knees up onto the back of the seat in front of me, clasped my hands under my legs to hold my knees in place. I grit my teeth, and made up my mind to remain thus positioned for as long as it took. There was definitely no way they were going to leave me behind to float back on a troop ship.

The plane touched down briefly on Iwo Jima for fuel, but we were not allowed to deplane. From the window I saw the only two trees on the island at the time. Everything else had been killed during the war. They were two Banana trees and there was an armed guard protecting them twenty four-hours a day.

By this time I don't think I could have gotten up if I had wanted to. I had been cramped into one position for so long I was beginning to lose the feeling in my extremities.

The next stop would be Hawaii. I could hardly wait. I figured if I managed to get to sleep it would help. With this in mind I forced myself to sleep, it wasn't easy. Just as sleep was about to wash over me and kill the pain, someone shook me. I looked up into a smiling face of the stewardess who asked, "Would you like some coffee, tea, milk, or orange juice?" She moved quickly away sensing the urge to kill which swept over me like a huge wave.

Once again I tried to get to sleep and once again, this smiling face reappeared to ask if I wanted anything. For the next eight hours this happened over and over again until I was sure the hostess was there to add to the torture rather than sooth the pain. I even fantasized she had been hired by my former Supreme Commander, to harass me on the trip home.

Time and time again, I explained to this worthy soul I was trying to get to sleep. Each time I would be assured I would not be bothered again, then a short time later, "How about a pillow?" or "Would you like a nice cold cup of orange juice?" In the back of my mind, I knew these people were only doing their job as described in the Airlines Handbook, but it sure didn't make it any easier to take.

At long last, the man on the aisle next to me went to the stewardess and explained my problem to her. I guess he just couldn't stand seeing me in pain any longer, even though it was my pain and not his.

I will never know how the stewardess did it, but she managed to get a little short officer, who was sitting by the emergency door, to switch seats with me. The seats next to the emergency door had just a little more foot room than the seat I was in.

It took three people to get me out of the seat I had so carefully wedged myself into. I had to be carried because there was just no way I could walk. I couldn't even feel my legs, much less walk on them. My arms were cramped from being in the same position for so long holding my legs up. In short I was a bent up mess.

By the time we reached California, I was able to walk again. I walked back to this little short officer who had given up his seat for me and tried to thank him. He growled something at me and turned away. I don't think he was very happy about having helped me. I felt real bad about this, I had never wanted my problem to become anyone else's. I could do all the suffering needed by the situation all by myself.

In California the military offered to fly me on to New York on another Military Air Craft at no cost. I guess not having been on the flight from Japan with me, they had trouble understanding why I declined their offer.

Nopo San

Chapter 35

New York Air Force Base

When I arrived at New York A.F.B. I found myself in a type of limbo, I had less than a year to serve in the Air Force. On reporting in to the Photo Lab I was told there were at least 150 other photographers on the base and the Base Photo Lab was only authorized three.

With less than a year to go, I could not be cross trained for another job so I was placed, along with 147 hapless souls of all different ranks, in a holding pattern called, "In Transit".

At this point, let me digress a moment and explain this holding pattern; It meant we were confined to base. No passes. No leave. Not even a chow hall pass. We were truly hung out there in limbo.

We could not be cross trained because of the short time we had left in the Air Force and, because of our rank, we could not be assigned to labor details. In short we had nothing whatsoever to do . We began volunteering for various jobs just to break the boredom.

On one occasion, we took a set of lockers from one of our barracks and put them in a "Block House". The Block House was part of the early warning radar system which has long since been replaced by a much more sophisticated system.

I have long wondered about the block house. Security around the place was tight. No one got in out of the place unless they were festooned with all sorts of security badges. Yet here we were, a bunch of short timers with no security badges moving steel lockers into and out of the building.

Later I found the power and communications lines which fed the entire complex ran over the top of a hill about a quarter of a mile away. They were only about five feet above the ground. The site was unfenced and unguarded. There was however, a big sign which said, "Danger! Keep Away! High Voltage!"

We took the lockers had been in the Block House and put them in the officers quarters. We took the lockers from the officers quarters and put them in the N.C.O. quarters and those lockers were moved back to our barracks. Then, a week later, we did it all over again in reverse.

At one time, I was given a detail of four men and told to make a two-inch wide by two-inch deep trench along side all of the cement walk ways in the area. It took three weeks to dig all those little trenches, put the dirt in cans and haul it to the dump.

It took another four weeks for another team to go to the dump, pick up the dirt, bring it back to the area, and refill the trenches. It seems, when the base safety officer saw what we had done he determined the trenches were a hazard. He ordered them filled in again.

Then the C.O. ran out of things to give us to do. Finally, in desperation, he gave us several pairs of scissors and told us to mow the one and one-half acre field outside his window. Just to give you an idea of how things were going at this time. I had become a Buck Sergeant (Three Stripes) by this time. It meant I was not supposed to do any manual labor. I was assigned three men to use the scissors. I was not to touch the scissors except to pick them up in the morning and hand them back to the C.O. in the evening. It was stupid but what else was the poor C.O. to do.

During all this, time marched on. Winter moved in and the grass stopped growing. Soon there were no more details to be done, so we sat around and caught up on our reading.

Before anyone knew it, Christmas was upon us and here we were stuck on the base with no passes or leave. We griped long and loud about this but the military regulation governing this sort of thing was quite specific. No passes or leave, for short time, transient personnel! And this was very definite.

Fortunately, we had among us a Master Sergeant. He had been overseas for the last six years without a chance to see his family. They lived out in the Mid West somewhere. He sat about in the day-room with a scowl on his face.

Each day he would go to our area H.Q. and beg, plead, argue or demand a pass to be home for the holidays with his family. He could get nowhere with it. After one exceptionally stormy encounter about the pass and leave issue,.he became unusually quiet.

There were a bunch of us assembled in the day room watching a Soap Opera on TV. We has sunk to this lever because there was nothing else to do. Suddenly and quite without warning, he jumped to his feet and yelled, "**That does it!** We are going to get out the Hell of here, if it's the last thing I do as a Sergeant. Get the men together, here in the day-room, and be quick about it!"

The word went out all over the area like a fire storm. Something was up and we should all assemble in the day room, and it was to be done very quietly. A loud speaker system could not have done the job quicker or more affectionately. Within moments, everyone to whom it made any difference was there in the day room.

Once assembled, the sergeant explained his fiendish plot to us, "You **will** go **quietly** to your rooms. You **will** pack your field packs with your civilian clothing. You **will** let no one see you do this!"

He paused a moment or so as if to let it sink in, then he went on, "You **will** dress yourselves in your combat gear and assemble for maneuvers outside this building at exactly 09:00 tomorrow morning. You **will** speak to no one about this!" Thus was born a code of silence, among 147 men, could not have been broken with torture. No one knew exactly what he was up to but we could guess. We didn't even speak about the plan among ourselves.

At exactly 09:00 all 147 of us lined up outside our barracks and stood at attention for the Master Sergeant. To us he was like a General but I doubt if any General could have gotten the kind of loyalty this Master Sergeant got out of us on this auspicious day.

"**Right face!**" He yelled, "**Forward march!**"

As we marched smartly by the Company H.Q. I saw the C.O. stop the Sergeant and ask him where he was going with all of us. His answer was loud and clear for us all to hear, "Bivouac, **Sir!**" It was hard to suppress the lumps of laughter welled up in our throats as we heard those words.

Someone heard the C. O. mumble, "Bivouac? At this time of year?" Straight faced and stoic, we marched on past the C. O. and out the Main Gate of the base. We really played the part to the hilt. We even did a little grumbling for the benefit of the guard at the Gate.

The Sergeant called out, "Column Right, **March!**" And down the road we marched. It wasn't long before the Sergeant found a suitable wood lot.

"Column Right, March!" He yelled. Then as soon as we were far enough into the wood-lot so as not to be seen from the road, "Column Halt!"

Then in a quiet but unmistakably authoritative voice he said, "Now listen up! You **will** change into your civilian clothing. You **will** put your combat gear into your field packs and go home. You will stay out of trouble, because if you don't stay out of trouble the whole bunch of us will get the ax!

You will be back here at this spot, in your combat gear, no later than 16:00 on January third. By the way, you will have a Merry Christmas and a Happy New Year! Now get the Hell out of here and don't mess up!"

It was a bit hard to get the steel helmet into the field pack so it didn't show. We all helped one another and in a relatively short time we were ready to disburse. One at a time we filed by the Sergeant. Each one of us gave him a warm handshake and wished him the best Christmas and New Year he would ever have. He sure made ours for us.

We dispersed like oil on water, each man going his separate way. I had a great time at home with the family. Then promptly at 16:00 on January third the Sergeant yelled, "Fall in!"

He counted heads to be sure we were all there before he said, "Attention! Right face! Forward march!" and we went back to the base.

Everyone showed up. Everyone was on time. No one messed up. It was a flawless military operation. As a matter of fact, I think it was the first and only time in the whole three and a half years, everything went as it should have gone.

A few days after our return the C.O. stopped me and asked, "Where were you the other day? We looked all over the place for you."

I could see the Sergeant out of the corner of my eye, he had stopped short when the C.O. stopped me. I answered with a salute, "Bivouac, **Sir**!"

The C.O. looked puzzled, shook his head and muttered, "At this time of year?"

"**Yes Sir**!" I replied.

Shaking his head again, a very confused looking officer moved on. Just as soon as he was out of sight and ear shot, the Sergeant and I both exploded with laughter. I think, the C.O. was the only person on Base who didn't know what had happened. Then again, maybe he did know and just had a little compassion for a group of men in a nebulous situation.

It really wasn't the fault of the C.O. at all. The man had his orders and he carried them out. It was just one of those things where the book simply didn't cover the situation. I would like to think the C.O. knew what had happened and ignored it, however as an officer he could never admit it.

It was near the end of my enlistment and the Air Force decided they didn't need me any more. I was offered a six month early discharge. This was fine by me so I made ready to go home for the last time in my military career.

I was not alone, there were a whole bunch of us going home for the last time. We got together in the day room and asked the Sergeant if he wanted to march us off the one last time, he smiled as if he was actually thinking about it, but he declined.

What a shame, it would have been a fitting end to my military career.

A few days later, as I was sitting in the operations room awaiting processing, I noticed a huge pile of papers with red flags all over it. It looked strangely familiar. When the clerk, who had left his desk for a moment, returned I asked about the file.

He looked straight at me a moment then he said, "I have never in my whole military career seen a file like yours. We sit around here, in the evening, and read it rather than go home and watch TV. It's a military record, so these things must have really happened. It's still hard to believe. It's a wonder you're still alive! You should write a book someday But if you do, for God's sake don't mention any names! No one in their right minds is ever going to admit these things really happened."

He showed me a copy of my medical record and told me, "If you take this to the Veterans Administration you got it made for the rest of your life." Unfortunately, I was young, stupid and in a big hurry to see the last of the military. I didn't go to the V. A. it was a monumental mistake.

Now, many years after the fact, the maladies visited on me in the military have resurfaced. Currently I'm at war with the V. A. trying to prove they happened in the service. Of course without the records I can't prove much of it. The things I can prove, they had told me there was no cure for and I'd have to get used to living with them. Many of the civilian doctors who have examined me agree on this point.

Shortly after I got out of the service I asked for a copy of my file. It arrived in a plain brown envelope a few weeks later, it had shrunk to about six pieces of paper. I never saw or heard about the rest of the file again. I often wonder what the file would have looked like if I had taken the Air Force up on their offer to make me a Staff Sergeant and send me to the Libyan Desert for six years.

Like I said before, I liked the service and there have been many times since I got out I have wished I had stayed in the Air

Force. But I didn't, hind sight is always 20/20.